THE HAYTON COLLECTION

# WE MET IN PARIS

SHANNON STEEVES

# Copyright

# Dedication

Paris, you taught me the language of love.
London, you are the heartbeat that moves my pen.

# Chapter One

The aroma of fresh pastries enveloped the Mayfair London bakery, where Executive Pastry Chef Cordelia Dyer imagined each one as a handcrafted love letter delivered on a silver tray. She and her team of bakers worked behind a glass wall as admirers peered through marble-lined cabinets, anxious to indulge in one of Bastien Larue's creations. Every day, the kitchen hummed—a symphony of mixers, ovens, and scrapers, each manipulating the dough into something new.

Cordelia tossed a handful of flour onto the worktable and watched it settle like snow on the landscape. The cool texture offered relief in the hot kitchen. For a moment, she was four years old again, standing on a wooden stool beside her mother. Coated in flour her small hands pressed into cookie dough. "Not too hard, Cordelia," her mother whispered, the scent of vanilla extract on her cheek. "We don't fight the dough, we shape it." Cordelia blinked the memory aside.

Sam Hardy, the head baker, watched from across the table as she rolled and stretched buttery dough. She wondered if he'd been born with that smile, broad and cheeky, framed in day-old red stubble. A useful tool in kitchen politics.

"This is how the dough should look. Thin but not transparent. Smooth. A combination of both recipes." Cordelia pressed her fingertips against the edge and felt a slight resistance. She knew the gluten had perfectly developed. "Here, feel that? That's what you're looking for." She patted her hands together, letting flour fall to the floor, and then wiped them on a nearby towel.

"Yes, Chef." Sam reached across and felt the texture of the dough. "I never made a financier sable biscuit. Can we eat them after they're baked?" His boyish tone amused Cordelia. The Kensington native must have surprised everyone when he announced his school of choice was in Paris and not a posh university.

"Oh, sure. You guys need to know these. I mean, perfectly. No more mistakes." The wall clock grabbed her attention, "That can't be right?"

Sam glanced over his shoulder and then at his watch. "Late for something?"

Cordelia sighed. "Yes. And I need to see Jasper and Lucy before I leave." She refocused on the dough. "Right. The black cherry jam is in the cooler, and we'll finish these off in the morning. You work tomorrow, right?" She didn't wait for a response. "Go ahead and bake them off. And be prepared to teach Lang how to make them." She looked around, "Where's Jessica?"

"Out front with a customer."

"Why? Where's Suze?" Cordelia wiped her hands across the apron.

"She left early. Brad couldn't get their daughter from school. Remember? She needed to leave?"

Cordelia ignored Sam's eyes, studying her. She didn't want to admit she'd forgotten and have a repeat of last week. Jessica would love nothing more than to tell Bastien his executive pastry chef couldn't cut it, and she couldn't risk Sam telling her. That's what best friends do. "Yes, she did say that this morning." She fussed with her apron and tossed it into a nearby basket. "Anyway, you have plenty of help."

"Yes, Chef." Sam scribbled notes on a pad.

The phone in her pocket chimed. Richard, her tennis partner, sent a photo of his watch. Message received. He had an uncanny way of being obnoxious and funny, while clueless that he was either one. "Okay, I'm leaving. Have a nice evening."

"Night." Sam nodded and flashed a charming smile, more focused on snapping photos of the dough than his boss.

"Gees, it's baltic out there. Froze my ass off when that lady opened the front door." Jessica Meier—Sous Pastry Chef with a pink pixie haircut and gloomy facial expressions. A mismatch that Cordelia found frustrating yet fascinating. Bastien described her as adorable. Sam and the team defined her as funny. Cordelia's experience with Jessica, frosty. But her baking was impeccable, and that deserved respect.

Cordelia hurried into her office, a reprieve from the noisy, hot kitchen. The space, the size of a closet, had a window that peered onto the alley. She paused and listened to the persistent storm as it settled in for the night, orchestrating a dance of wind and rain between the buildings. A pastry box sat on the corner of her desk with *Jasper* and *Lucy* scribbled on top. She grabbed the box, her coat, and a racquet bag from behind the door. One day, I'll make it on time, she promised herself.

As she breezed through the kitchen, Jessica and Sam debated the differences between biscuits and sables. "Technically, a sable is a biscuit," Cordelia said.

"See, I told you, Jess."

"Well then, why the fancy name, Sam? Showin' off?"

"Jessica. Let's meet tomorrow before I leave town, say 9:30?"

"Sure. Yes, Chef." Her acidic smirk landed on Cordelia like burnt sugar on the hand. The same smug smile had surfaced at the team meeting three weeks prior, in response to Cordelia's holiday menu. Everything about it questioned Cordelia's creativity and capabilities.

Cordelia turned to leave, slinging her racquet bag across her body. "And Jessica, no more wrinkled coats, especially in front of customers."

Moments later, Cordelia popped open her turquoise umbrella and walked out from under the awning's protection. Raindrops splattered against the fabric and plummeted to the ground. A streetlamp's golden hues dispelled pockets of blackness as Cordelia rushed into the side alley that ran alongside the bakery. The thought of getting lost in the passage that wedged itself between buildings unnerved her, but she needed to find Jasper and Lucy.

Cordelia called out and listened. Her pulse quickened, and she prepared to flee. Going into the alley on a rainy night might prove to be foolish, definitely risky. Two shadows emerged and walked towards her. Her fingers gripped the umbrella, just in case.

"Are you mad, girl? What are you doing here?" The familiar Irish cadence of Jasper Mack's voice calmed Cordelia's nerves. He and Lucy Cobbett, his longtime companion, ambled towards her. Their hunched bodies clung to one another under a single umbrella, and the frayed edges dripped rain onto their worn boots.

"I could say the same thing to you, old man." Cordelia handed the box to Lucy, feeling the weight lift from her arm. "I know they're a day old, but with this weather, you two deserve a treat." Her protective nature considered them more as her chosen London family than strangers, but familial feelings or not, they enjoyed their *little independent life.*

"Aww, dear, we ate at the church tonight." The shadowy, weathered lines on Lucy's face softened in gratitude. "But we'll enjoy them tomorrow."

"Then why didn't you stay? They have beds." Her voice stumbled, with the memories of another couple she'd helped in New York. For five years, they happily endured the frigid cold and blistering heat, but Cordelia watched as the streets consumed them. She feared the same fate for Jasper and Lucy.

At her first bakery job after graduation, Cordelia met Martin and Ellie, who lived in a nearby alley. Their weathered faces greeted her every morning and she watched their decline. First Ellie and then Martin, their bodies broken and tattered, as worn as their tent after that many seasons on the street. One day, their possessions were gone. Cordelia searched shelters throughout the city for days, every moment she wasn't working, but they became ghosts. Regrets that lingered.

"We can't leave our tent." Jasper pointed down the alley. "It'd be gone in the morning, and that's our home."

"Jasper." Cordelia tightened the collar of her coat, feeling a chill that didn't come from the weather. "That's not a home, it's a tent." The words emerged sharper than intended.

"My dear, we are doing all right. Now you should be inside."

Cordelia's phone vibrated again, and to answer it would take too much time and effort. She knew it was Richard.

"Oh, look Jasper, macarons. With your favorite flavors—raspberry and pistachio."

"Oh, um, those are strawberry. The raspberry is redder." Cordelia treasured the quirky couple: Jasper in his old brown suit jacket, baggy high-waisted jeans, and brown fedora that resembled one of the jazz crooners her father listened to on Saturday nights; and Lucy, less old school but toughened by life, with silver hair that draped across frail shoulders. Her bell-bottom jeans flared underneath the oversized wool coat.

"I love strawberry. They remind me of my mum's jam." Lucy savored every nibble.

Jasper grabbed a macaron and smelled it. "Coffee and." He smelled it again. "Rosemary?"

"Thyme. Wow, Jasper, you've been holding out on me."

Footsteps splattered in a puddle behind Cordelia, giving way to laughter and whispers. She glanced back and caught a glimpse of a petite, loud woman nuzzling her head into a man's chest as they paused to kiss in the rain. *Oh my god. It's one of our customers.* Cordelia turned around and hid in her umbrella, positioning her body protectively between two worlds.

Jasper finished his macarons and meticulously wiped the corners of his mouth. "Well, my dear girl, thank you for these delectable treats. We'll enjoy these for days to come."

"I know you'll probably say no, but why don't I put you up for the night. There's space in the stockroom and."

"No, no, we're fine."

"But Jasper it's warm. And drier than your tent."

"You're such a doll." Lucy patted Cordelia's arm.

"I'm serious, you can keep an eye on your tent and stay dry. How perfect is that?" She examined their faces. "Come on, take me up on it."

Lucy squeezed Cordelia's hand. Her weathered, soaked fingers felt cold against Cordelia's skin. "Don't worry about us, we've slept in worse. Besides, we have our blankets, these wonderful desserts, and each other."

"I must say, Lucy's correct." Jasper wiped raindrops off his cheek as they seeped through a tiny tear in their umbrella.

Cordelia's phone vibrated again. Richard. "Listen, I'll be in Paris next week. If you need anything, ask for Sam, he'll help you."

The couple listened intently, curious about Cordelia's plans. She listed off several museums, including the Musée Cluny, but left out one detail—she planned to spend most of her time researching the history of French pastries for her upcoming cookbook. As lovely as Jasper and Lucy were, Cordelia hesitated to share the details before it became a reality.

After a few reserved hugs, they slogged back to their tent, fading into shadowy figures. Cordelia sprinted down the sidewalk, splashing through puddles, and called her tennis partner. "I'll be there in five, hold the court."

A black cab approached, its headlights streaked against the rain-slicked pavement. The city lights glowed, bouncing off the foggy night sky.

# Chapter Two

The library's heating system groaned and roared to life, creating a tunnel of wind around the room. Royce Brownell scanned the worn pages of a book and hastily wrote in an academic journal littered with multi-colored sticky tabs, each a clue, a thread connecting him to long-forgotten people. Stacks of books, strewn across the table, surrounded his laptop and notebook—organized disorder.

Royce stretched his six-foot-two frame and released the tension from his back. For five hours, he'd perched himself over the table, but the successful research outweighed a few sore muscles. There would be time for a massage back in London.

The smears of black ink on his notebook matched the ones on his left hand, leaving ghostly words on his tan skin.

Within minutes, the small reading room sweltered, forcing him to loosen the top two buttons of his crisp, black shirt. He wiped his forehead with a monogrammed handkerchief. His mind was unable to concentrate. Why the museum flooded the library with intense heat when across the courtyard, galleries with thousands of French artifacts enjoyed frigid temperatures baffled him.

Royce contemplated the consequences if he opened the window. Would it be so bad if he cracked it? No one would be injured, and he'd close it before leaving, although he risked deafening alarms and removal from the library. Probably not the smartest idea. He wiped his face and shoved the handkerchief into a worn, brown leather satchel. The library closed in two hours. Determination propelled him forward.

A few minutes later Royce's phone rattled against the table, the sound reverberating against the walls. Thomas Brownell, The Earl of Thornbury. He called three times. Another example of how patience eluded his father as the world moved too slowly for his liking.

"Hello, Pop." Royce swiveled in the chair and knocked his knee against the table leg.

"Royce, I've been trying to get a hold of you." Thomas emphasized the last two words with a clipped tone.

"Right. Can I call you this evening?"

"Why are you whispering?"

"I'm in a library."

"Right."

Royce's shoulders tightened. The Earl's weighted pauses could collapse time and space and revert his thirty-six-year-old son into a schoolboy.

"Well, I spoke with Ronald. He informed me you're no longer using his services. He's concerned, rightly so, about your decisions."

"Hey Pop, I, I'm in the middle of research, can I call you tonight?"

"What are you thinking, son?"

Royce tapped his pen across his notebook, leaving a winding stream of tiny dots. "I'd prefer to discuss this later. Maybe when I get back?"

"Now is a perfectly good time for me."

"Of course." Royce sat up and straightened his back. "I decided it was time work with someone new. It's nothing personal, but he's your age, and times change, investing changes."

"Sounds like a gamble to me, which as you know, I never condone. We didn't get here."

"Respectfully, I disagree."

The Earl sighed. Whenever he prepared a lecture, he exhaled and paused, gathering his argument as if he were back in Parliament's halls. "As you know, Royce, our family has sacrificed and established."

"And established its prominence and influence for hundreds of years—yes, I remember. You imprinted it on our brains."

"Exactly where it should be. Now, I told Ronald it was a mistake. That you were most certainly not forgoing his services."

"Pop. Why do you always think you can speak for me? You need to stop."

"I should have been consulted."

Royce stood and relieved the tension in his neck. "You've been notified."

"There was a time when you cared about your legacy."

A lifetime of lessons, of self-restraint and obligation. It always came back to that one word—legacy. "Okay, Pop, this isn't the time."

"First, you leave academia, and now this. What's next?" He had an uncanny way of inserting the past into conversations, disguising it as *a concern for one's well-being.*

"Listen, I need to go. We'll talk when I'm back, alright?"

The Earl spent a few more minutes pressing the issue before reminding Royce about Sunday dinner, the weekly tradition where the family debated society and politics. In ten years, Royce had only missed a handful, maybe two, but his brother

Marcus offered a stream of excuses. First professional polo, then marriage, and most recently, a baby.

As quickly as the call began, it ended, dwindling Royce's research time to one and a half hours. The door swung open and Melisent, a museum librarian, smiled, her arms hugging two leather-bound books against her chest. "We close soon, but I found these and assumed you might be interested." Her sand-colored hair framed her eyes, and with the tip of her finger, she pushed strands behind her ear. A practiced and deliberate gesture meant to draw Royce's attention to her eyes. It worked.

"Fantastic." Royce created space on the table, maintaining professional distance. "Thank you. You're a gem."

"It's my pleasure." Her French accent twirled across the words, each syllable carrying a subtle invitation. She lingered in the room, hoping to engage in conversation. She asked about his progress, discoveries, and offered her research assistance.

"Umm, No, it's all good, thank you. And thank you again for pulling these." He returned to his notes, his movements deliberate and restrained.

Melisent hesitated. Royce looked up. Their eyes met. A risky move for him, especially since Paris had been his sanctuary from entanglements, a refuge from London's press. Here he had the opportunity to be valued as an intellectual, rather than title or appearance, and he had no intention of complicating life, no matter how helpful or attractive the complication might be.

"Will you be working here tomorrow?" she asked. Her eyes transmitted desired hope, a look that historically meant disaster for Royce or, at the very least, drama. "I'll be happy to help you find more."

"Yes, but I have plenty here to keep me busy."

She kept the conversation going, running her fingers through her hair and smiling at Royce's responses, ignoring the five times he thanked her, picked up his pen, and looked away.

"Well, I won't keep you."

"Yes, yes. I'll leave you to your work and return in an hour."

"I'll be here until you kick me out, although I'm hoping you won't." He chuckled, knowing it was best to stop talking. "Thank you." Royce darted his eyes back to the book and concentrated on the words. The door clicked shut, and Royce leaned back in his chair. If he considered dating again, she might be a viable candidate, but the well-worn path of doubt diverted his thoughts back to research.

Exactly one hour later, Melisent returned. She creaked the door open, sending a gust of cool air into the room. Relief. Royce typed quickly, pushing his fingers across the keys, eager to record a few more lines of information.

"I'm sorry, but we are closing. I waited as long as possible, however, I'm afraid I must place some of the books back." She retrieved two of the books.

"Five more minutes? I'm almost done."

"No, I'm afraid George is ready to leave, and to be honest, I'm meeting friends for wine. Would you like to join us?" Her fingers ran the edges of a book, carefully brushing the frayed fabric.

Royce considered her offer, hesitated, and closed his laptop. Since when did a drink violate his rules?

By the time they reached a small restaurant near the university, regret settled in his back, a reminder that impulsiveness usually led to disappointment. Like many women Royce had known, Melisent, a pleasant and intelligent woman, wasted no time expressing loneliness despite her successful career. And like all the others, she wanted more, suggesting more of his time. The reality settled like a cold stone hitting pond water.

Drinks turned into dinner, and safe conversations passed

with recommendations for lesser-known cafés and, of course, the differences between Paris and London. Royce maintained a polite engagement, but his mind drifted to his research and the solitude of writing. When the bill arrived, he insisted on paying for Melisent, a token of appreciation for her assistance at the library. She accepted and leaned closer, momentarily resting her hand on his arm. Being a gentleman came with regrets, the second of the night.

Minutes later, they stepped outside into the cool Parisian evening, where streetlamps cast a golden glow over the cobblestones, and in the distance, an accordion entertained tourists with a melancholy tune. The pair politely shook hands and wished each other a good night. Royce paused long enough to ensure Melisent's safety down the street. Just as she turned the corner, he saw her look back and wave.

The walk back to his hotel was peaceful. The crowds thinned out and ancient buildings cast themselves in shadows, revealing Paris stood as a graceful woman who shared her soul. He detoured at the Seine, drawn to the silhouette of Notre Dame, and watched a tour boat glide past. Before leaving his favorite bridge, he called Richard, his mate from prep school.

"You assume everyone is Katherine."

"No," Royce said, hardening his voice. "Some are Vivian. Or Caroline. Different name, same story."

"You know you're as bleak as crossing the channel in a rowboat."

"I'm a realist."

Richard chuckled. "One day, mate, one day. That girl's going to overturn your theory."

"Who?"

"No idea, but she exists. And you don't stand a chance."

Royce debated Richard's points with practiced cynicism,

and despite his unlucky record, privately he entertained the idea of a *Ms. Right*.

# Chapter Three

The next morning, Cordelia stared out the train window, watching the sleepy English countryside whiz by. She boarded with minutes to spare, dropping into her seat as the train pulled away from St. Pancras Station. The scent of strong coffee drifted from across the aisle, a reminder she'd skipped breakfast after oversleeping her alarm.

The near-miss with a taxi replayed in her mind, a suspended moment reminding her why they tell kids to *look both ways*. Another step, and her next piece of jewelry would've come from the hospital, not Paris.

Her phone vibrated again. Daniel. A familiar tightness crept across her shoulders. She couldn't imagine what he wanted or needed after discovering his affair six-and-a-half months ago in New York. Her finger hovered over the notification, almost afraid to touch it.

I need to talk to you. It's important.

Classic urgency.

Just five minutes. Btw, I saw you in the NYC spread. Congrats.

And there it was, sandwiched in with Daniel's needs, recognition of her, but only long enough to get what he needed.

Cordelia clicked off her phone, dropped it into her tote, and began sketching pastries with flavor profiles scribbled on the side.

"Excuse me, is this seat taken?" The woman gestured at the empty seat across from Cordelia.

"No, please."

"Thanks. The train is surprisingly full for a Tuesday." The woman settled into the seat, placing a designer tote between her feet. "Business or pleasure?" She twisted her shiny black hair into a top knot and sipped water from an orange stainless bottle.

"Oh. A little of both. You?"

"All business, I'm afraid. First, a conference at the Sorbonne, a second one at Oxford, and with any luck, home."

"Where's home?"

"Boston, but originally San Diego. And you, you're clearly not from this side of the pond?"

Cordelia laughed to herself. This question tripped her up. Did she call London home? New York, where she'd spent thirteen years, including culinary school? Or one of the seven university campuses she'd grown up on during her father's teaching career? "Originally out west, but now I live in London."

"Nice. I'm Robbie, by the way." She extended her hand. "No ring on the finger, work?"

Cordelia introduced herself and indulged Robbie's prying questions. She discovered her train companion held a PhD in Computational Linguistics and spoke four languages, accomplishments that overshadowed Cordelia's culinary achieve-ments. She fidgeted with her necklace and listened.

For the next hour, the train raced through the dark tunnel, and the pair bonded over food, travel, and Parisian men—Robbie's non-academic pursuit.

The train pulled into the station and Cordelia gathered her belongings. Back in Paris. The distinctive sounds of Gare du Nord station gave way to scents of fresh bread, igniting her creativity.

Not long after, Cordelia arrived at Bastien Larue Paris, the flagship patisserie, thirty minutes before their scheduled meet-ing, a feat she rarely accomplished. The thought of indulging in one of his specialties, the trio croissant, seduced her appetite. It was only available in Paris. The scent permeated the boutique—almond and pistachio cream, finely chopped hazelnuts, and chocolate on a buttery pillow.

Bastien honored French design at his Parisian store, with Belle Époque mirrors and marble countertops aged from decades of usage. The morning light gleamed on glass cabinets. A different mood than his BL London shop, where clean lines blended with innovation, and pastries were more Picasso than Monet.

"Cordelia!" Bastien emerged from the kitchen, flour dusting the front of his navy apron. "You are early, my dear." At sixty-three, his salt-and-pepper hair and laugh lines suggested a life devoted to love and passion. He embraced her warmly, kissing both cheeks. "Did you arrive this morning? How is your holiday so far?" Bastien fired off questions faster than she could respond. His energy bubbled.

She followed him up two flights of stairs as he shared his enthusiasm for life. They passed through a windowless hallway with pale blue wallpaper. The sconces emitted a cool white light that gave the corridor a frosty chill.

Finally, they emerged into Bastien's office. The expansive room with high ceilings and double crystal chandeliers felt sparse, almost incomplete, with two black sofas and a marble coffee table. The seating faced an ornamental grey stone fireplace, almost forgotten. And in the corner, a whitewashed desk with an oversized leather chair. A modern sculpture of lovers in white stone commanded the room's attention.

"Ah, yes, Jeannie's work." Bastien helped himself to the coffee and cookies on the coffee table. "Please, help yourself."

Cordelia settled for two cookies before taking a seat across from Bastien. She craved a trio of croissants, fearful they'd be sold out by the time she got back to the shop.

"Now, about your cookbook, tell me your plans."

Cordelia pulled a notebook from her bag and handed him a copy of the outline. In detail, she explained the concept—French and English pastries and desserts.

"I know exactly which ones I want to include. You can see it won't be a huge book, only ten or twelve recipes."

Bastien nodded, keeping his focus on the outline.

"And I've done my research, there's nothing like it on the market."

"What about your publisher? They agree?"

"Yes, they do. They said we can include all my historical research into the book. I even showed them my sketches for the layout, and they loved it."

"Excellent."

Cordelia pushed her hair to one side and then the other, sitting up straight to sip her coffee. "So, do you like my idea?" She hesitated. "Do you mind if I do this on the side? It won't interfere with my job because I'll work on it at night."

. . .

Bastien nodded and flipped through Cordelia's journal, scanning the pages of historical notes. "Fascinating. You know Madame Rici in the sixth?"

"Yes." She twisted a thread on her watchband.

"You do? Excellent. She tells everyone it's her husband who taught her to bake, but really, she learned from her grand-mother. Talented woman. She makes the best macarons in Paris. But if you tell anyone I said this, I'll deny it." Bastien chuckled and dusted the crumbs from his shirt. "We all know, I make the best macarons in Paris."

"Are you saying you want me to visit your competition?"

"Ah, see, in history, there is no competition, only preserva-tion. She can tell you how her family survived during the war, selling them off market."

"Seriously? That's amazing."

"Yes, yes." Bastien handed the notebook back to Cordelia. "About your request, perhaps it's time to trust Jessica more. I think she's ready for the responsibility."

"Jessica? She...I can manage."

"Is there a problem?"

Cordelia's stomach knotted. Tension crept upward. Did she tell Bastien the truth, that Jessica is a talented chef who's ruth-less and conniving? And she doesn't trust her? Her eyes darted around the room, contemplating what she'd say next.

"Cordelia?"

Cordelia sighed. "Yes, you're right. I'll delegate some things to Jessica. With oversight."

"Perfect. I trust you to work everything out and keep me informed."

Their meeting concluded, and Cordelia made her way back through the ornate patisserie. An icy dread spread across her chest. The prospect of Jessica gaining power made her wonder, could more responsibility crack Jessica's façade? She savored the idea. But as much as she wanted to envision Jessica's downfall, optimism whispered, suggesting the two might find common ground. Not likely.

That same morning, Royce leaned over a book and mumbled to himself, writing coded notes that to the untrained eye appeared indecipherable. Melisent appeared with armloads of books—three times, and during each interruption, she hovered longer, arranging and rearranging books.

"Melisent," Royce accepted the inevitable, "perhaps we could speak?" He gestured for her to sit in a chair near the door.

"Yes, of course." Her eyes brightened, and she pulled the chair away from the wall. Her clog dangled from her foot and swung in a rhythmic motion.

Royce cleared his throat. "You've been invaluable this week, just wonderful."

"My pleasure." She brushed her fingers through her hair.

"I've enjoyed our professional collaboration, and thank you for inviting me to dinner the other night." Royce stumbled over his words. He lost count, but at least three words were repeated twice. "I believe I gave you the wrong impression."

Her expression shifted, and the warmth from her eyes faded to disappointment. "No, no. I understand." She stood. "I have no impression. We had a nice evening, that's all."

"Right. And I value our professional relationship."

"Yes, of course. I didn't think."

"Oh, good. I'm glad. I thought." Royce's words trailed off. He adjusted his collar and leaned back in his seat.

Melisent placed the chair back against the wall, grabbed a stack of books off the table, and assured Royce there was no misunderstanding. Although she didn't make eye contact with him, the rest of the day.

Royce spent the afternoon immersed in research. The morning's awkwardness dissipated as the stories pulled him into another time and place. When the museum closed, Royce retreated to a quiet bistro on the Boulevard Saint-Germain, where the waiter recognized him with a nod. He led him to his preferred patio table, left the menu, and walked away with only a smile. This spot, this corner of Paris, provided the perfect sanctuary for a glass of Burgundy and his thoughts. Here, he enjoyed anonymity.

# Chapter Four

The next morning, Cordelia dashed across Boulevard Saint-Germain. Her neon blue sneakers pounded the pavement, alerting pedestrians of her presence. She had less than five minutes to make it to Pont Saint-Michel if she wanted to break her Paris record. The last time she ran the river was with Daniel, right before the French Open. Now the city reawakened her memories and her competitive spirit.

She weaved past a silver-haired woman with a cane and wondered if she should stop to help her cross the street. Despite the woman's age, she seemed to keep pace with most pedestrians. Cordelia kept running. Strands of ponytail stuck to her moist cheek. She pushed ahead toward her goal. Cordelia had her routine to maintain, even on vacation, and day two in Paris would not break a sixteen-year habit.

Unprepared for a sudden break in rhythm, Cordelia stumbled around a family of four who stopped and huddled over a phone, appearing lost and confused. She bounced off the patriarch of the group. "Excuse me."

"Hey. Watch out!" The words slammed like sleet against a stone façade.

Cordelia gave a wave over her shoulder. People needed to be more aware of their surroundings and move out of the way. It was about respecting those who needed to get somewhere.

The scent of warm yeast and butter drifted towards her. Hunger pangs rumbled in her stomach, and she wanted nothing more than to stop and eat. Instead, she drove her feet into the roadway and counted. One. Two. Avoid the queue. Three. Four. Run past the door. On the last step, Cordelia broad-jumped and planted a foot on the sidewalk. A man in line at the bakery caught her attention. Their eyes latched onto each other. He smiled. She returned the gesture. Her mouth felt parched. She glanced at her watch. Four minutes left. Cordelia sprinted away.

In a split decision, she selected the Rue Hautefeuille as the path to success. The quiet side street provided quick access to Place Saint Michel and one of her favorite views of the river. The route was perfect, no one slowed her down or held her back from personal victory.

Cordelia used the quiet to her advantage, running recipe ideas through her mind. Even though she had a list of twelve, so far, she needed to make sure every recipe in the cookbook reflected her culinary journey and historically made sense.

"My dear, you're here!" A lean, older woman waved at Cordelia. Her lips pooched when she smiled.

"Bonjour Madame Rici." Cordelia panted. "I'll come by tomorrow." She tapped her watch and ran faster.

The woman stood in the doorway of a patisserie. Hundreds of bite-sized cakes and macarons, all brightly colored and adorned with edible flowers, dotted the window display. She wiped her hands across the white chef jacket and clapped. "Danielle will be so happy." She blew Cordelia a kiss.

Seeing Madame Rici again brought back memories of Cordelia's best friend, Marnie. They'd known each other for fourteen years and immediately bonded at culinary school. They had traveled to Paris after graduation and discovered the family shop by chance. In one week, they sampled their way through every pastry at Maison Rici and called it an orgasm for the sweet tooth.

Cordelia pressed her chest forward and weighed into the last few minutes of her run. A delivery truck turned onto the road, rambled towards her, engulfing the sidewalk in fumes and dust. She swatted the air and coughed. A dust particle landed in her eye, halting her progress. "No!" She dabbed her eye. "Come on." Her eyes watered.

"Do you need help?" A man asked. His warm British accent comforted her.

"What?" Cordelia forced an eye open and glanced at the raven-haired man. "No. But thank you." She brushed the tears and dirt from her face. "Something's in my eye, and I'm out of time."

"Out of time?"

Cordelia stared at him with one eye. "Yes. Time." She wiped the sweat from her forehead as her eyes fluttered to stay open. "I was running and this damn truck." She grunted and wiped the tears pooling on her face.

The man pulled a handkerchief from his leather satchel. "Here, this might help?"

"Thank you." Cordelia pressed it against her eyes and sighed. "This really sucks." She leaned against a building and dabbed her cheeks. "Sorry. I'm not normally like this. It's just."

"Understandable."

Cordelia blinked rapidly, relieved not to feel grit in her eyes. "Live around here?" She chuckled, knowing how it sounded. "Don't worry, I'm not hitting on you."

His cleft chin jutted out as he laughed. "Ah, no. London, actually." Handsome enough, but she decided not to tell him she also lived in London. Who needs stalkers, especially well-mannered ones?

"Well, listen, I don't want to keep you." Cordelia wadded up the handkerchief and shoved it into her jacket pocket. She glanced at his shoes: classic white court sneakers. Interesting. Fits him. "Yeah. Thanks for your help. You don't find many that would stop." She cut her eyes at him, brushed back strands of hair stuck to her forehead, and smiled. "I need to finish my run."

"Right. I hope it works out for you wherever you're headed."

"Yeah, you too." Cordelia blinked in rapid succession, making sure her eyes were dust-free, and scooted past him. Her watch indicated she had two minutes to make it to the bridge. An impossible feat, but worth a try.

She jogged a few steps when a lingering tear rolled down her cheek. That's when she realized she still had his handkerchief. Cordelia spun around and dashed up the street, but the man had vanished. She scanned the crowd, searching for his tall frame, dark hair, and white sneakers, but he'd disappeared. As if he never existed.

Her fingers ran across the cloth, running over the embroidered initials "RGB" in one corner. It smelled warm and spicy, like aged wood after a shaman ceremony.

After one last scan of the crowd, she tucked the handkerchief into a pocket and jogged toward Pont Saint-Michel. *London*, he said, what an odd coincidence. The city seemed determined to swallow up her mysterious gentleman with old-world tastes, but something about the encounter softened her run.

The morning light streamed into the Musée Cluny courtyard as Royce and his curator friend, Jean Allard, walked toward a medieval exhibition hall. The tapping sound of their shoes against the ancient stone floor reverberated off the pillars, and their voices echoed upward. Royce followed Jean through a door, stepping back in time.

"These fragments," Jean gestured toward a lab table with several tarnished metal pieces, "were discovered during the renovation of a cellar on Île de la Cité. Carbon dating places them in the mid-ninth century." A technician stood to the side and observed.

Royce leaned closer, examining the intricate pattern etched into what appeared to be a brooch clasp. "Incredible." His mind should have been absorbed in the historical significance, but images of the American woman with flushed cheeks flashed in his mind. The tear that streaked down her face and her unapologetic attitude. Jean's voice brought him back to the brooch, back into the room. "Impressive discovery."

"Yes, yes, and there's more, a wealth of treasures. Come." Jean guided Royce to another table where a small, kite-shaped shield rested. "I believe you will appreciate this one."

Royce slipped on gloves and gripped the shield in his fingertips, feeling the fragility of history in his hands. The metalwork reminded him of artifacts he'd studied during his doctoral thesis at Cambridge. He immersed himself in eighth and ninth-century Anglo-Saxon history and became the youngest tenured professor at a former London university. That's why his decision to resign a year ago stunned his colleagues—a departure based on creativity and ethics.

"The iconography is distinctly Frankish, but the shape and size are not," Jean said.

Royce nodded, forcing his attention back to the artifacts.

"And the intertwining patterns resemble those found in court records."

Royce set the shield back down. "Clearly, it was designed

for a child. Have you considered it might have been made for a woman?"

Jean adjusted his wire-rimmed glasses. "Very good."

They talked for almost an hour, continuing to examine the brooches and shield. But the image of the runner intruded on his thoughts, again and again. Her brown ponytail, the long strand of hair stuck to her face, and the way she'd dabbed her green eyes. He caught himself smiling. "I swear, I'm not hitting on you," she'd said with a laugh. He adjusted the collar of his white shirt.

"Royce?" Jean stared at him.

"Sorry. You were saying?" Royce straightened his back, attempting to refocus.

"I was asking about the potential connection to the Viking raids of 845." Jean studied him with the same scrutiny he applied to his artifacts. "Perhaps we should take a break. The café is open, and we can grab a coffee, yes?"

Royce cleared his throat and agreed.

As they walked through the museum's vaulted corridors, Royce found himself scanning the clusters of tourists, almost expecting to see her again. He pushed the thoughts away. A chance encounter, nothing more. Whoever she was, he hoped the handkerchief served as a reminder of their unusual connection.

Thirty minutes later, the men sipped the last drops of their coffee. Royce bit into a madeleine, one of his favorite desserts, especially dipped in chocolate, and said, "Is there time to see the textile fragments?"

"You are welcome to stay until we close, if you like. Maybe I should offer you a position."

Royce chuckled. The thought of returning to academia, even in a museum setting, made his palms sweat. He preferred bringing history to life through stories rather than lectures, through pages rather than display cases.

As they made their way back to the lab, cutting through the medieval garden, the scent of herbs and flowers created a bridge to the past. This was where Royce belonged, exploring history's remains. The mysterious runner receded in his thoughts, becoming nothing more than an odd encounter on a normal day.

# Chapter Five

Refreshed from her morning run, Cordelia explored the neighborhood streets around Boulevard Saint-Germain. At every corner, the smell of coffee mingled with fresh baguettes. People pushed past each other, ignoring those who came to experience an ideal Paris or get lost on quaint streets. Cordelia wandered. She walked east, then west, weaving on and off both sides of the boulevard, going as far as Luxembourg Garden before returning to the boulevard.

Cordelia found an open table at a bistro facing the tree-lined sidewalk. Around her people settled into the green and white chairs, finding a welcomed relief after a busy day. Her phone read 36,797 steps—not as high as she planned, not after that run. She could do better.

Within minutes she sipped on a glass of Sauvignon Blanc and people watched, admiring the stream of fashion, including a striking young couple. Their arms and fingers intertwined. The girl's straight white-blonde hair reached the top of her high-waisted jeans. The flare, something Cordelia could never pull off, swished with a catwalk rhythm. Her purple crop top and oversized wool coat complimented her Scandinavian complexion. But it was the guy who caught Cordelia's attention. He had luminous, deep brown skin with a slight stubble and brooding eyes. He walked with a swagger like John Travolta. He made the street his personal catwalk. Cordelia watched him. That face, that stoic gaze hung above Time Square in New York.

"Would you say they're models?" A man two tables to Cordelia's left leaned towards her and smiled. His velvety British accent reminded her of home, and his smile revealed dimples that softened his deep eyes. Another familiar face. Had she seen him gracing Time Square too?

Cordelia smiled. "Oh, for sure. The last time I saw him, he was half naked on a billboard in New York." She cut her eyes back to the couple as they continued down the street.

"Then I guess we can say we had a celebrity sighting."

She raised her glass in agreement. "I guess we did." Cordelia sipped her wine, desperate for a witty response, but with strangers humor usually fell out of her mouth like an under-cooked cake—promising but soggy. She looked at him, he glanced at her. She started to speak but nothing came to mind.

"If we sit here long enough, we might see more."

"Maybe, but that'll require another glass of wine."

"Then, I suggest we order a bottle and wait."

Cordelia gave the man a sideways look. "What's the catch?"

"Does there need to be one?"

"No. But a stranger offering my wine in Paris. There's gotta be a catch."

The corners of his mouth rose, forcing warmth into his dark eyes. He dressed like a banker or lawyer with a white shirt and black jacket, but his two-day old stubble didn't fit the image.

"Is the bottle red or white?"

"Whatever the lady prefers."

"I'll split a white with you if you tell me your name. I don't drink with strangers."

He laughed and joined her. "Royce Brownell. Mind if I sit?"

"Sure."

He situated himself and said, "Actually, we already know one another."

Cordelia examined his expression. He appeared nice enough, but broad shoulders and a great face meant little, look at Daniel—deceptive.

"I believe you have my handkerchief."

"Oh my god, that's you. Yes, it is." Cordelia pulled it out of her tote. "RGB, that's you?"

Royce fingered his jet-black hair. "You found me."

"How did you, how did you find me?"

"Me. I believe I was here before you."

"True. Sorry. Oh, here, I'm sure you want it back."

"Yes, thank you." He shoved the handkerchief into his brown leather satchel. The bag. She remembered it from earlier. And he wore the same sneakers too. "And you are?"

"Cordelia Dyer."

"It's nice to meet you, Cordelia. I see your eye is better."

She nodded.

Royce ordered a bottle of white wine and a charcuterie in French. He even thought to ask her if she was vegetarian or vegan. Not a bad start for showcasing gentlemanesque qualities.

"Oh, look, I think we have our next sighting." Royce followed Cordelia's eyes.

Three teen girls, at the most sixteen, glided towards them. Their legs, longer than most men's, strutted in multi-colored suede trousers and chunky heels. They talked over one other and ignored the abundant looks as they passed by.

"Don't tell me, you recognize them as well?"

"I think so. I'll guess Hermes, spring collection. Yeah, I'm sure it's them."

"Impressive." Royce swallowed the last of his red wine.

"Why are you in Paris? Alone?" His voice elevated, exposing his curiosity.

"Mmm, work and vacation. And yes, I'm solo." Cordelia looked down before glancing at him. She wanted to see his reaction, but hesitated, and missed catching his expression. He had turned to look for the waiter. "What about you? Why are you here?"

"Research for my upcoming book."

"Wow. You're an author?"

"Yes, among other things." There was something deliberate in his response, restrained, but she brushed it off as still strangers to one another.

"Would I know it? Your book?" The waiter returned with their wine, told Royce the food would be out soon, and poured Cordelia a fresh glass. She leaned back in her seat and listened to Royce's voice shift from refined, mellow English into rapid, clipped French. He and the waiter chatted like old friends.

Minutes later Royce shifted in his chair and refocused on Cordelia. His gaze created an unfamiliar feeling for her, a fluttery sensation she hadn't felt in years. She dismissed it as the wine.

"Sorry for that." Royce animated as he opened up about his books, tracing invisible patterns on the table as he described plots and characters. "The first book is set in ninth-century England during the Viking incursions." His voice deepened when he explained the hours of historical research, and Cordelia found herself captivated by his passion. As an afterthought, he shrugged and mentioned The New York Times bestseller's list, along with a few other awards that left Cordelia wondering how she'd missed seeing his first novel on the bookshop shelves. "Book two drops in the spring, and to answer your question, I'm in Paris researching for book three." His eyes revealed a modest pride.

"I think my reading list just changed. Any suggestions on where I can get a copy of your infamous book?"

"I do. There's someone here who can help with that. Although, acquiring it would require dinner."

"Tempting offer, but is this person worth spending an entire evening with? I'm selective, you know." She maintained eye contact, moistening her lips with the wine.

"I've been told he's an exceptional dinner companion. Witty conversationalist, extremely knowledgeable, excellent taste in wine, and I can't forget, a charming smile." A persuasive smile appeared, highlighting his disarming dimples.

"We'll see." The playful energy hung in the air as silence settled around their table. Cordelia traced the stem of her wine glass, aware the warmth spreading through her had nothing to do with the wine. Their attraction was undeniable, and she hadn't planned for this. Yet, her pulse quickened when he moved closer. How could it be? Their conversation flowed, like they'd known each other for years. Part of her wanted to explore their connection, the other half reminded her Paris was a holiday, and so was the connection.

Royce topped off his wine and nodded as a waiter placed the charcuterie board onto the table. "Tell me about your work, what do you do?"

"I'm a pastry chef, executive pastry chef, to be exact. I attended culinary school in New York and then worked for several high-end chefs, including Sean Dulcy's Bakery."

He raised an eyebrow and nodded. "Impressive."

"You've been there?"

"Pretty much every time I visit the city."

"Well, if you ever had the chai-spiced eclair with white chocolate crémeux, then you can thank me." Cordelia smirked, still proud of her thirty-under-thirty accomplishments, which began with that one pastry.

"I have. Here's to the genius behind one of my guilty pleasures." Royce lifted his glass to toast her. "Are you still in New York?"

"Umm, no, I'm in London, Mayfair. BL London Patisserie." Cordelia brushed a leaf off the table and repositioned herself, avoiding full eye contact.

"London? You kept that a mystery. My flat's around the corner from BL."

"Why am I not surprised?"

As the evening progressed, their chairs moved closer together, and their conversation, along with the wine, flowed effortlessly. She found herself drawn to his enthusiasm and ability to tune the world out and just listen. She noticed subtle details about him, like the scent of soap and spice, and the way he acknowledged people with a slight smile and nod, as if he observed them through a different lens.

Royce poured the last of the bottle, and they realized the restaurant had packed in around them. Streetlights illuminated their faces, and out of the corner of her eye, she watched him explore her. The wine amplified her senses. She enjoyed his company, but things needed to end before they became something. She needed a clear head.

Cordelia thanked him for a nice evening, suggesting they split the bill, which he declined. She slipped on her coat and grabbed her tote. "Well, it's been fun. Maybe we'll see each other again." Her voice lifted, hopeful for another opportunity to see him. A friendly dinner can't hurt.

"How about tomorrow?" He stood and extended his hand.

"Maybe." Their hands lingered, and the warmth of his skin made her want to draw closer rather than pull away.

"And for the record, I'm an exceptional dinner companion." There, right there. The disarming smile that made her heart leap.

"We'll see." Her mind halted what she wanted to say—yes, definitely, yes.

"Just in case, I plan to be here, same time, with a bottle of wine. And a copy of my book."

Cordelia's cheeks flushed. "It's been nice."

"Good night, Ms. Dyer. See you tomorrow."

Cordelia grinned and left before she changed her mind, deciding to see where the evening took them. As she navigated the streets back to her apartment, she realized it had been hours since she had checked her phone. The thought thrilled and terrified her.

# Chapter Six

Royce and Cordelia walked along the Port de Montebello. Their bodies were reservedly close, yet close enough for him to catch the floral notes of her perfume. Notre Dame loomed above them, silhouetting the night sky. Around them, the rhythmic sounds of strollers blended with nearby street musicians as multi-language whispers echoed against ancient stones.

He'd looked at his watch three times, second-guessing his decision to wait, when Cordelia approached from the sidewalk. Her dark hair showcased a teardrop necklace and rested softly against her collarbone. His eyes followed the sweater's lines, a plunging black pool that dipped into a silky pink skirt. She'd left him speechless.

Despite his declaration to Richard that dating led to inevitable doom, Royce had spent the day in anticipation, anxiously glancing at his watch, distracted from his work.

"You said you're researching the Vikings in Paris?" Cordelia said, her hand brushing against his.

"It's on a Dane in England, actually. Guthrum, you probably heard him called Athelstan, if you remember your history on the Saxons and Vikings. Some scholars suggest he and the Viking Rollo, the first Duke of Normandy, had a friendly alliance. Although my book is set in East Anglia, Rollo is an important character." Royce recounted details of his research, information that fascinates a historian more than a fiction reader. "Do you need clarification?"

Cordelia stopped. "No. Not at all. You just explained, in great detail, that you've been researching Guthrum, a Dane who converted to Christianity under Alfred the Great, ruled East Anglia, and maintained a friendship with Rollo, another Viking who converted after their invasions. Does that sum it up?"

Royce smirked and rocked on his heels.

"Are you always this rude?"

"Am I being rude?" he shoved his hands into his pockets.

"I shouldn't say rude, just condescending."

In his world, people didn't speak so candidly, except for The Earl, but Royce found her jarring and refreshing. "I'm sorry. Haughtiness is a family trait, I guess."

"God, I'd hate to be at your family reunions."

Royce laughed and explored her eyes, her body. She enticed him. But he held back. "Tell me more about your afternoon with Madame Rici."

Cordelia moved her hands in expressive arcs as she described the lively family and the recipes that had built the patisserie into an icon. She effervesced a passion for food history, evident in every word, and matched his own enthusiasm for historical evidence—both thrilled at connecting centuries of people.

They continued walking along the Seine and an hour later found themselves back in the Latin Quarter. Crowds of tourists pushed past them, occasionally giving Royce the opportunity to brush against her hand, feeling the softness of her skin. He listened while she told stories from New York, including recognition by several food magazines. He realized the emotional distance with Cordelia narrowed the more time they spent together. The conversation meandered, like the river, without the calculations that typically controlled his dates.

"And your family? Where are they?" Royce said as they passed through a cast iron gate and entered a quiet garden park. For a moment, their eyes met, and the inches between them dissolved. Both retreated.

"There's only my brother, James. He's an attorney in Seattle." She paused, pulling her coat tighter around her waist. "My father was a historian and professor of indigenous folklore. Most kids learn to read with Dr. Seuss, I learned on legends of the stars." Her voice caught on the word *was* but continued without further explanation. "We moved a lot so he could work among the cultures, which meant he never tenured anywhere." She described her childhood as an adventure, a world unhindered by city life.

Royce contemplated the differences in their upbringings. His on a sprawling country estate where Sunday dinner was a lesson in traditions and the evolution of English politics. She attended public schools. He attended a prep academy.

When she asked about his family, he said, "My father is a lawyer, my mother manages a non-profit, and my brother, Marcus, is a professional polo player." Fortunately, his career distracted her from inquiring further about his parents.

They strolled the outer paths of the park before venturing between rows of hedges. The warm glow of lamps filled the park with a sense of wonder, animating her expressions with playfulness. The trees buffered the outside world, and time suspended without responsibility or expectations.

"Let's check this out." Cordelia grabbed his hand and encouraged exploration, a game of discovery. Her purposeful touch lingered. "Come on."

They scooted left and right, weaving through hedges and following sandy paths into pockets of darkness. Eventually, he wrapped his arm softly around her waist and tugged her towards a lone lamp standing between three trees.

"What's over here?" Royce whispered.

"I don't know. Maybe a portal to the past. Ooh, maybe we'll meet some Vikings." Her giggle hinted at her childlike imagination.

"I hope they're friendly."

"Don't worry, if not, I'll protect you."

He laughed. Despite his intentions to maintain emotional distance, Royce found himself drawn to Cordelia's authentic ability to express life freely, passionately, without an agenda.

When they reached the clearing, Cordelia said, "Oh my gosh, it's a ping pong table in the middle of the park."

"Haven't you ever seen table tennis outdoors?"

"Of course, but I didn't know they had them in Paris."

They walked closer to inspect the table. It was a sturdy concrete structure with a metal net, weathered but functional. To their surprise, someone had left behind two paddles and a ball. A gift from the Parisian gods, Cordelia thought.

"They're quite common here, dozens around the city."

Cordelia picked up a paddle and tested its weight. "Care for a game?" She dropped her tote to the ground, watching as Royce's book shifted to the side.

Royce grabbed the other paddle and bounced the ball. "Do you play?"

"A little."

He juggled the ball on the paddle, perfectly controlling it in the center. "I'm warning you, I'm pretty good."

His challenging tone triggered her competitive instinct and sparked her curiosity.

"Ladies first." He tossed her the ball.

Cordelia's first serve landed fast and precise, catching him off guard. He returned it, but she whizzed it back faster than he reacted.

"You call that just a little?" Royce raised an eyebrow. She could tell he assessed his approach as he paced from side to side.

"Okay, maybe more than a little. I played a bit in high school."

"Since when is a bit more than a little?" Royce took off his coat and rolled up his sleeves.

"Since I was the tennis team captain." She laughed and strutted, rolling up her coat and setting it on top of her tote.

"I see. So, the high school captain thinks she can beat the club champion? We'll see about that." Royce served and aced the ball past her. "I believe that's one point each."

The park lamp cast long shadows across the table as they played, and shadows mimicked their competitive dance. Cordelia proved her athletic ability, lunging, pivoting, and reacting quickly to every shot Royce threw her way.

"Point!" Cordelia shouted as she landed another perfect shot outside his reach. She did her victory dance, channeling her best Brittany Spears moves.

Royce laughed, a good sign, considering he was losing. "You're enjoying this too much."

"Beating a club champ? Absolutely."

"The game isn't over yet." He served with a force she hadn't seen from him.

A small group of teenagers gathered, encouraging them in French and quietly applauding Cordelia's wins. Their impromptu audience heightened her competitive nature. She admired Royce's cut-throat gameplay, but even more, she enjoyed watching his muscles flex. His broad shoulders commanded his side of the table, and a few times she got a glimpse of his tight abs as he lunged for the ball.

Their audience grew when an older couple stopped to watch. The man offered a running commentary in French to his wife, who nodded and followed every ball as Cordelia skidded over the short net.

"He's telling her you're going to win," Royce said.

"Smart man." She cut her eyes at the man and grinned, thanking him for their support.

Royce seized the moment and executed a spin shot that bounced on the far corner. "I wouldn't celebrate prematurely, Ms. Dyer."

"Game on, Mr. Brownell." Cordelia struck a commanding pose at her end of the table and tapped the paddle against her hand. "Are we playing or talking smack?"

"We're definitely playing. And you might want to step back slightly, so you don't miss again."

"Don't worry about me, just serve."

The game continued, each of them winning points. Neither conceded. At match point, Royce led by one. Cordelia served. He lunged. The ball hit the corner and bounced. Royce leaped for the ball, his shoulder colliding with the table's edge.

"Are you alright?" Cordelia ran to check on him.

Royce cradled his shoulder. "It's only a bruise. Let's continue."

"Let me see." She pulled back the corner of his shirt and felt around. "Does that hurt?"

"No. Slightly, but I'm fine." He flinched when she pressed on a red scrape that ran alongside his collarbone."

"I think we should call it quits." She felt the heat of his skin and a rush of breath on her cheek. She glanced up, and his mouth lingered close, moist and open. Their eyes met, and the charged air narrowed the void between their lips. An invitation. A wish. All she had to do was lean up and taste him. "People are watching us," she whispered, an echo of caution from her past with Daniel. But Royce felt different, honest, and unassuming.

I know."

Cordelia realized her hands were pressed against his chest. "I think we're even." Her voice cracked, and she stepped back slightly.

Royce pulled her close. "We shouldn't disappoint our audience. One last point, and then we'll leave."

"You know I'll beat you." Cordelia didn't resist his hold on her waist. She memorized their closeness, the intimacy, and the silent agreement between them.

"As I said, ladies first."

She felt unsettled, excited. This was just the beginning. Paris, a city that orchestrated chance encounters the way she crafted sugar into art, tempted her again.

# Chapter Seven

Royce parked in front of Hayton Manor, the imposing early Tudor home of his family loomed against the evening sky. For him, the anticipation and anxiety of Sunday dinner never lessened, regardless of his age.

Once inside, he followed the rich aroma of roast lamb back to the expansive kitchen at the rear. The spicy scent permeated the house, adding life to the dark paneled hall.

"It smells delicious." Royce approached his mother with a kiss on both cheeks. He breathed in her signature scent of jasmine and bergamot mingled with the savory herbs from the oven.

"There you are." The countess wore a sage-green apron over navy joggers and a tee shirt. Her infectious laughter lit up the room. "Perfect timing. Take these to the table, please." Without hesitation Royce did as she asked, wishing he had a fork handy to taste test the buttery mashed potatoes.

His brother, Marcus and sister-in-law Emma moved together in synchronized fashion, setting the antique table family style. The Earl, sat at the oversized kitchen island, sipping a gin and tonic with two lime slices, watching the countess cook like a lovesick puppy. After forty-two years together, his Pop softened in her presence.

"I saw your interview in the Guardian," Emma remarked, rubbing her rounded belly absently as she arranged napkins. Her burgundy dress outlined her pregnancy without emphasizing it. "Very impressive. Though they made you sound rather stuffy and prudish."

"If they only knew the real you." Marcus joked. "Oh wait, it sounds like they do."

"Speaking of the Guardian," The Countess interjected as she whisked gravy at the stovetop, "the Foundation Gala is December twenty-first. I expect all tuxedos to fit properly this year." She cut her eyes at The Earl.

"I do not know why you look at me when you say that?" The Earl said, swirling his drink.

"You know exactly why, dear." She poured up the gravy. "I say this in all charity The Earl, if you want to wear your usual tuxedo then you need to visit the gym more frequently."

"You must have me confused with your other husband, I visit the gym daily."

The countess patted him on the cheek, blew him a kiss, and said, "Let's eat, dear."

A short while later, stacked dirty dishes littered the kitchen island. Royce and The Earl sat in oversized club chairs where a side table divided them. Marcus looked after Emma, who rubbed her belly and paced. She assured him she didn't need a visit to the hospital.

The countess curled up on the sofa and peered at Royce over the rim of cup. "I assume you'll attend the ball with Cassandra?"

Royce wobbled his tea. "Is that a question or statement?"

"Both, actually."

"No. We're only friends."

Marcus guided Emma to a straight-backed chair beside the sofa. "What's the big deal? You're not seeing anyone else."

"Why the sudden interest in my personal life?"

"I don't think there's anything sudden about it." Emma winced.

"Or personal. We all saw the photos of you with the young actress. What were you thinking, Royce? An actress?" The jovial look on The Earl' face contradicted his tone.

"Don't worry, Pop, she's a client of Cassandra's, and I did her a favor."

"I heard she patronizes everyone on set." Marcus massaged Emma's shoulders.

Royce's mind drifted to Cordelia's expression when she called him condescending. He'd been labeled difficult before, but she said it without malice. Her tone, her eyes bypassed his indifference and left him unsettled.

"Royce?" The countess said. "Where did you go?" She studied him. "You've been distracted all evening."

"It's nothing."

"Problems with the book?" The Earl sounded hopeful.

"No."

"Better confess. You know he'll find out." Marcus said.

"There's nothing to confess. I'm tired." Cordelia's laugh echoed in his memory. "I should head home."

"Royce, find someone nice, like Emma, and bring her to the ball." The countess smiled, but her motherly gaze came with hint of worry.

"I'll consider it." Royce wondered. Would Cordelia understand his family's normalcy? The formality of Hayton Manor juxtaposed with their relaxed closeness.

"Marcus, we need to leave." Emma stared at her lap. A small puddle encircled her feet.

. . .

Cordelia sorted laundry in her London flat, but her mind remained in Paris. It had been a week since their night in the park, and Royce's breath still danced across her skin. The city's scent—a blend of spicy vanilla and chardonnay—held her memories hostage.

She had thought about calling him twice, but changed her mind. The first time was when she arrived at St. Pancras Station, after mistaking a stranger for Royce. The second time happened last night, after finishing a plot-twisting chapter of his book.

London required a different version of herself, someone methodical and in control. She folded sweaters and tucked thoughts of him away.

"Yes, I'm listening." Cordelia snapped at Marnie through her earbuds.

"Then what did I say?"

"You said the opera azalea."

Marnie squealed, "Cordelia Dyer, that's not what I said. Pay attention, please."

Cordelia matched colored socks together, "Okay, I'm listening. Go."

Marnie repeated herself, but her voice faded into chatter.

"Wait. Back up. What did you say about Maisie?"

"I knew you weren't listening."

"Well, I am now, so tell me again."

Marnie's voice drifted across the line. "For the third time, Australia. I'm opening a cake shop in Sydney with Edward. Can you believe it? Sydney!"

"Australia? That's far away. That's like moving to Mars."

"I mean, we always talked about visiting. Who knew I'd

open a shop there for Edward Gild." Marnie's voice pitched higher.

Cordelia smiled and pictured her best friend's ice-blue eyes sparking with enthusiasm. "But what about Maisie?"

"That's what I said, if you'd paid attention. My dad will stay with her while I'm gone."

"But she's five. She needs you."

"She'll be fine. My dad's great with her."

"I know, but."

"Well, Auntie Cor isn't here. And I can't tell Edward no."

"Wait. What happened to slowing down and spending more time with her? Aren't you the one who said she'd only be five once and you were missing all those precious years?"

"Yeah, I did, but New York's expensive. Remember? I have bills to pay: rent, childcare, food."

"Then hire a nanny and take her with you." Cordelia leaned back on the sofa and scrolled through muted TV channels.

"If you're that worried, then come play nanny."

"You know I don't have time."

"Mmhmm. That's what I thought."

Cordelia stopped on a sports channel with tennis highlights. "Have you told Darius yet?"

"I will. But don't change the subject."

"Marnie, it's been six years, you've had plenty of time." On TV, two men battled in front of a packed center court stadium. One smacked the ball with an overhead swing. Cordelia sat up. "Have you considered that this might be the second unfair decision for Maisie?"

"No. This has nothing to do with that. Besides, this is for her."

"She'll miss you."

"I'll miss her too, but I'll make a shitload of money in three months. And then I can slow down."

"But."

"Did anyone ever tell you, you're annoying?"

Cordelia playfully gestured, "Certified pest at your service." The TV grabbed her attention when one of the tennis players collapsed onto the hard court. "Oh, my god. That's Daniel." Her heart constricted even after months of no communication—six months, three weeks, and four days to be exact. During that time, she'd removed traces of their eight years together, focused on a new life, but betrayal or not, seeing him motionless on the court left her feeling knotted. A reminder that some things are hard to delete. "Did you know about this?" His voice from their last fight rang in her head, telling her she cared more about pastries than people. The irony that he'd tell her she was heartless, when he cheated.

"Yeah, I heard they rushed him to the hospital."

"Why didn't you tell me?" The question emerged sharper than intended.

"It's not like you guys talk anymore."

"That doesn't matter. You guys should've told me." Uninvited memories cascaded in, and she resented that after everything, her first instinct was concern rather than detachment.

"I thought you'd heard, by now."

"Has Ben talked to him?"

"He said Daniel has a concussion after heat exhaustion. Supposedly, he's fine. But he said something about Daniel doing rehab in England."

"England?" Cordelia's voice hung on the word.

"Probably nothing. You know how rumors fly. Anyway, back to Australia."

"But Daniel doesn't get injured. Ever." The first time Cordelia watched him play was at the French Open. He raced across the court like a gazelle, never tired or weak. While most players expended energy in a match, Daniel bottled it up, releasing it later in the bedroom. That's how he dominated the rankings. Always a master of control.

"Cordi? Please tell me you don't regret…"

"Oh god, no." A vast ocean stood between sympathy and affection, and it was one she had no intention of traversing. "It's just a shock, that's all."

# Chapter Eight

Cordelia dragged herself into the bakery after a sleepless night. She blamed Marnie and their marathon call. The kitchen lights shocked her eyes into submission. Sam and Lang hunched over sheets of pastry dough, their skillful movements synchronized in the early morning quiet.

"Morning, Chef," Sam said without looking up. His fingers crimped the edges of a tart.

She waved and shuffled towards her office. Shoved against her desk, two cardboard boxes blocked a path to her chair. She dropped her tote on top and strained for the desk lamp. Her elbow whacked against the filing cabinet. "Owwww."

Sam glanced up. "You alright in there?"

"Yeah. I'll survive." She collapsed into her chair, flipped on the computer, and peeked at her phone. The last message she received from Royce, two days earlier, read "Busy tonight. Dinner at the club with Marcus and Pop. Thinking of you." Interesting. Whenever Daniel cancelled, he peppered the text with emojis and exclamation points, but Royce didn't hesitate.

His cancellation came honest and precise. Although, she couldn't decide if it made his message easier or harder to face.

Jessica's voice cut interrupted her thoughts. "Delivery short again." She appeared in the doorway handing Cordelia a clipboard. "It's the third time this month."

"Did you call the supplier?"

"Of course I called the supplier." Her tone suggested Cordelia asked if she knew how to breathe. "They said the invoice matches what they sent."

"Let me see." Cordelia grabbed the clipboard.

Jessica hovered in the doorway as Cordelia compared the invoice and receiving form.

"Now we're out of Madagascar vanilla again, and Bennie says they can't deliver until Thursday."

"Thursday? That's almost a week. We can't operate without vanilla."

"That's what I said." Jessica leaned against the doorway. "He suggested Mexican vanilla as a substitute."

Cordelia shook her head. "Are they kidding? The flavors are completely different. People will notice."

"Right?" Her voice lifted slightly. "Some of us know the difference."

The unexpected agreement caught Cordelia off guard. After six-and-half months they finally agreed on something.

Jessica suggested two options, none of them ideal, but Cordelia thanked her the solutions and told her to finish her tasks. She pulled up the supplier list on her computer, hoping to find someone who could deliver asap.

A text arrived. Royce.

Good morning. Free to meet for coffee?

Mr. Brownell, you're up early ;)

Sam popped his head around the corner. "Chef, can you approve this test batch before we go further?"

"Sure." Cordelia set her phone down and followed Sam into the kitchen.

"It's the cardamom apple-pear tart you wanted to sell for the holidays."

"Right. I forgot you were testing those this morning." Cordelia tasted the poached apples and pears, coated in a sweet-spicy glaze. The flavors were warm, sensual, and comforting. "It's perfect. Let me grab Jessica. She needs to taste this." Cordelia headed for the storeroom, but failed to notice that the cleaning station sink had overflowed. She went airborne.

Time slowed. Cordelia's arms windmilled, her hands desperate to grab hold of something. She watched her feet rise above her head. The inflexible concrete floor sent shockwaves up her spine as her tailbone landed first, followed by her head. It bounced with a thud.

"Chef!" Sam's alarmed voice sounded a million miles away.

Cordelia stared at the ceiling, stunned and spread-eagled on the floor. She stared at the ceiling, transported back to culinary school when she'd accidentally locked herself in the walk-in fridge while hiding from Jeremy. After five minutes of knocking and shouting, Chef Branch opened the door, welcoming her to a roomful of applause. At least this time, she wasn't shivering in a forty-degree prison or running from a disastrous night of boring sex. She became acutely aware of her surroundings, the water seeping into her shirt, and the pain. "Owwww."

Sam's face leaned over. "Don't move. You might have a concussion."

"I don't have a concussion." She attempted to sit up, but a sharp pain forced her back onto the floor. "I think I broke my ass."

Sam cracked a laugh.

Cordelia laughed, wincing in pain. "What next?"

Royce stared at the incomplete sentence on his laptop. The cursor blinked in unison with the ticking desk clock, inherited from his grandfather.

A cold cup of coffee stood in the middle of his research notes, which covered the desk in four organized piles. Across the room, ceiling-high, beige curtains hid the panoramic view of London and buffered the city noise. A coffee table book lay on the oversized sofa, untouched for days. An oversight by the housekeeper.

His phone chimed. It had been hours since he'd heard from her.

Can't make it. Soon?
I'll hold you to it, Ms. Dyer. ;-)

He stared at the cursor, typed a few words, and deleted them. Royce struggled to clear his mind, hungry for creative inspiration, but staring at the screen paralyzed his efforts. The words had flowed effortlessly in Paris. The chapter summaries had clarity and creativity. Now, every sentence was a battleground, scrambling his thoughts. The muffled sound of vacuuming started in the hallway. Thursday. He'd forgotten. The noise fractured his fragile concentration.

He slammed the laptop shut and carried the stale coffee to the kitchen. The spacious room gleamed with unused appliances. Royce dumped the coffee down the drain and watched it spiral into oblivion.

Royce: Free for dinner tonight?
Cordelia: I doubt it.

Royce: Saturday?
Cordelia: Dinner? Definitely.
Royce: Perfect.

His phone rang. "Cassandra." He leaned against the counter.

"Oh, good, you answered. How's the new book coming? You wouldn't believe the backlog of manuscripts I have right now. Everyone wants to be a writer these days. I mean, how many books on business and politics do we need?"

"I'm glad you're not my agent."

"I'm not your agent because I don't do fiction. But that's not why I called. I have an extra ticket to tonight's symphony, and you're coming with me."

"Why?" Royce squeezed his temples.

"Because you need a break from your cave. And I have an extra ticket."

"Everyone else turned you down, didn't they?"

"No, you're my first call. Royce, it's the opening of the season, and this'll put you in the mood."

"Tonight's not good. I have stacks of research to sort."

"No, you don't. Those stacks are meticulous. Besides, I mentioned this performance last month at your parents' dinner, remember? The Mendelssohn project with Grovesson. You said, and I quote, count me in."

Royce returned to his office as Cassandra continued pushing her agenda. He grabbed a remote and the curtains, allowing muted sunlight to flood the room, a welcomed break after three days of rain.

"You can't write if you're burnt out," she said. "An evening away will do you good. And several Scandinavian scholars are attending. I could make an introduction."

The vacuum cleaner moved outside his study door. Royce

imagined another evening alone, a lukewarm takeaway for dinner, and a battle between his thoughts and the keyboard. "What time?"

"Seven." Her voice softened. "And wear the charcoal tux. It complements my gown." Cassandra's invitations had been a standard in his social calendar since childhood, and usually included their fathers in attendance, reminiscing about the good days at Oxford. But the symphony was a rare invite, something she had done with Noah before the breakup.

After ending the call, Royce went out and spoke to Kay, who dusted bookshelves and carefully placed everything in its original spot. She'd worked as his housekeeper-assistant for three years and knew the location of every book, corkscrew, and cufflink.

"Morning, Kay. I'm going out tonight, are my shoes polished?"

"Yes. Would you like me to pull a suit?"

"Not necessary." He turned for the kitchen. "On second thought, yes, the charcoal tuxedo, if you don't mind."

"Don't worry, I'll set it all out for you."

"Perfect." Royce returned to the kitchen. The symphony meant another evening of careful conversations, being the future Earl who *behaved accordingly, not impulsively.* "Why did I agree?"

His phone buzzed with an email from his agent—a reminder about an upcoming book engagement with the Kensington Bookstore. Connor flagged it priority, but Royce remembered the event was booked for January. Plenty of time to prepare. His mind occupied with more pressing matters, Cordelia, and getting over his writer's block.

Despite swearing off relationships, Royce couldn't deny the chemistry with Cordelia. He grinned, anticipating their date on Saturday. But he wondered, could what they shared in Paris survive London's realities? Whatever happened with her was secondary, his books came first. An idea sparked, and he hurried to his computer.

Cordelia shifted uncomfortably in her chair. She'd spent the past three hours at the clinic, only to be told she had a bruised tailbone. Her bottom disagreed. No matter the position, pain shot into her back, and she anxiously waited for Sam to return with her cushion.

To her surprise, Jessica had managed the kitchen with efficiency, even solving the vanilla crisis with a quick exchange of sugar. It seemed everyone had order mishaps.

Cordelia checked her phone again. Nothing new from Royce. At least they'd see each other Saturday night, a well-earned break from work's pressures. Her cookbook loomed in the back of her mind. Her passion project was overshadowed but not forgotten.

She retrieved a pink linen-bound notebook from her tote, the one Royce had given her on their last day in Paris. "I hope you can use this for your recipe project," he said, sliding the burgundy paper-wrapped journal across the table. He'd even thought to add in a white fountain pen, with her initials 'CD' engraved on the cap. She barely knew him, but she swore he'd monogram everything if allowed. Cordelia ran her fingers across the top, the soft texture a reminder that he understood her dedication, her passion.

Cordelia heard Bastien's distinctive laugh in the kitchen. She stood, winced at the pain, and attempted to look less disheveled as he appeared in the office doorway with Jeannine.

"I heard what happened. How are you, my dear?" Bastien leaned down to kiss her cheeks. He looked impeccable in a tailored, yet relaxed, navy suit. Jeannine, his wife, squeezed into the office and greeted Cordelia, without smudging her red lipstick. Their appearance reminded her of how they'd become like family, offering professional and personal guidance. Even though they had children, they treated her like one of their own.

"You're here? I hope you didn't come because of me?"

"No, Jeannine had a gallery meeting, and as luck would have it, friends gave us tickets to tonight's symphony. And here we are." Bastien talked boldly with his hands.

Sam stuck his head in and quietly handed Cordelia an inflated cushion. "Thank you." Her eyes cut to Bastien, offering him a sheepish grin. "I can't believe I did this."

"It happens to all of us."

She eased herself onto the donut-shaped cushion and silently thanked modern pharmaceuticals and design.

"Bastien, she needs a better chair." Jeannine glanced from her husband to Cordelia, "Why aren't you home resting?"

"It's nothing serious, just a bruised tailbone."

Bastien winced. "She's right, you should relax."

"That's my plan for tonight."

"I have a suggestion." His face lit up with a broad smile. "Why don't you come with us tonight?"

"To the symphony?" Cordelia shook her head. "Thank you, but I." She hesitated. Her instinct to decline was as routine as her morning coffee ritual, and Daniel said she had an inability to enjoy life outside the kitchen. Her body screamed for rest, a life away from work.

"You'll relax, listen to the music, and dine with us. It'll be good for you."

"Bastien." Jeannine touched his arm, but he continued talking.

"You can bring your cushion and enjoy yourself. Jessica can manage for one night."

"I appreciate the offer, Chef, but I don't even have anything to wear." Cordelia glanced at Jeannine. "What do people wear to the symphony?" Her eyes pleaded for a way out. She hoped Jeannine would notice.

"Surely, we can get you a gown off the rack. You are slim. We can find you something." She looked at her watch. "Bastien, let's take her shopping before everything closes."

Bastien added with a mischievous smile. "Trust us, you will forget about your derrière and have fun."

Normally, an evening out would be preferable to sitting alone in her flat, but attending her first symphony with an inflatable cushion, as her date sounded embarrassing. Bastien and Jeannine appeared ready to whisk her away if necessary. Saying no was not an option. Cordelia laughed. "You're not going to take no for an answer, are you?"

Together, they replied a stern "No."

Cordelia nodded and gathered her things, including the cushion, and said, "Alright, let's go dress shopping."

As they made their way out, Sam shouted, "Enjoy the symphony, Chef."

"Thanks. They say the music will help. Let's hope so." Across the room, Jessica pulled tarts from the oven. She waved and smiled, revealing the gap between her front teeth. Compelled by her kindness, or maybe the drugs, Cordelia approached her, hoping to avoid the oven's heat. "Thank you. For everything today."

Jessica shrugged, and a hint of satisfaction with a hint of humility crossed her face. "Just doing my job." She slammed a hot pan onto a rolling rack. "Hey, feel better."

They had a breakthrough. It took an injury, but they managed a conversation without frustration. Life took an unexpected turn, and she survived, even without a contingency plan.

# Chapter Nine

Cordelia arrived at the symphony hall coat check window alone. She struggled to balance on three-inch heels the sales lady convinced to wear, while the cushion under her arm protruded, bumping against a few bystanders as she moved up the line. Despite her best efforts to conceal it, her evening companion gathered unwelcomed glances.

The tension in her legs increased as she waited to exchange her coat for a ticket. Her heels clicked against the marble, and she remembered tushes are fragile. She feared one bystander bump could send her into another mortifying tumble, but one for the day was enough. When she made it to the front of the line, Cordelia gripped the brass edging and handed her coat to an avant-garde attendant. She considered lingering, but the woman glared with impatience. As she walked away, anxious to find Bastien and Jeannine, she swallowed a pain pill, hoping it wouldn't lodge in her throat.

In the expansive lobby a crystal chandelier taller than herself, heels included, hung above the sea of shimmering black and red gowns, showcasing everyone's favorite jewels. Ornate columns rose to the ceiling adorned with gold leaf filigree. A temple, of sorts, that reminded Cordelia she came from a different world.

The symphony's prelude played out and opinionated voices collided against marble walls. Cordelia pushed her way to a column and leaned her back against it. The cool stone numbed the discomfort of her feet.

"My dear, you look lovely." Jeannine's French accent drifted toward her as she stepped out of a crowd, elegant in a silver-gray gown. Bastien followed, his black tuxedo impeccable, along with his brightly polished smile.

Cordelia smoothed her hands over the unfamiliar texture of her navy gown, the silky fabric very different from her chef's coat, yet both costumes requiring different performances. "Wow, so do you guys." She gave each a French greeting and forgot about her pain.

"I see you brought your cushion. Now, why don't we find our seats, so you can use it." His expressionate eyes amused Cordelia.

She nodded and looked around the room, unsure where to go. Her heart stuttered when she spotted a familiar face across the room. Royce. He talked with a petite, strawberry-blonde woman who rested her hand on his arm. When she laughed, she tossed her head sideways, revealing a diamond chocker on milky white skin.

A spasm of jealousy tightened in Cordelia's chest, a sensation she swore never to feel again after Daniel and Cary Anne publicly displayed their affair. She wondered if most men morphed from attentive to distant, lacking the ability for sincerity.

"Are you alright? You look faint." Jeannine followed her gaze. "Ah, someone you know?"

"Yes, I think so."

"Would you like to say hello before we take our seats?"

"Yes, we have plenty of time." Bastien looked at his watch and rocked on his heels. She'd worked for him long enough to recognize his restlessness.

"No. It's fine," she looked at Jeannine, "I'm ready."

They turned their attention to the central grand staircase. Bastien scanned the crowd and motioned at Jeannine and Cordelia.

"I thought you had to work."

Cordelia pivoted. Speechless. Royce. His eyes followed the lines of her neckline and dropped to her fitted waist. "Stunning." He leaned in for a friendly greeting, pressing his cheek against hers.

Cordelia held her breath. A deep, rich vanilla scent oozed off him and mingled with the saltiness of his skin. Her body wanted to embrace him, to feel the warmth of his touch, but her mind had alternative desires. She imagined strutting away, leaving him speechless and stranded with his pretentious date. But first, she'd deliver one smart line that exposed him as a player, letting his date know the real Royce. Then she'd walk away laughing, uninvested in their Parisian memory. But the state she was in, her feet and tush couldn't carry off that maneuver. Her back stiffened and she balanced herself on the heels. "How are you?" Her tone sharp, cold.

"I'm with..." He noticed her companions, including the cushion. "Good evening, Royce Brownell."

"Monsieur Brownell," Bastien gave him a two-handed shake. "Bastien Larue, and my wife, Jeannine Gosselin."

"Nice to meet you."

"Well, I'm sure we need to take our seats. I hope you enjoy the symphony, Mr. Brownell. Cordelia." He winked, grinned, and followed Jeannine into the crowd.

"Hold on." His hand slid down her arm and rested in her

hand. "Let me introduce you to my friend, Cassandra." The warmth of his palm against her skin sent a familiar flutter throughout her body despite being annoyed.

"Maybe later. I need to get upstairs." Cordelia released his hand. Their eyes met. The foyer lights flickered. His scent lingered on her cheek, and she craved to more of him.

"I thought you were working tonight?"

"Change of plans." She patted her cushion, prepared to share her mishap, but the boisterous pale ginger arrived, seizing the conversation. "Royce, dear, we need to take our seats."

"Yes, in a moment. Cassandra this is Cordelia Dyer, the Pastry Chef at BL London that I mentioned." He turned to Cordelia. "Cassandra Shaw is an old family friend, since childhood." His tone emphasized their platonic relationship.

"Countess." She emphasized her title as her eyes moved over Cordelia with practiced assessment. "It's nice to meet you."

Cordelia suppressed an eye roll, unimpressed by the inherited status, and her airy tone. "You too." Cordelia shifted on her heels.

"Royce tells me you are an excellent chef. I might be able to use you for an upcoming party. I could use someone creative."

"Oh, I don't do private..."

"She's a pastry chef, Cassandra." Royce stepped closer to Cordelia, resting his hand on the small of her back.

"It sounds like you need a caterer." Normally, she resisted others speaking for her, but she welcomed the caress of his fingers on her skin.

Cassandra squeezed Royce's arm. "We really must take our seats. It was lovely meeting you. Cordelia." Her pause deliberately condescending.

"Yes, it has been a pleasure."

"I'll call you about the party."

Royce pressed his fingers into Cordelia's back, as if reluctant to break contact. "It was a pleasure seeing you tonight."

She wanted his hand to linger, to feel his body pressed against hers.

He leaned closer. "And the seats, they're pretty comfortable." Royce playfully tapped the cushion.

She giggled. "Long story."

"I look forward to hearing it on Saturday."

Cassandra slipped her hand around Royce's elbow. "Darling, we must take our seats." Her hand slithered down his forearm.

"Right. One moment."

Cassandra didn't move, her fruity-floral cocktail of a fragrance invading their space. She tugged at his arm.

"I should go find my seat. It was nice meeting you, Cassandra. Countess. I can refer a caterer if you need one."

"We'll talk."

Cordelia brushed her lips on Royce's cheek. "I need to go."

"I'll call you tonight."

She eased her way into the crowd and heard Cassandra and Royce a few steps behind.

"Does she think the symphony is like their football games?"

"Cassandra."

"I doubt your father will like her, if that's what you have in mind."

Cordelia glanced back. The comment stung like a burn from a hot oven. She wasn't seeking anyone's approval, and she sure as hell didn't trust the word of a pompous Countess.


From below, Royce watched Cordelia ascend the staircase. Her navy gown showcased the lines of her body, exposing a small dandelion tattoo on her shoulder blade, and her hand glided up the railing. But there was an awkwardness to her movements, a tension in her back.

"I think a weekend in the country would be good for you." Cassandra's voice sliced through his thoughts.

"The country's too quiet."

"Yes, but London has noise and distractions."

"I do my best work here, you know that."

"I'm not talking about work, Royce."

Royce cleared his throat. "I heard Guy and Simone bought a house in Primrose Hill."

"I heard." Cassandra stopped, forcing the steady stream of concertgoers to part like water around an immovable rock. "She's a baker, Royce, an American baker."

"Executive pastry chef, and yes, she's American." He gently tugged at her elbow. "We'll discuss it later. Let's get to our seats."

Cassandra had been a fixture in his life, a nuisance most of the time, but beneath her annoying habits she genuinely cared about people. And the reality was, they'd always be neighbors. Her family's estate bordered Hayton Manor.

They reached the top of the staircase, and the usher greeted Cassandra, asking if she needed anything. Royce's eyes followed Cordelia, who'd caught up with her companions and walked in the opposite direction. She whispered to Jeannine, held onto her arm, and removed her shoes. He suppressed the urge to smile, but a grin forced its way out.

"She's pretty, in an obvious way, but."

"I don't recall asking for your opinion."

"No? "Cassandra laughed, void of warmth. "Then why did you introduce us, if you didn't want it?"

"Just being polite."

"Darling, I can see you're enamored with your hopeful schoolboy gaze, but she's only going to cause you problems." She held her hand up when he began to protest. "May I remind you, my record is twenty-two out of twenty-three, and I missed the mark on her because you were at university. This one, is no different."

"This one, isn't up for conversation. Can we get to our seats, please? It's about to begin." He gestured for her to walk. Tension built in his neck and shoulder. But Cordelia was different. Her directness, her passion for her craft, the way she called him out on his condescension—she challenged him in ways that felt both uncomfortable and necessary.

They made it to their box, slipped inside, and found Richard waiting inside, deep in conversation with an exotic, polished woman. The couples greeted one another as the house lights dimmed. On stage the orchestra strolled in and assumed their seats. Other than a slight ruffling sound, the hall echoed silence.

After a brief applause for the conductor, a solo violinist swiped her bow across the strings, but Royce remained lost in his thoughts of Cordelia's lingering kiss on his cheek. They'd restrained themselves in Paris, agreeing to keep things casual, but that kiss was anything but informal.

"Excuse me," he said, rising from his seat. He'd been taught proper behavior outranked emotions, that impulsiveness led to disastrous mistakes. But leaving things unsaid with Cordelia unsettled him.

"Where are you going?" Cassandra whispered.

Royce quietly navigated the corridors, remembering her seat was in Box F2. He slipped through the curtain as the violinist soared into a lively Mendelssohn concerto. Cordelia sat beside Jeannine, her profile illuminated by the stage lights. He slipped into the empty seat beside her.

He scanned the box, finding Cordelia seated between Bastien and Jeannine. Even her profile, illuminated only by the stage lights, she was breathtaking. His chest tightened with an emotion he hadn't allowed himself to acknowledge since Paris.

Cordelia's eyes widened. "What are you doing?"

"No more canceled plans."

"What?"

The music swelled around them, the violins reaching a crescendo. Royce studied her face in the dim light. Cassandra was wrong about Cordelia, and he planned to prove it.

"Let's agree, no more cancelling plans."

"Okay, fine."

"I know we agreed."

The music softened to a whisper. Cordelia grabbed his hand, and led him into the corridor, finding a quiet alcove away from prying eyes.

He continued, "I know both of us wanted to keep this friendly, but I changed my mind."

"Okay." Her eyes darted. "What are you saying?" Her voice elevated with uncertainty.

"I want us to give this a chance."

"I thought we already were." She stepped closer, her voice confident, unwavering.

"Yes, but we seem to have our fair share of interruptions."

Their eyes met. "Work's been busy..." She began to speak, but stumbled over her words, "Maybe you're right, maybe I want." Her eyes darted back-and-forth. She bit the corner of her lip.

"I'm tired of games and rules. Don't you want to step outside the lines and see where it takes us?" The confession felt risky, but something about her made him want to walk the edge.

The wistful sounds of violins drifted into the corridor. The sound hesitated between notes and married with her breath. He stepped closer, looking for a response, and waited.

Cordelia traced his lips with her finger. She tasted buttery, sweet. She nodded and closed the distance between them. Her tentative touch turned turbulent like a dancing bow across strings reaching a fervent pitch. Their kiss encapsulated the music, and Royce pulled her close. She winced and pushed away, pressing her hand against the wall.

"Owww."

"I'm sorry?"

"Don't be. I bruised my tailbone. It's why I cancelled this morning." She exhaled, releasing tension from her back.

"Why didn't you say so?"

"Embarrassed. Frustrated. I don't know. It sounds pretty stupid right now."

"Can I get you anything?"

"No." She stretched and stared into his eyes, resting her hands on his chest.

Royce held her face with a feather-light touch and kissed her. Cascading sounds of flutes mingled with cellos and the violins spiraled upward, before softly falling into silence. They examined each other's faces.

"I think we just crossed the casual line." She whispered. "And I don't want to go back."

# Chapter Ten

In a dimly lit dining room, Royce longed for Cordelia's touch. She sat across from him, engaged in animated conversation with restaurant owner Darius Blume, whose wild hair and matching eyebrows made him look more like a mad scientist than a culinary genius. When she talked, her elegant fingers moved through the air with the precision of a maestro. Candlelight flickered on a single pearl draped around her neck, accentuating the classic lines of her black dress. And the constellation of freckles across her cheekbones glowed like a map with untold stories.

As he looked around the room, the converted vault's old stone walls arched upward, echoing murmurs of forgotten voices. The atmosphere inspired an idea—the perfect setting for Saxon monks immersed in prayer, hiding from Viking invaders. He should've been taking notes, but instead found himself mentally cataloging the melancholy of phantom chants beneath the clinks of modern silverware.

"Thank you for accommodating us," Cordelia said. "I know Saturday nights are hectic, especially on short notice."

"Of course, anything for you." Darius' rugged Scottish

accent seeped through. He kissed Cordelia's cheek and then extended his hand to Royce. "Nice to meet you, mate. We'll take care of you guys tonight." After a solid exchange, he patted Royce on the shoulder and rushed back to the kitchen.

Darius' restaurant, Wonder, had become the hottest reservation in London. Located in West Smithfield, the converted medieval ruins offered guests intimacy, with sixteen tables and an enchanting lounge. Everything about the place represented him and his elevated Highland cuisine.

Cordelia reached across the table and caressed Royce's hand. Her touch aroused something more dangerous than physical desire, it made him susceptible to trusting again.

"How's your writing going?"

"Until yesterday, I hadn't written a complete chapter." He sipped his drink, "Usually I'm a fast writer because I spend the majority of my time on research and outlining." He withheld mentioning the family archives he'd grown up exploring, the stories that had shaped him long before Oxford. "But this week I couldn't write anything satisfying. Then yesterday, I sat down and wrote the first two chapters without any problems."

"What changed?"

"I'm not sure." He hesitated to admit thoughts about her had consumed his writing time. "What about your cookbook? Any progress with the research?"

Cordelia's eyes lit up. "Yes. I reached out to some of the old English families, the ones that are dukes, with big estates, and asked if I could research their culinary files. You'd be amazed at the recipe collections some of them have hidden away in their libraries. Some even go back to medieval times."

Royce swirled his gin and tonic. "Oh, which families?"

"So far, I've written to the Bradley House, which is owned by the Duke of Somerset, and Knowsley Hall. The..." She tapped her finger against his hand.

"The Earl of Derby."

"Yes, that's who it is. And I also wrote to Hayton Manor."

"The Earl of Thornbury?"

"Yes. That one I'm very interested in visiting. The lady at the archives said the Countess of Thornbury is friendly and generous."

Royce's fingers tightened around the cold glass. He took a measured, three-second sip. A technique he'd perfected at social gatherings, which allowed him time for composure whenever unexpected topics arose. "The Countess of Thornbury?" He steadied his voice.

"Yes. I've already heard from her secretary. She said the records are housed within the family's private library, so she'd need to coordinate with the countess."

Royce nodded and intertwined their fingers.

"She also said it could take months to get an appointment because the family is cautious about who gains access. I told her where I work and about my project. She seemed impressed. Hopefully, that'll get me in."

He squared his gin glass beside the water goblet. His eyes darted from the soft touch of her fingers to her face. "Right. The Countess of Thornbury." The words *my mother* sat on the edge of his tongue, but her enthusiasm for culinary research, unmarred by social games, made him rethink the timing of his disclosure.

"Yes, do you know her? Oh, god, don't tell me she's related to Countess Cassandra?"

He chuckled. "No. No, they're not related. But she's." Royce struggled to find the words. How did he explain that the Countess of Thornbury was his mother, and Hayton Manor was his childhood home? Or that he'd withheld this from her because, as soon as she knew his title, things would change? "They're traditional. Very nice people, but their history makes them conventional. What I'm saying is, don't expect too much."

Before Cordelia could respond, Darius reappeared, carrying two plates with langostinos placed on a vibrant herb sauce. He poetically described the first course and then hinted at what's to come. "Enjoy." After a few steps, he returned to the table. "You tell him about us yet?"

Cordelia laughed. "No, and don't make him think there was an us."

"Were you?" Royce asked, relieved the conversation had shifted.

"No." Her voice elevated. "Sorry, Darius, I didn't mean it like that."

Darius smirked. "I get it. No, mate, I dated her flatmate Marnie in New York. One night, I got up to use the bathroom, got turned around, and ended up walking into Cordi's room."

"And I woke up to find this naked guy crawling into my bed, so I hit him with the nearest thing I could grab, my water bottle."

"A full stainless steel water bottle," Darius said, rubbing his head. "Mind you, she gave me a concussion before I could explain."

"You were naked in my room, explanations weren't my priority."

"And now here we are," Darius gestured grandly. "Still friends."

"Only because Marnie didn't kill us both." Cordelia's eyes moistened from laughter.

"How is she?" Darius' tone deepened. "Did she take the job in Australia?"

"She told you about that?"

He nodded. "Yeah, she called a few weeks ago. Said she wanted to stop by on her way home from Australia."

Royce noticed Cordelia's fingers tightened around his hand. "Stop by? Who stops off in London from Sydney?"

He chuckled. "Good point. She said it'd been a while, and it sounded like a good excuse to take some time off myself."

"You two did always end up back together, in between everyone else."

"Maybe it's a sign." An awkward pause settled over the table. Darius cleared his throat. "Right, well, I should check on your next course."

Royce waited a few seconds. "Is everything alright? You seemed uncomfortable when he mentioned Marnie's visit."

"It's nothing." Cordelia took two short sips of wine. "It's just..."

"Are you jealous of her? Of him?"

"No." She sighed. "Marnie and Darius have history. More than just casual. But it's not my story to tell."

Royce nodded, understanding the desire to protect secrets, especially when it changes the dynamics. If he confessed his connection to the Countess of Thornbury, then Cordelia's impression of him would change. She'd treat him differently. "About those families, I might know a few people from university who can help. They have access to records in London."

"London? I'm interested in the family's collections, not government records. I want access to their cook's notes and recipes, especially the Thornbury's."

Royce lifted her hand, examining the soft curves of her fingers. "Yes, well, those families can be complicated." He hesitated to say more, worried his confession would spoil the evening. "We should eat before the next course arrives."

Cordelia agreed. With the arrival of each new plate, they discussed everything from molecular gastronomy to medieval manuscripts to chocolate tempering. Royce found himself caught between two desires: the urge to reveal everything about his family and his title, and the desperate wish to preserve this uncomplicated connection they'd built.

For now, he chose to remain simply Royce, the writer she'd met in Paris, the man who'd kissed her at the symphony, and the one who longed to study the curves of her body. The truth would have to wait.

# Chapter Eleven

Cordelia walked in a straight line to work. The cold, dark morning forced a brisk pace. She breezed past Sam and the team, offering an exuberant wave before slipping into her office. Between the symphony and their dinner at Wonder, the relationship had taken an interesting, overly comfortable turn. She caught herself planning shared mornings with Royce, his lips against the nape of her neck, instead of replying to supplier emails. An unnerving habit for someone who, at the age of seven, had watched her mother leave with a suitcase and never return.

For fifteen minutes, she drifted between her task list and imagination. Warmth spread through her chest, fresh hope—a sensation that exhilarated and frightened her. She finished the last of her tea, fired off the emails, and escaped to the kitchen. She found the simplicity of flour, sugar, and butter soothed an unpredictable heart.

Before long, she wrapped her hands around a cold, baseball-size clump of dough and dropped it onto the table, manipulating the pastry into a thick square. The rhythmic movement provided mental solace for Cordelia, even in a noisy, bustling kitchen.

In the far corner, a machine hummed as Sam flattened, stretched, and layered dough with butter. The rollers compressed and groaned. Delicate dough trapped between pins.

"Chef." Sam wiggled a knob, then another.

"It's fine. Try turning the pins. Or see if one slipped out of place."

Sam did as suggested. No luck.

"Umm, try rebooting it."

"Yes, Chef." Sam unplugged, waited, and re-plugged the machine. "That didn't work."

Cordelia wiped her hands and darted over, pushing and pulling on the rollers. The machine went silent. "No! Shit." She flipped the switch off and on. Nothing. "Dammit." How many more sheets did you need to roll out?"

"Five."

"Five? It's six-thirty. I don't think we'll get them all done, but we'll try."

"Try what? Rolling manually?"

"We have no choice." Cordelia wiped her hands on her jacket. "They did it a hundred years ago." She grabbed a knife and sliced what she could of the stuck sheet. "Grab your team. I want everyone in here rolling, unless they're in the middle of mixing. These sablés have to go out today. We've marketed them for the holidays, including custom orders. Okay, go, get everyone in here."

Two taps on the storefront window grabbed Cordelia's attention. "Someone, please see what that woman wants."

Seconds later, Lang, a young baker, returned. Her voice cracked. "Umm, it's a journalist. She said she needed to speak to you."

"Now?"

"Apparently." Her girlish voice trailed off to a whisper.

"Okay. I'll be there in a second. Tell her to wait out front. No, have her wait in the shop." Cordelia glanced at Sam. "Get everyone rolling. There are at least ten pins in the stockroom. And I'll call Jessica in a second." Her watch revealed time had barely passed. She grunted. "Damn, company's not open yet."

After a couple of composed breaths, she greeted the mysterious reporter. The woman dressed as if she'd finished a session at the gym, shoved her hand at Cordelia. "Taylor Henson. It's nice to meet you, Ms. Dyer."

"Can I help you?"

"I know you're busy."

"That's an understatement."

"I wanted to talk with you about Daniel Montali. He said."

"What?"

"Daniel Montali. Your ex?"

"What about him?" Cordelia glanced over her shoulder, making sure her staff were in the kitchen working, not eavesdropping, and then squared her shoulders at Taylor. Her pulse quickened. She'd put time and space between the past and present, yet Daniel continued to demand attention. Didn't he get enough from his fans?

"He said you would be a good person to speak to."

"Well, he's wrong. Listen, this is an inconvenient time. Give me your number and I'll be in touch."

"Sure." Taylor searched her jacket pocket for a card.

A crash from the kitchen jolted Cordelia.

"That didn't sound good."

Cordelia smirked and shook her head, startled again when a shadowed figure knocked on the shop door. Royce. He pressed his nose to the glass and held up two cups of coffee. The sight of him, a reminder of life's thoughtful gifts.

"Well, I can see you're busy. I look forward to your call."

Cordelia rushed her out the door and greeted Royce with a quick kiss. "You're a lifesaver, thank you."

"Who was that?"

"Nobody." Cordelia gulped her coffee.

"Everything all right?"

"No. Our sheeter machine quit right in the middle of rolling dough. And we're on a time crunch, but I've got them manually rolling until I can get someone out here."

"Is there anything I can do to help?"

"Fix my machine." She grinned, appreciating his offer.

Jessica appeared in the doorway, tucking her pixie into a hair net. "Morning, Chef."

"Jessica? When did you get here?"

"Just now. Sam rang, so I thought I'd come on in and help."

"Thank you."

Jessica nodded. "No worries." She glanced at Royce and gave a half-smirk. "How are ya?" She returned to the kitchen before he could reply.

"I should get back in there. Thanks for stopping by." She kissed him on the cheek.

"See you tonight."

"Tonight?"

"The book signing event."

"Oh, right. Yes, I'll be there. For sure." A flash of guilt settled into determination. She knew the importance of the night and assured him she wouldn't be late. They said their goodbyes, and Cordelia returned to the kitchen, wondering what other unexpected events would unfold. To her surprise, Jessica had five bakers lined up, rolling in unison.

"Come on, guys, light pressure, but make that dough stretch for you." She stood with her back to Cordelia, facing the group and rolling as she coached. "That's it, Lang, massage it with your pin."

Cordelia threw on her apron and stationed herself alongside Jessica. Two hours later, the kitchen had transformed into an efficient operation, and what began as a crisis evolved into friendly teamwork. Jessica impressed Cordelia, and she found time to laugh at her jokes.

As the staff began to clean up, Cordelia approached Jessica. "You're a good leader."

"You mean it?"

"I wouldn't say it if I didn't mean it."

A flicker of surprise turned into pride. "Thanks. Ya know, you are too, Chef." She peeled the hair net off and shoved it in her back pocket. "So, you know, I set aside some chocolate croissants, the ones Jasper and Lucy like. They're on your desk." She shrugged and stretched, speaking to a passing baker.

"That's really nice, Jessica, thank you."

"It's nothing. Besides, it's cold out." Jessica tugged her sleeve down, covering her wrist. "Cold's harder on some than others." A bowl dropped and rattled against the floor. "All right, all right, who's damaging stuff?"

Cordelia returned to the office and collapsed in her chair, staring at Taylor Henson's card. What could Daniel possibly want after all this time? The question nagged at her more than the broken machine—they can be fixed, some relationships can't. She tossed the card into the trash and watched Jessica continue to organize the kitchen staff. An unexpected alliance revealed itself, and new relationships in London proved to be her future, but her past edged itself closer. She decided to confront things and texted Daniel.

We need to talk.

Despite the time difference, he responded instantly.

Tell me when and I'm there.

City streetlight poured through the bookshop's windows, casting cream hues onto tables neatly lined with rows of books. A hallway-like aisle lined with bookshelves invited visitors to explore further into the heart of the shop. There, a group of historical novel enthusiasts listened to Royce as he gave a reading from his first novel. When he finished, the hush lingered, and he examined their faces, looking for signs of approval. Their expressions ranged from somber to mournful, emotions he'd hoped to draw out of his readers, but to experience it first-hand unsettled his nerves.

His thumb rustled the pages of his book, emblazoned with a Saxon sword wrapped in delicate blue ribbon. "Well then, thank you for coming."

Applause rippled through the crowd, leading to an explosion of support. Royce nodded in gratitude and scanned the room for Cordelia. He'd spotted her midway through the Q & A, slipping into a chair in the back row. She listened and draped her hair to one side, exposing the elegant line of her neck. The sight of her derailed his thoughts.

"Excellent presentation, Mr. Brownell." The man at the front of the line tapped the open book. "Would you sign this for my husband? He loved your book so much, he's read it twice."

"Of course. What's his name?"

"Warren. He's working at the hospital tonight, so he sent me instead."

Royce signed his name and thanked the man for attending, gifting him a copy of his own. With each person, he maintained a methodical approach as if they were students under his guidance, pausing for eye contact before signing. Yet, his attention remained split. Cordelia wandered the shop, having tactile interactions with the books. She immersed herself in mystery.

As the queue shortened, Cordelia approached the table, her expression complex and playful. She placed his book on the table. "Your book comes highly recommended." A smile rose at the corners of her mouth.

"Glad to hear it. And you are?"

"Cordelia."

"You're very mysterious, Cordelia. Any chance I can rectify that over a drink?"

"Maybe." She ran her hand through her hair. "Depends on how poetic you are, in my note." Her fingers paused and adjusted the pearl necklace that rested against her porcelain skin.

Royce opened the book and wrote a personal message: Cordelia, the most memorable stories begin unexpectedly, with characters that linger on the mind. That is you in Paris. I hope our story continues. He handed her the book, "Poetic enough?"

Cordelia read his note and blushed. "Yes, it is." Her finger traced the letters. "I'll wait up front."

As she walked away, a bearded man in a sports jacket approached the table. Royce recognized his former mentor, Gavin Andrews, immediately. His stomach clenched.

"Royce Brownell. From lecturer to bestselling author." His hardworking Northern accent still lingered, even though he'd been in London for more than thirty years. "Quite the transformation." His tone remained cordial, but his smile avoided his eyes.

"Gavin. I'm surprised to see you." Royce kept his voice neutral, aware Cordelia and the shop owner were in earshot.

"Why wouldn't I keep up with my top protégé?" Gavin glanced around the room, noticing Cordelia. His eyes followed the curves of her body as she browsed books. "Especially one who left so abruptly. The students still ask about you, you know."

Royce stood and straightened the remaining copies of his book on the table. "Do they?"

Gavin crossed his arms. "Yes, the department never recovered after that unfortunate business with."

Royce shoved a book at him. "Are you here for a copy or not?" He and Gavin locked eyes. Royce searched for some semblance of remorse but found only a void.

"No. Just stopped by to see for myself." He tapped the table and walked a few steps away. Royce waited, anticipating that Gavin had more to say. "Oh, Dean Palan said there might be a place for you, should the fiction writing fail."

"You can tell the Dean it's not necessary. Better yet, I'll tell him myself." Royce tucked his fountain pen into his black wool coat and gave the books one last straightening.

"I guess some of us can't use our name for leverage."

"That's enough, Gavin."

He stepped closer, squaring off to the table. "It's a real shame, Royce. You always seemed to be running from something rather than toward it." Gavin leaned closer and lowered his voice. "Evie's doing well, by the way. Completed her PhD over the summer."

Royce shoved a stack of books into Gavin. "Guess you need to back up."

The bookshop owner approached. "Everything alright, Mr. Brownell?"

"Yes. He's an old acquaintance, and he's leaving."

"She mentioned you're the only one." Gavin's eyes contained a darker intention than mere professional interest. He always liked to play games with people.

"It was good seeing you, Gavin." Royce grabbed his coat and

walked around the table. "Give my regards to your ex-wife." He motioned towards the front door, encouraging him to leave.

Gavin nodded and brushed past Cordelia with a cordial goodbye. She gazed at him and looked back at Royce inquisitively.

A few minutes later, Royce said good night to the shop owner and located Cordelia among the cookbooks, reading about Middle Eastern desserts. A weight of silence hung in the air.

"Old colleague?" she said, her tone curious but cautious.

"You could say that."

"Well, I guess some stories are better over a bottle of scotch." She tucked her hair behind her ear and smiled. He read her eyes, a bridge, an invitation to leave the past behind and be invested in the present with her.

# Chapter Twelve

Hayton Manor looked nothing like Cordelia imagined, imposing itself onto the green, rolling landscape with neatly shaped trees flanking the front door. Above it, a family crest, carved into stone, reminded guests of the owner's lineage. The impressive medieval house with mullioned windows and sharp roofline peaks appeared timeless and resolute.

The taxi that had driven her to the estate from the train station pulled away. It disappeared around a bend in the private road that wound through sprawling fields. Cordelia double checked her tote, making sure she hadn't forgotten her notebook and design ideas. Her fingers paused on the journal Royce had given her in Paris. She felt around the bag, pulled out the white fountain pen he'd given her, and kissed it for good luck. Confidently, she approached the massive oak doors and rang the bell. It chimed like church bells after a wedding. *Just as Royce said, traditional.* It amused her.

A middle-aged woman in a muted yellow sweater opened the door. "Ms. Dyer," she said.

"Hi, yes. I'm here to see the Countess of Thornbury."

"Of course, the Countess is expecting you." She smiled and gestured, her teeth whiter than her skin.

Cordelia stepped into the entrance hall that could have housed her entire London apartment. An ancient tapestry hung on a wood-paneled wall, adding color to the otherwise quiet room, while a small portrait of a Tudor-Esque man appeared to guard the house from above the fireplace. The space smelled of beeswax, wood polish, and the subtle fragrance of fresh flowers arranged in massive urns.

"I'm Amy Kelley, the Countess' assistant. You can leave your luggage here." She didn't wait for formal greetings. "Please follow me."

"Oh, sure. Thank you."

They passed a sweeping, wood-carved staircase and entered what Amy called a study, emphasizing this was one of several throughout the house. A moment later, a slender woman with jet-black hair appeared, moving with the poise of a ballerina. Her inviting smile seemed at odds with the formal setting.

"Ms. Dyer," she extended her hand. "I'm Countess of Thornbury, Alia Brownell, but please call me Alia."

"Thank you for inviting me. Did you say, Brownell?"

"Yes." She motioned to Amy, who nodded and left the room. "I thought we might start in the library. I had three volumes pulled, but there are at least five more if needed."

"That's perfect, thank you."

Amy returned with a tray of tea and assorted cookies. Cordelia and the Countess talked for thirty minutes, with the conversation revolving around the cookbook and pastries. She maintained a warm smile throughout, showing genuine interest in the project.

"If you're ready, we'll go to the library." The countess stood and placed her neatly folded cloth napkin on the tray. "I think you'll find the cooks here were meticulous in their records."

"That's great. I'm excited to see what you have."

Cordelia followed her through the house, in awe of the historical features. Her hostess proved to be a knowledgeable guide, pointing out several family heirlooms, including a suit of armor in one sunlit corridor.

"My husband's family has occupied Hayton since 1583. Prior to that, it was a monastery. It's been modified over the years, with the east wing being added in the eighteenth century. And of course, modern conveniences have been incorporated."

She counted three formal living rooms and one hall, which housed two more sitting areas and a billiard table. They ended up back in the study, and Cordelia wondered how anyone ever got used to that many doorways. "It's incredible, like walking through living history."

The countess motioned for Cordelia to sit. "That's precisely what my son says. He's a historian, actually."

Voices in the entrance hall interrupted their conversation. Her face brightened. "Speaking of my son. Let me introduce you."

"Mother?" A familiar figure appeared.

"Royce, you're just in time. I want to introduce you to Ms. Cordelia Dyer. She's a pastry chef in London, doing research here for a couple of days. Cordelia, this is my son, Lord Royce Brownell."

She froze. Her mind struggled. The truth had been there all along, and she'd foolishly overlooked it. His knowledge of Hayton Manor. Childhood friends with a Countess. Hesitation about her onsite research. It all hid in plain sight.

His eyes widened, darting around the room, and settling into a polite demeanor. "Ms. Dyer." He extended his hand as if they were strangers. "A pleasure to meet you."

She accepted it with a practiced smile. The icy touch of his skin felt more formal than in Paris. It stung. "Lord Brownell."

Her mind calculated escape routes back to the safety of the kitchen, where posh titles wouldn't uproot her. But the cookbook was her dream, and the opportunity might slip from her fingers if she left too soon. Success battled with betrayal, and ultimately, achieving her goal won.

"Please, call me Royce."

She smirked. "The countess has been telling me about your family's history." She cleared her throat, hoping the shake in her voice would fade.

"We're not formal, just Alia." She looked at Royce. "Perhaps you can assist with interpreting some recipes."

"Oh. I'm sure he's too busy."

"I'd be happy to assist, Ms. Dyer." His tone showcased good manners, but his eyes pleaded for forgiveness.

"Excellent." The countess said. "Cordelia, I'll show you to the library, but I thought we'd have lunch before settling into the books." She headed towards the door, with Cordelia following behind. "Royce, will you be joining us for lunch?"

"I hadn't planned on it, but I'll rearrange my schedule."

Cordelia cut her eyes back at him, just as she turned the corner.

"As a matter of fact, I think I'll join you now."

Cordelia maintained a deliberate distance from Royce. He walked behind her, his sneakers resistant against the wood floors. Each step reinforced the aspects of himself he'd hidden from her.

They reached the library, with its soaring shelves filled with thousands of books, ranging from contemporary to leather-bound covers. A rolling staircase allowed them to access the upper shelves. The room smelled of bergamot and sweet tobacco, the odor of a time when women were discouraged from imagining anything other than a pious life.

The countess directed Cordelia to a large oak table where

several antique cookbooks resided. "These volumes date back to the 1700s." She opened one of the leather-bound books and slid it in front of Cordelia. "The family believed in meticulous documents."

"The condition is remarkable." Cordelia focused on the yellowed pages that were bound in leather and wrapped with twine, a welcomed distraction from her emotional turmoil. For several hours, she immersed herself in a disciplined regimen of note-taking, allowing her fingers to go numb from the grip of her pen. Whenever footsteps passed the library door, her shoulders tensed, anticipating Royce's return. But he never did, and gradually, recipes absorbed her mind, even as skepticism simmered in her heart.

Royce's gaze burned against her cheek, but she refused to look at him. If she did, she'd reveal her sadness, and she refused to give him the satisfaction of his game.

The afternoon passed with Cordelia and the Countess bonding over recipes, while Royce avoided the library altogether. Her hollow stares compounded the heaviness of his guilt. Instead of dealing with the self-imposed charade, he retreated to the east wing study and buried himself in writing. Or the appearance of it. The words refused to come, his mind replaying Cordelia's shocked expression. He knew the moment would come when she'd learn the truth, but he'd hoped to control the circumstances. His father had taught him to strategize for every contingency, yet he'd failed to prepare for the hurt in her eyes.

At seven o'clock sharp, Royce and his family gathered around the kitchen table. Cordelia entered. She wore the same outfit from earlier, except now half of her cream blouse hung over her jeans, and her hair was tossed in a messy ponytail.

"Wonderful, you decided to join us." The countess said. "Thomas, this is Cordelia Dyer."

He stood and offered his hand. "Very nice to meet you, Ms. Dyer. I'm the Earl of Thornbury."

"You too, and please call me Cordelia. Should I call you Earl?"

Amused, he grinned. "Sir is fine, unless I see you in public, then it's Lord."

"Pop, don't overwhelm her," Royce said.

Cordelia cut her eyes at him, looked back at the Earl, and said, "Nice to meet you, Sir."

"And this is our younger son, Marcus, his wife Emma, and their daughter, Ada Rose."

They warmly greeted each other, and Royce watched the tension subside from Cordelia's shoulders. Yet when he pulled her chair out, the softness in her voice vanished, replaced with a formality that cut deeper than rage.

"Ada is named after my mother." The Earl said, returning to his seat.

"It's a beautiful name." Cordelia sipped her water as they passed dishes of food around the table. "Thank you for sharing your recipes with me. They're remarkable." She held eye contact with the Earl and Countess.

"Well, if you ever need to know the rainfall amounts of 1620, he has those too," Marcus said, passing her a basket of freshly sliced bread. "And I'm not joking, our library records contain bizarre trivia."

"As you know, organization reflects respect." The Earl said.

"Respect for history. Yes, Pop, I know." Marcus smirked at Royce.

He quietly pushed food around on his plate, and as she interacted with his family, Royce felt a silent indictment, an awareness he'd denied her the opportunity to prove she fit into his world.

"Speaking of which, were you aware, Cordelia, that our family has occupied this estate since before the founding of America?"

"Pop." Royce dropped his fork onto the plate. "You don't need to make Ms. Dyer feel uncomfortable."

"I assure you, I'm not." Cordelia locked eyes with him. "I find it fascinating." Her chin dipped. Her fingers laced around the fork and knife, cutting through a chicken breast in one motion.

Royce felt the subtle rebuke in her response, and the control of her words provided an obvious message for him. He had work to do, to repair their relationship.

The conversation eased after their initial tension, and the Earl entertained her with tales of Brownell ancestors who'd entertained kings at the house. Royce listened to the subtleties of her voice, surprised by her attentiveness. He'd never seen someone, other than his mother, that interested in his father's stories.

An hour later, empty dessert plates dotted the table. The countess poured tea while Marcus shared a recent polo accident, revealing the bruises on his arm. Ada Rose stirred on the monitor, distracting both Emma and Marcus.

"If you'll excuse me, I need to review my notes before bed." Cordelia folded her napkin and placed it on the table. "Thank you, both of you, for a lovely dinner."

"I'll escort you." Royce stood, his chair scraping against the wood. "It's easy to get lost in the east wing."

"Oh. No, I can manage," she said.

"He's right, without a map you might wander for days, and this house is known to have a ghost or two." The countess laughed and insisted it was a joke.

"Actually, there are." Royce caught Cordelia's sigh. "Come with me."

They walked in silence through the first corridor, their footsteps brushing against antique rugs.

"We'll take the second right and then a left at the armor."

"Is that the British equivalent of 'turn left at the McDonald's?" She said with spirit.

He chuckled. "Should I tell the Earl you just compared his house to a fast-food restaurant?"

"Why would you? I thought you liked keeping secrets."

And there it was. Royce halted and faced her. They squared their bodies to each other. "Cordelia."

"Lord Brownell."

"Don't."

"Why? Isn't that your name?" She crossed her arms. "Or just a minor detail you forgot to mention?"

"I never lied to you."

"Did I use the word lie? No." Her body moved with each word. "Do you feel guilty? Yes."

"You're overreacting."

"Really? In my book, omission is lying, and you omitted the fact that you're the heir to a title." Her voice remained low, controlled. "Were you ever going to tell me?"

"Yes. Of course."

"When? After we slept together? After I met your family?" Her body shifted to one side. "Or were you waiting for your coronation?"

"We don't have coronations, just inheritance." He winced at the automatic correction.

"Exactly. You know the difference. This is your life. Yet, you presented yourself as a humble author with a lawyer father."

"And I am an author."

"Who happens to be Lord Brownell, future Earl of Thornbury, ruler of all this." Her arms gestured wildly.

He ran a hand through his hair and crossed his arms. "Is it so bad that I wanted you to know me before my title interfered?"

"Again, my point, your title is part of you. This house, your family, these expectations, they're who you are, very different from the Royce I knew."

"Hear me out, people change when they learn who I am." The words burst from his core with unexpected force. "They're either impressed or dismissive. They interact with the title, not me, not Royce, who likes to eat chocolate ice cream in the middle of the night, or loves an early morning jog when it's foggy outside."

She rested her hands on her hips. "Is that what you think of me? That I'm so shallow I wouldn't see anything more than a title? And by the way, you shouldn't eat ice cream that late, really bad for you."

"I know, it's a bad habit. And I never accused you of being shallow."

"Then why didn't you give me a chance?"

He leaned against the wall, searching for words that would fix things between them. "With you, everything felt genuine. You're genuine, and it was refreshing."

"So, you risked hurting me?" Her voice softened.

"I had planned to tell you this weekend, minus the ancestral stories and armor. And the ghosts."

Her lip twitched, and she smiled. "Are there really ghosts?"

He moved closer to her. "At least a dozen."

She leaned against the wall and scanned the hallway. "Seriously, do they come into the east wing?"

"That's their favorite part of the house, especially the blue room." He laughed wide-eyed and menacing.

Cordelia covered her face. "Oh my god, I'll be awake all night, thanks to you."

Royce reached over and touched her hand. She flinched and stepped backwards.

# Chapter Thirteen

That night, Cordelia couldn't sleep. The unfamiliar softness of the four-poster bed in the blue room, the silence interrupted by floorboard creaks, and the whirlwind of revelations of the day conspired against her.

At one a.m., she gave up on sleep, slipped out of bed, and threw on a plush guest robe over her pj's. The chilled air felt like a ghost's breath. Why did Royce have to tell her the house had resident goblins? She grabbed her phone flashlight, hoping they feared modern technology.

A noise in the hall startled her, and she looked for a hiding spot, wondering if ghosts could see through objects. Royce would pay for his mental prank, assuming it was probably him lurking in the hallway, hoping to scare her. But to her surprise and disappointment, the hallway was empty. Staggered night-lights lit the corridor along with two small sconces, just enough light to navigate without her phone.

Hayton Manor appeared different at night. The palatial feel softened, and the historical heaviness quieted. The house became intimate, minus the threat that ancestral ghosts lurked.

Cordelia wandered. She admired paintings, tapestries, and

intricate wood carvings that she'd missed earlier in the day. The east wing seemed larger than she remembered, and she began following a faint sound, a baby crying. The hushed voice drew her down a connecting hallway, through a cracked door, and into a room on the right. Warm moonbeams spilled onto the green corridor rug.

"Shhh, I'm here, my little love." Emma held Ada Rose and kissed her cheek.

Cordelia hesitated. She didn't want to intrude, but the door creaked as she turned to leave. Emma looked over, tired but smiling.

"I'm so sorry," Cordelia whispered. "I couldn't sleep and decided to take a walk. And then I heard Ada crying. I'll just go."

"No, please, come in." She waved Cordelia closer. "I could use the company, if you don't mind."

"Not at all."

Decorated in soft yellows and lighting that cast stars on the ceiling, the nursery became a little girl's dream. Emma settled into the rocking chair near a window and soothed Ada, encouraging Cordelia to relax in a winged chair near an oversized giraffe. Ada Rose had a thick patch of black hair and her mother's complexion. A month old with the beauty of a Persian princess.

"She's beautiful."

"Thank you." Emma's face glowed with pride. "So tiny, but she already has everyone wrapped around her fingers."

"Royce never mentioned."

Emma lifted her eyes, nodded, and brushed her fingers through Ada's hair. "Now it makes sense." Emma grinned. "You're real. Royce has been keeping secrets."

"You can say that."

"He's pretty private, especially with his parents. But he means well."

"How can secrets help anybody?"

"Look around. Wouldn't this make you secretive?"

"I guess. But."

"I don't envy him, and neither does Marcus." Emma explained to Cordelia the differences between being a first and second-born son, that the oldest carried the weight of the title, which meant preserving centuries of tradition. More expectations. Less freedom. More responsibility.

Cordelia listened and absorbed Emma's words. Royce had presented himself in Paris as an academic, a writer who defined his life by intellectual and creative pursuits rather than someone who succumbed to endless scrutiny. "But he concealed his true identity."

"Concealment or protection?" Emma tossed a towel over her shoulder and softly burped Ada Rose.

Cordelia shrugged.

"Don't get me wrong, Royce is private, but he has good reason for it. What I've learned here is that sometimes keeping your distance isn't about hiding who you are, it's about protecting yourself from being reduced down to a one-word description."

They sat quietly, and Cordelia watched as Emma patted and rubbed Ada's back. The little girl's head rested against her mother's shoulder, and she fell asleep.

"Would you like to hold her?" Emma said.

"Oh, I don't, I'm not." Before she could object further, Cordelia felt the delicate weight of Ada Rose in her arms. Her chubby hand waved and settled, tucking into Cordelia's chest. A wave of awe washed through her, causing her heart to swell. "She's so perfect."

"We think so. Although if she's anything like her father,

she'll have a stubborn streak as big as this house. It's a Brownell trait." Emma rocked, folding and unfolding a burp cloth in her lap.

"Were you born into a family like this?"

Emma laughed. "Not at all."

"So, what was it like? Coming here?"

"It was," She considered her words, "an adjustment. My parents are immigrants, doctors in London."

"Then how did you two meet?"

"We were on the Olympic team together. I was competing in archery, and my roommate knew Marcus, who competed in equestrian." Emma became expressive, moving her hand in a fluid motion. "We didn't like each other at all, in the beginning. I thought he was pretentious and arrogant, just rude. But we kept running into each other, even back in London, and I began to see a different side of him. Once I understood this side of Marcus, it didn't matter. It works itself out."

Cordelia considered things as Ada Rose shifted in her arms and sighed in her sleep. Other than Maisie, she hadn't held many babies. Unlike baking, they required nurturing and intuitive instincts. She feared she lacked those abilities. Her mother had taught her independence, not caregiving. What if she couldn't provide the emotional stability a child needed? She knew those wounds well. Ada's tiny fingers wrapped around Cordelia's, and the little girl's scent brought a simple sweetness to the night.

Their conversation faded. She said good night and made her way back to her room. The time with them became an unexpected reprieve from her emotions. She still questioned his dishonesty, but Emma's advice gave her a new understanding. Maybe she'd rushed to judgment without listening to his reasons. As she fell asleep, the floor creaked, but exhaustion took hold of her body, and she decided trust was the best option.

# Chapter Fourteen

The following morning, Cordelia ran her fingers along the pages of a recipe collection dated 1837. She marveled at the precise measurements written in a fluid handwriting, with a note stating *Third edition of Mr. Cooke's receipt. His Lordship now partakes of East Indian sugar only.*

The countess briefly explained the significance of the note, giving historical context to it, and marked the page with a silk ribbon. "Proof that revolutionary thinking occasionally penetrates these hallowed walls." Her right eyebrow lifted, pulling the corner of her mouth upward in an expression of sarcasm.

Cordelia copied the recipe, distracted by a crash of thunder that rattled the windows. Rain had threatened all afternoon as clouds gathered in haunting formations. She debated whether to leave for the train station before the storm settled in, but her research kept her bound to the chair. Besides, immersing herself in recipes offered a welcomed distraction from the complications with Royce. Emma's insights had helped her understand him better, but she needed time to reconcile the two sides of him.

Time dissipated, and Cordelia lost herself in transcribing recipes. What felt like thirty minutes became two hours, only setting the pen down when Amy brought in afternoon tea—a teapot, two floral mugs, homemade shortbread cookies, and tri-folded napkins. She and the Countess quietly spoke, discussing an upcoming foundation gala.

Cordelia turned her attention back to two recipes, Victoria sponge cake and Rout cakes. She tapped her pen against the notebook, wondering if she should go Georgian or Victorian. Either way, she'd want to modernize it and add her own flair. But the book didn't have enough pages for both. She flipped through the pages, reading the chef's notes.

"Would you like some tea?" The countess said as she filled both mugs.

"Yes, thank you."

During their tea break, the women bonded over the nomadic qualities of their childhoods. The countess' father, having been a diplomat in several countries before obtaining the London post, required his daughters to study the host country's culture. The countess laughed and shared a story. At the age of nine, her family moved to England, and she told her parents there was no reason to learn British. Mary Poppins had taught her everything she needed to know. Cordelia saw Royce in his mother, the way they threw their heads back when they laughed, or told stories with hidden life lessons built in. Her influence was obvious.

Cordelia left one detail out of her childhood—the absence of her mother.

Thunder rumbled, and a distinct pattern of rain tapped against the windows. Cordelia glanced outside, her view of the garden obscured by the downpour. The storm intensified with a vengeance.

"The weather service warned it might be severe, but this

looks dreadful." She stood beside Cordelia, watching as bolts of lightning flashed in the distance.

"How long will it last?"

"It's uncertain, a day or two. It's September, and these storms are always the worst. Last year, we lost two trees."

"That long? Maybe I should call a cab and leave before it gets worse?"

"I don't recommend it. Country roads become deathtraps in weather like this due to flash flooding. You're more than welcome to stay."

The idea, as generous as it was, distressed Cordelia. She and Royce hadn't revealed their facade to his family, and Emma promised to keep their secret. "I wouldn't want to impose."

"Of course not. We all enjoy your company. And if you need anything, I'm sure Emma will lend it to you."

The countess left Cordelia little room to refuse, so she graciously nodded and returned to her notes.

"Lovely. I'll let Amy know. And you'll be in the blue room again. All right, dear, the library is at your disposal. If you need anything, just pop your head out. There's usually someone walking about who can assist you." She slipped out, and the heavy oak door clicked shut.


Royce hesitated outside the library door, his hand hovered about the brass knob. He swiftly knocked and opened the door. The hinges creaked, a sound he'd known since childhood when he'd sneak in to read after bedtime.

Cordelia sat at the main table, surrounded by open books. Her posture hardened like an armored suit.

"I thought you might enjoy a cup of tea."

"I already had some. Amy brought it earlier." She set her pen down. "But thank you."

"Finding any good recipes?" He sat on the arm of a club chair and sipped the tea.

"Yes, take your pick of options. There's Tudor, Georgian, and Victorian. It's clear your ancestors loved cake, especially cakes with jams and berries." Her face animated. "Have you ever looked through this stuff? It's incredible."

"I can't say I have."

"Look at this." She waved him over. "There are techniques and preferences. It's incredible."

"Yes, you mentioned that." Royce smiled, grateful he had a moment alone with her, and even more so when she returned the smile.

A crack of thunder punctuated the moment, as if nature wanted to interject itself into their lives. The library lights flickered and stabilized.

"The estate's electrical system is temperamental during storms."

"I see." The lights flickered again, and she moved closer to him.

"Don't worry, we have generators, if needed." Royce settled into a chair across from her, maintaining a respectful distance while close enough for comfortable conversation.

"I'm not scared. I've worked in worse conditions in New Mexico. There was a blackout, and we spent two days cataloging pottery fragments by flashlight. At least you don't have scorpions."

"No, but we have ghosts."

"Stop." She tossed a small, ball-shaped thread at him. "You're horrible." She laughed, a nose-crinkling, lip-biting laugh. He hadn't seen that expression since dinner at Darius' restaurant.

He seized the opportunity and approached, squatting in

front of her. Royce reached for her hand, but her touch felt distant. His heart pounded like thunder rattling the windows.

"I should have told you, I'm sorry."

"You don't have to apologize again. But I need time."

Royce caressed the back of her hand and searched for words. "I appreciate your honesty, so I'm going to be open with you." Her fingers twitched in his palm.

"I'm listening."

"I was selfish. I wanted to preserve what we have in Paris, and I should've told you before the symphony."

"Don't you think you should've told me in Paris? I mean, you had plenty of opportunity to just say, 'Oh, by the way, I'm a Lord and one day I'll be an Earl. And my family owns one of the most historical houses in all of England.' Would that have been hard?"

"Obviously it was, or I would've told you."

Cordelia tilted her head and paused. Her eyes cut away from Royce's face. "I think you underestimated me."

"I would never."

She continued, "It's not the first time someone has, but it still hurts."

Outside, the storm howled, creating a roar in the chimney.

Royce stood and squeezed her hand. "Come here, I want to show you something." He guided her to a corner shelf, pulled out a black leather binder, and showed her a collection of yellowed letters in two distinct handwritings. "These are letters between my great-grandparents, Elizabeth Tyebury and William Brownell, the 15th Earl." He turned the binder toward her. "They weren't supposed to end up together."

"Why?" Cordelia leaned closer, curiosity momentarily displacing her hurt.

"Elizabeth was promised to the Duke of Pelford, a marriage that would have elevated her." Royce removed a letter and handed it to Cordelia. "She met William here at Hayton during a summer party. They spoke briefly and danced once, but that day changed their futures."

She examined the letter. Feminine script filled two sheets of paper with passionate confessions.

"He realized pursuing her created a scandal, but he risked his title for her." The next letter he handed Cordelia, in William's handwriting, had controlled loops and tails. "Elizabeth refused the duke, and convinced her father that marrying an Earl, while a lesser title, would preserve their standing and make her happy. You'll enjoy this one."

*My darling William,*

*Father has consented at last. Your last letter left me trembling with such fierce longing that I slept with it pressed against my heart, dreaming of the day when it will be your hands upon me instead of mere words.*

*With love beyond measure, Elizabeth*

Cordelia chewed on her lip, staring at the letter. "All she wanted was happiness."

"That's all they both wanted. They continued writing letters to each other years after their marriage. It's all here, and here." Royce pointed to two more binders.

"My god, what a treasure to have these."

A gust of wind pushed and howled outside the windows, followed by a crack of thunder. The lights flickered twice and went out.

Cordelia bumped into something, let out a yelp, and said, "Royce? Now what?"

# Chapter Fifteen

Awake and restless in the blue room, Cordelia listened to the storm's assault on Hayton Manor. Frequent lightning illuminated the room, casting strange shadows across the bed.

Frustrated to see one a.m. again, she wrestled with her blankets. A cold draft hovered in the room, and she cursed the failed generator. Without the heating system, the house's nighttime sounds became more pronounced, especially an unidentifiable rhythmic tapping that came from inside the walls. Which wall? She recalled too many movies with storms and old houses, and bad endings. Cordelia jumped out of bed and fumbled for her robe. The chill seeped through her t-shirt, and goosebumps rippled across her skin. The wood floor was icy under her bare feet.

Guided by lightning flashes, she felt her way to the door and searched for the flashlight she'd tossed onto the lounger. Thunder cracked overhead. She ducked as it invaded the room. Her instincts had told her to leave before the storm hit. If she'd listened, the sounds of London would be drowning out the storm and soothing her to sleep. Instead, she braved the manor's darkness, faced with centuries of secrets.

Cordelia moved through the hallway, breaking up the darkness with her flashlight. One hand trailed the wall for guidance —left at the tapestry, right onto the staircase, left through the hall and dining room, and into the butler's pantry. The storm provided additional light, revealing interesting patterns in the grand hall, ones that swirled like wine poured into a glass. The room felt magical.

A faint glow caught her attention as she approached the kitchen, spilling from under the doorway. A kettle whistled. Someone else had the same idea.

Royce stood beside the gas stove, holding a small container of ice cream. Two flashlights rested on the kitchen island.

"Couldn't sleep?" He silenced the kettle and reached for a second mug.

"How can anybody sleep through this? And there's something tapping in my wall. Really annoying."

"That's the water pipes contracting. You get used to it." He placed a steaming mug of tea in front of her. "Don't worry, it's herbal."

Cordelia wrapped her hands around the cup, grateful for the heat against her cold fingers. The earthy aroma of chamomile mingled with the metallic scent that hung in the air from the storm. She mimicked the way he pronounced herbal. They laughed and compared the British vs. American variations. Their linguistic debate ended in a friendly stalemate, each determined to convert the other.

"You know, you really shouldn't eat that this late at night," she said as he put the ice cream away.

"I believe you mentioned that."

"It's obviously worth mentioning again." Her eyes followed him as he approached where she sat at the kitchen island. He wore a black V-neck tee and plaid pajama bottoms. The shirt's fabric outlined his muscles and highlighted what his formal clothes had always hidden. Cordelia caught herself sighing and looked away.

They sat next to each other in silence for a moment, drinking their tea. Royce's knee pressed against hers. This was the first time since arriving at Hayton Manor that Cordelia coveted his touch.

"Anything else keep you awake?"

"Do you mean tonight or in general?"

"Both, I guess."

She wanted to say *you, you keep me awake,* but she resisted sharing that much of herself under the circumstances. "If I'm being honest, fear."

"Of the storm?"

"No." She smiled faintly and rested her hand on his knee. "Fear of failing this cookbook, fear of." Her words trailed off, and she sipped her tea.

"I find that hard to believe."

"Well, it's true."

"Cordelia, you're amazingly talented."

"Amazingly, huh?"

"Yes, amazingly talented. I've watched you in there, you light up with those recipes."

"But can I recreate them? Can I do them justice?"

"What are you talking about?" Royce squared their chairs to one another. "You do everything you make, justice. More than justice. You make them craveableum."

"Oh my god, what does that mean?"

"Crave-worthy yum."

"Where do you come up with all these words?" Their eyes smiled at each other.

"I guess you're my muse."

A warmth spread through her core. Was it the flattery? Arousal? Probably both. She saw herself through him, feeling an urge to kiss him, to express herself physically. Yet, uncertainty plagued her mind, wondering if it would be wise to cross that casual line again. "What about you? What keeps the future Earl of Thornbury awake at night?"

He swirled his tea and stared into the mug. "Honestly?" Royce cut his eyes up, the corner of his mouth smiled, showcasing his dimple.

"After this week's revelations, I think I've earned your unedited honesty."

"Touché." Royce braced himself, almost afraid the truth would consume him. Lightning flashed, illuminating his features. "There's something daunting about being the eighteenth link in this chain that has been recognized since the Tudors. What if I don't measure up to centuries of legacy?"

"Okay, that's a bit heavier than my cookbook anxiety. You win." She leaned forward, placing her hands on his knees, and looked into his eyes. "Seriously, you'll be fantastic as the Earl. Probably better than all of them put together."

"That's a tall order, especially when medieval armor clashes terribly with my wardrobe."

She laughed and sipped her tea, enjoying the comfortable moment with Royce. It reminded her of Paris and the ease of their conversations. Thunder rattled the house, and Cordelia flinched, spilling tea onto her robe. "Sorry. Violent storms make me jumpy." She used a napkin to dab it up. "Childhood thing."

"Really?"

Cordelia sat back and assessed Royce's expression. "My mother left during a storm. I was seven. I came home from school and found her suitcase by the door. She hugged James and me goodbye, promised to return, but when she walked out the door, she never looked back."

"I'm so sorry."

"It's ancient history, as you say." Her eyes watered, and Cordelia wiped them away before they could reach her cheeks. "My father and brother became my world, and it's because of them I became a baker."

"That explains a lot. Thank you for sharing this with me." His hand brushed her arm. "Do you have contact with your mother?"

"No. But she taught me a valuable lesson, everyone has secrets, and in time, they're all revealed." She listened to the rain running through an outside drainpipe. "And what about you? What's your excuse for keeping secrets?"

He didn't flinch from her challenge. "Prep school. It taught me to question people's motives. Boys befriended me because their parents saw an advantage in getting close to my father."

"So, you learned to hide."

"Right. My circle stays narrow." He brushed the hair off her face, gliding his fingers over her cheek. "And what's your big dream? When you're not worrying about career failure."

"Connection." She answered without thinking. "Real connection."

Royce moved closer, the charge of electricity between them stronger than the storm.

"I've seen you since Paris."

Her heartbeat sped up. "I thought I saw you, too." Her eyes examined his face.

"You have, you still do."

"And?"

"And you're still here."

His hand moved to her face, his touch so delicate it made her breath catch. The distance between them vanished, and their mouths met in an unrestrained kiss that matched the storm's intensity. All doubt subsided.

Cordelia wrapped her arms around his neck and pressed closer, eliminating any remaining space between them. She surrendered to the pleasure of his hands roaming her body as they slid from her breasts to her hips. Effortlessly, he lifted her onto the kitchen counter and dropped the robe from her shoulders.

She gasped against his mouth at the sudden movement, then smiled as he settled between her parted thighs. "Very smooth, Lord Thornbury."

His mouth trailed kisses along her jaw to a sensitive spot beneath her ear. "I have my moments."

Anticipation flooded her body, releasing a soft moan.

Outside, the storm unleashed its fury, pounding rain against the house. Stark flashes of lightning highlighted their entangled form before casting them back into an intimate shadow.

Cordelia's hands found the hem of his shirt and slipped beneath, eager to explore the warm skin of his back. The muscles tensed under her fingers as she traced the length of his spine.

He pulled back, enough to meet her eyes. "Are you certain?" She could see the intensity of his gaze, the control he maintained despite his desire.

"Definitely." She removed her robe, feeling the cool air rush underneath the thin t-shirt. "Are you?"

He answered by pulling her forward until their bodies aligned, his hardness pressed against her core. Only a thin layer of clothes divided them. "Since Paris."

Cordelia smiled and gasped as his hand moved underneath her shirt, trailed her ribs, and cupped her breast. "That soon?"

"That soon." He drew her hardened nipple into the wet heat of his mouth, teasing her through the fabric.

Thoughts became difficult, and sensation overtook her ability to read him. He explored her body with the same attention he brought to everything, observing and learning what made her gasp, what made her moan, what made her arch against him in silent demand for more. And when he slid inside her, Cordelia yielded to something far deeper than physical pleasure.

Outside the storm raged, but within the kitchen's walls, they created a shelter, their universe. Together, they moved with urgency, and like the storm, released the building pressure.

"Well," Cordelia's voice breathy, "I won't ever look at this kitchen the same way."

Royce laughed, the sound vibrating against her where their bodies remained connected. "Nor will I." He brushed damp hair from her forehead and softly kissed her. "Stay with me tonight."

"I'd like that." Cordelia sensed a peace, a resolution to her unease.

He helped her down, and they embraced in a kiss. The rain softened outside. She no longer perceived his world as a stranger. She saw him, she saw Royce.

# Chapter Sixteen

Four days after her stay at Hayton Manor, Cordelia worked in the kitchen of BL London, constructing a Victoria sponge cake. Despite her focus, memories of that night with Royce lingered—the scent of his skin, the storm, and how everything had changed between them.

Jessica sidled up with a clipboard. "The new distributor arrives at eleven."

"I'm aware, but I'm almost done." She looked at her. "Thanks anyway for the reminder."

Jessica lingered. A month ago, her hovering would've annoyed Cordelia, but now she valued their supportive relationship. "Was there something else?"

"No. Yeah, what did they do to you out there?"

Cordelia poured a jam on top of a cream layer and smoothed it out. "What are you talking about?" Her lips twitched, trying to smile, but she forced them into a grin.

"That. I don't know what it is, but you're different."

Cordelia laughed. "Maybe the storm." Before Cordelia could elaborate, Suze poked her head through the door. "Chef, there's someone here asking for you. It's a woman who mentioned something about meeting you on a train?"

"Robbie? Tell her I'll be right out."

Jessica glanced at the wall clock. "Do you want me to start with the distributor or keep him busy till you're free?"

Cordelia wiped her hands on a towel and removed her apron. "Umm, start without me. Thank you." Out of the corner of her eye, she caught Jessica's reaction. "And yes, you're doing a great job." She hurried into the boutique and greeted Robbie, who bubbled with enthusiasm.

"Oh my god, look at this place. It smells heavenly. I can't believe you get to work here every day. You'd have to shove me in a barn if I worked here." She laughed and hugged Cordelia a second time.

"I can't believe you're here. I thought you were jammed all week."

"The conference got rescheduled," Robbie said, adjusting her designer shoulder bag. "Which is fine. My brain was on overload after Paris and Munich. I could use some R & R."

"I'm so glad you stopped by. Do you have time to grab a coffee?"

Robbie glanced around the crowded shop. "Do you have time?"

"I can make time."

"Excellent. Well, let's go, babe." Robbie gestured, rushing Cordelia along.

"Let me grab my bag." Cordelia turned toward the kitchen, dusted flour off her shirt, and wondered if she had a backup outfit in her office.

"I'll wait. Hey, any word from that guy in Paris? The one with the bridge fetish?"

Cordelia shushed her as she stepped closer. "It's not a fetish, it's research. And yes, I'll spill the details in a minute." The shop door chimed, and a floral delivery person entered, carrying an elaborate arrangement. He paused, looked around, and approached her. "Delivery for Cordelia Dyer?"

"Oh, that's me, thanks." She accepted the arrangement, unsure why Royce would send flowers to a bakery.

Robbie smirked and wiggled her shoulders. "From him? Quite the grand gesture."

Jessica stuck her head out of the kitchen door. "Chef. Wow, that's huge."

Aware of the growing audience, Cordelia awkwardly gestured. "Jessica, would you mind taking these to my office?"

"Sure."

She handed them off, but grabbed the card as Jessica walked away with them. "Wait, never mind. I'm going that way, anyway."

An hour and a half later, Cordelia returned. She retreated to her office, where the enormous arrangement dominated her desk. She retrieved the unsealed card from her bag.

*Thinking about you. Remember Paris? Call me. — D*

Daniel. Not Royce. Intuitively, she recognized the dramatic show of attention, similar to what he did when they were together. But now, it felt like a deliberate reminder of their history rather than a respectful reconnection. She crumpled the card in her fist. Memories of Paris no longer belonged to him. He presumed more than he should have, a skill he'd mastered.

"Not this time." She tossed the card into the trash as Jessica knocked on the open door. "Can you have someone take these flowers to the local senior center?"

Jessica's eyes widened. "You're not keeping them?"

"They're wasted here."

Jessica nodded and removed the flowers.

The rest of the afternoon, Cordelia bounced between memories, the French Open with Daniel, and table tennis with

Royce. One filled with glamour, the other genuine and intimate. She felt Royce's mouth on her neck and his breath in her ear. The connection left her stronger, yet exposed, like walking a mountainside trail with the summit in sight. She reached for her phone and texted Royce.

Thinking about you. XX

Since their night at Hayton Manor, Royce measured time differently, cataloging moments with Cordelia rather than days on a calendar. Moments that came in stolen kisses, late-night calls, or take-away meals in the BL kitchen.

Royce shifted the weight of a food bag in one hand, and a wrapped package in the other. He began to knock, but paused, observing her through the storefront window. Her dark hair was piled haphazardly on top of her head. Flour dusted her black chef's coat, and she bit the corner of her lip as she worked in the kitchen. In her element, she personified beauty.

He tapped gently on the glass, amused when she startled and then smiled with recognition. "I hope you're in the mood for Thai," he said as she opened the door.

"Perfect." She stepped back, let him enter, and wiped the flour from her cheek.

In the kitchen, the worktop resembled a battlefield, and it appeared the flour had won. An oven hummed in the background. "Sorry about the disaster zone."

Royce pulled her close, enjoying the way her arms wrapped around his neck. "And I thought archeology was messy." The taste of sweet cream lingered on her lips. He brushed flour from her face, letting his thumb linger against her skin. "Stay at my place tonight."

"It'll be late."

His fingers ran down her neck and traced her collarbone. "I'll wait up."

"You're such a distraction."

He pretended to walk away. "I can leave then."

She pulled him back. "Not yet." Her tongue teased his mouth, reminding him of the night at Hayton, and deepened the intensity. But the kiss ended as quickly as it began, her plump lips moist and lingering just out of reach. "Maybe I can stop by."

"I'll take that as a yes."

"I need to wash my hands. I'm starving."

Royce squeezed her hips. "So am I."

As she washed her hands, Royce cleared space on the worktable, arranging the takeout containers in precise order, rice before curry. They ate sitting on stools and caught up on each other's projects. The rich aromas of Thai spices mingled with the lingering sweetness of baking and emphasized the warmth of the kitchen, a retreat from the autumn night.

Cordelia shared her successes and frustrations with various flavor profiles, detailing her thought process. "I haven't been able to get the cognac and raspberry ratios right, or at least the way I want them. And I need the recipe perfect for Bastien's visit on Monday." Her shoulders slouched. "He's expecting something original, and right now, all I have is ordinary."

"How many times have you run the recipe?"

"Three. But something's off. It's either too tart from the berries or too spicy from the cognac. It shouldn't smell like an oak barrel."

"Where are your notes? Let's look at the numbers. I'm sure you're closer than you think."

Cordelia grabbed her notebook, and together they recalculated ratios, unaware that their food grew cold. Soon after, she threw herself into making a test batch, wanting to prove they'd figured it out. Royce watched her work with scholarly appreciation, observing an innovator immersed in her element.

As she strained the hot liquid into a bowl, he slid a blue and white patterned package across the table. "I brought you something."

"What's this?" She asked, wiping her hands on her jacket.

"Open it and find out."

"The paper's so pretty." Cordelia used a knife to slice through the tape, doing her best to preserve the paper. She uncovered an antique cookbook stand. Her gasp and eyes said it all. "Oh, Royce, where did you find this?" The edges of the hand-carved stand showed evidence of use. One side was smooth and worn, while the other appeared to have a knife gash in it. On the back side, her finger ran across the inscription—Hayton Manor, 1887. "Are you kidding? You're giving this to me?"

"It hasn't been used in years."

"Are you sure? I mean, it's a part of the estate."

Royce moved around the worktable and stood behind her, wrapping his arms around her waist. "This way you'll never forget."

She placed the stand back in the box and rested her head on his shoulder. "Forgetting isn't my issue."

He kissed her neck and whispered. "Then what is?"

"Distractions."

"There's a wise man who teaches that distractions are a beneficial part of life. They make us resilient."

She giggled, her laughter warmed his body. "Is that right?"

His lips moistened her earlobe. "I'll agree to helping clean up this war zone, and you agree to stay at my place tonight."

"Appealing proposition." A smile tugged at her lips. The industrial refrigerator kicked on with a groan, and she turned to face him, resting her hands on his chest. "You've got yourself a deal, Mr. Brownell." A sharp, frantic knock at the back door startled them. Cordelia walked towards the back. "We're closed." The knocking intensified.

Royce followed her, grabbing a knife off the workbench. "It's best to ignore them this late at night."

"But it sounds urgent."

"It always does, but I think it's best not to open the door."

The pounding continued. She moved to the door and listened. "Jasper?" She flung the door open.

The man, weathered, pale with panic, squeezed a fedora between trembling hands. "Lucy won't wake up." Water from the roof dripped onto his brown jacket. " She's in the tent and won't wake up."

Cordelia pulled him out from underneath the gutters. "What happened?"

"Don't know. She was fine earlier. We shared tea at the church, and then she said she felt tired and wanted to sleep." His voice cracked. "I can't get her to respond. Please, dear, can you check on her?"

Cordelia grabbed an oversized coat that hung by the door. "Did you call an ambulance?"

"No phone."

"I'll call." Royce set the knife down and dialed emergency services while Cordelia grabbed a flashlight from a cabinet.

"Stay here. You're soaking wet and shivering. I'll check on her." She turned to Royce, who gave their location to dispatch. "The alley beside the bakery. Tell them the tent is about thirty meters in."

Their eyes met. The night's plans evaporated, but something deeper than disappointment registered between them, a different kind of urgency. "They're on their way."

"Jasper, stay here with Royce." She darted out the back.

Royce assisted Jasper inside. "Hi, Jasper. You look a bit cold. Why don't I help you with your jacket?"

"Thank you."

The shivering subsided, and Royce wrapped his coat around Jasper's shoulders. "The ambulance will be here soon. I'm certain they'll be able to help, Lucy, was it?"

"Yes, Lucy Cobbett." Jasper stared at the floor. "She went to sleep, and I couldn't wake her."

"Why don't I make you a cup of tea while we wait?"

"Lucy loves a good cup of breakfast tea if you have any."

"Sure." Royce filled an electric tea kettle and told Jasper he'd return in a moment. He hurried outside and located Cordelia crouched inside the tent.

"Lucy, emergency services are on their way. Hang on." She leaned out. "She'll be okay. Tell Jasper she'll be fine."

Paramedics guided Lucy's stretcher from the alley, and Royce watched as Cordelia lovingly reassured Jasper. He'd admired her drive in the kitchen, her intellect in conversation, and experienced her passion, but her instinctive compassion without hesitation cemented his growing certainty in her.

# Chapter Seventeen

It had been over a week since Lucy had been admitted and released from the hospital. The event rattled her and Jasper, convincing them their tent would no longer be their home. After a few calls, Royce found them a room at a center, one that allowed them to stay together. Unfortunately, it was fifteen miles from Mayfair.

Cordelia promised to visit them regularly, but work and the cookbook consumed her days. The publisher had moved up her deadline, creating a pressure that hummed in the background of her thoughts. As she dripped chocolate onto parchment paper, she wondered why she'd agreed to bake for the Murray's high-profile wedding. The demands of the event had compounded her stress and created disruptions with Royce.

She pulled the design sheet closer, double-checking measurements for the swirls—the last and simplest of her chocolate forest creation. The kitchen smelled sweeter than normal, with an additional essence of candy-coated walnuts cooling on racks. Off to the side, Jessica, Sam, Lang, and other team members constructed an elaborate winter-themed castle cake for the couple. Jessica piped and Sam led, assembling it like the construction of the Tower of London. Jessica worked with unusual focus, her phone persistently buzzed in her pocket. She ignored it, darting her eyes at others.

"Chef, shouldn't we start on the sugar work now? Sam can handle the rest of this." Jessica's tone carried a blend of inquiry and challenge.

"Keep piping. You guys can work on the sugar after the structure sets." Cordelia replied without looking up. "Besides, we need to bring the humidity down first."

"I was thinking, can't we use the walk-in as a controlled environment? The temperature and humidity are consistent in there."

Cordelia paused, chocolate dangling mid-air. "That's not a bad idea. Let's test your theory. Set up two stations, one here and one in there." She tossed the spoon into a bowl streaked with chocolate and stretched her back.

"On it."

"But after you're done." Cordelia checked her watch and felt a familiar tightness in her chest, the anxiety of competing priorities. Royce had invited her for dinner at Cassandra's house, a small gathering of nine, he said. Under normal circumstances, she would've stayed at the bakery until everything was perfect, regardless of personal plans. But recently, she'd begun to question the price of perfectionism.

Her phone buzzed in her pocket.


Royce: Pick you up at 7.


She glanced at the chocolate and calculated her timing. Another hour would ensure flawless execution. But another hour would mean flustered and unprepared for whatever social challenges Cassandra threw her way.

Cordelia's thumb hovered over the keyboard. To her

surprise, she told him she'd be ready and hit send. No hesitation. No afterthought. She set her phone down and exhaled, releasing a breath she'd held for years. Somewhere between Paris and London, a shift happened, a presence Royce nudged awake.

"Chef, is everything okay?" Sam said.

"Yes." Cordelia surveyed the kitchen. "Actually, I'm leaving soon. I have a dinner I can't skip. Jessica, I want you to oversee the final chocolate works. Sam, you handle the sugar. Can you do that?"

Jessica froze. She and Sam met eyes. "You want us to finish off the entire project?"

"Yes." The kitchen quieted.

"But, Chef, this is your vision."

"Yes." Cordelia folded her arms across her chest. "Are you incapable of executing it?"

"No, Chef."

Sam leaned closer to Cordelia. "Chef, I know you didn't ask my opinion, but Jessica is better at sugar work than me."

"Good point." She noticed the time on the wall clock and removed her apron. "Fine. Jessica, you're on sugar. Sam, you're on chocolate. Lang, you and the team finish assembling the cake." Cordelia felt an unexpected ease. The world survived. The bakery flourished. Jessica deserved the opportunity to prove herself.

She rushed to leave, knowing exactly which dress she'd wear, hoping to impress Royce. He'd been vague about the dinner details, which normally would trigger her insecurities and pleas for Marnie's help. But this time, she felt oddly prepared.

When she passed through the kitchen on the way out the door, she said, "I'll stop by after dinner. Text me if you run into problems."

"You don't need to. I think we can handle it." Jessica stumbled over her words.

"See you later."

As she stepped into the street, she texted Royce, sending him a single pink heart. The late afternoon sun faded behind buildings, contrasting with the kitchen's-controlled chill. For once, guilt didn't follow her through the door.

Royce studied Cordelia across Cassandra's dining table, admiring the way her burgundy dress contrasted with her milky complexion and deepened the earthy tones of her eyes. He wanted to tell her they reminded him of a rare scotch, but worried the metaphor sounded unromantic. She shared secret glances with him, focusing on him between bites and polite conversation. A slight furrow in her brow suggested she analyzed social dynamics, reading people the way she read recipes.

"This Bordeaux is exceptional." Connor Stafford said, swirling his glass with practiced precision.

"I know. It's from our vineyard in Côtes de Bourg." Cassandra smiled. Royce recognized the practiced modesty, a gift from her mother, and a performance he'd witnessed countless times. "It's small, but most agree we've had remarkable results. Royce, you remember the summers there?"

"Vaguely."

"Of course you do." Cassandra turned to Cordelia. "Royce's father believed he was destined for academic or political leadership. Their excellence spans generations."

Royce watched as the tension began in Cordelia's shoulders and moved its way up to her brow. He shifted in his chair, intentionally tapping her foot. The gesture, subtle enough to go unseen, yet felt by her, softened her expression back into neutrality.

"Cassandra, you may not be aware, but Cordelia has been doing recipe research at Hayton. She discovered several that will be in her upcoming cookbook."

"Is that so?" She cut her eyes at Cordelia. "Well done."

"Thank you." Cordelia sipped her wine.

"Speaking of impressive work, Connor was telling me earlier about the upcoming art exhibit he's planning. Quite revolutionary."

Connor cleared his throat. "Yes, we're creating a holographic experience, allowing viewers to become the craftsmen. Or craftswomen."

"And I believe you said, Royce's paper on contextual archaeology influenced the department's approach. Isn't that correct, Connor?"

There it was, her trap laid like breadcrumbs to the slaughter, an orchestrated intervention instigated by his father.

"Yes, that's correct. Your paper has been instrumental."

"I would say it was a collaborative effort. Professor Andrews should get the majority credit." The name slipped from his lips, bringing with it a tightness in his chest.

Cordelia's eyes double blinked at him, asking questions about a story he wanted to leave in the past.

"Darling, everyone there knows the innovations were yours," Cassandra said.

Connor sheepishly gulped his wine, looking at everyone around the table except for him.

"Such a shame about that situation. But he's still my client."

"Cassandra, that's enough." Royce set his fork on the plate, controlling the urge to walk away from the table. She referenced Gavin's actions as a casual event, forgetting that it shattered two women's lives. Evie's most of all. The image of her collapsed in the hallway still invaded his mind.

"More wine, anyone?" She said.

When he looked at Cordelia, he recognized that compassionate expression. She'd offered it to Jasper when he thought he'd lost his precious Lucy.

Connor cleared his throat again. "Royce, I'd be happy to bring you on board as a consultant. It would be my privilege." Connor smoothed the few strands of hair across his balding head.

"I appreciate the offer, but I'm not looking to consult." Royce's tone was courteous but firm.

Cordelia tapped his foot under the table, and her expression lifted like the beauty of a clear night sky. "I personally admire Royce for leaving the university and doing what he loves, writing. It's admirable."

Cassandra laughed. "That's so sweet. Very American, but sweet."

"Kindness is a virtue, whether American or British."

"Yes, but we have our reputations to consider before being cavalier with our careers." Cassandra folded her napkin with care, each crease a silent rebuke.

"Royce, Ms. Dyer, are you suggesting a career can only be enjoyable if one seeks non-traditional avenues?" Connor smoothed his creaseless shirt.

"Not at all. I'm merely agreeing with Cordelia. Success can be obtained through various avenues. That's innovation."

"And I'm an example of using traditional and innovative methods. Look, all I was trying to say is that Royce's choice is admirable."

"All I'm saying is, I believe there are opportunities for you to bring your innovative ideas into our museum. You tell your stories, and we use them for holographic experiences. No ties to the university. It's a win-win."

"I don't mean to be rude, but haven't you listened to the man?" Her direct voice startled everyone, including Royce.

The table fell silent. Glasses clinked. "Thank you, Connor, for the opportunity, but as I said, I'm not looking to consult." He placed his napkin on the table. "Now, if you'll excuse us, we both have early starts tomorrow."

"Darling, don't leave yet." Cassandra fiddled with her earring. "Cordelia, surely you can stay a bit longer?"

"It's getting late, but thank you for dinner, Cassandra. It's been illuminating."

Cassandra conceded and stood. In her heels, she stood eye level with Cordelia. "As one of his oldest friends, I applaud your support of Royce, but a little advice, don't misspeak when there are things you don't understand."

"Cassandra, that's uncalled for." Royce walked around the table and stood beside Cordelia, placing his arm around her waist. He'd endured socially opinionated judgements and had offered plenty himself, but watching them directed at Cordelia crossed a line.

In her directness, Cordelia had done what years of therapy failed to accomplish—clarity. He turned to Connor first. "I'm honored by your interest, but my decision to work independently wasn't made lightly." Then he turned to Cassandra. "Or without consideration of my responsibilities. Some experiences change your perspective permanently." Lastly, to Cordelia. Her quiet, supportive eyes felt more valuable than any position his father could negotiate. "Shall we go?"

Later, in the darkness of his Mayfair flat, Royce traced the curve of Cordelia's shoulder, unable to believe she stayed after the disaster at Cassandra's. The cotton sheets whispered as she turned toward him, her eyes reflecting the city lights that filtered through the half-drawn curtains.

"You surprised me tonight," he said, watching the shadows dance across her collarbone. His pulse increased as she shifted closer. She smelled of gardenias, sweetness after a summer rain.

"I should've been more diplomatic." Her voice carried no regret.

"Diplomacy is overrated." Royce drew her closer, his hands remembering the contours of her body with fresh urgency. The walls he'd maintained crumbled beneath her touch. "You're dangerously good at cutting through crap." He whispered in admiration and desire. "First secrets, then games. What next, Ms. Dyer?" His teeth grazed the sensitive junction between her neck and shoulder, a playful bite that made her gasp and arch against him.

Their mouths found each other less tentative than they'd been at Hayton. Her kisses tasted of cherries and liberation, with lingering notes of wine and certainty. When her teeth grazed his lower lip, he tasted the raw edge of his desire, sending electricity down his spine.

"I thought about this all night," she said, her breath hot and uneven against his neck. "Royce?"

"Mmmm."

"When I'm with you, I forget about control."

The corners of his mouth revealed his dimples, and in one fluid motion, he flipped their positions, pinning her beneath him on the bed. "I'm happy to oblige." His mouth dropped to her breast and drew her into the heat of his mouth, letting his tongue tease her nipple. Cordelia gasped and arched toward him. His hands moved down her body, exploring her with intent. His lips traced a path across her ribs and across the sensitive skin of her abdomen.

"I see you," he whispered, "All of you."

Her body curved against his like a question answered with absolute certainty. When she took him inside, Royce experienced a newfound trust, a vulnerability that should've terrified him, but instead felt like home. They moved as one, discovery softened into something profound, yet urgent.

He cataloged everything about her, the flutter of her eyelashes, the arch of her back, and the way she gripped his shoulders as if she anchored herself against rising tides. And the sounds she made, half-whispers that drove him past reason, burned into his memory.

When release came, it surged with an intensity that left them breathless, and his name rolled off her lips.

Outside, the city played its nighttime symphony of distant sirens and mumbled voices, but within his bedroom, nothing existed but them. Cordelia rested her head on his chest, her hair spilling across his skin. He listened to her breath, feeling her heartbeat pressed against his ribs.

She traced patterns across his chest, her touch soothing and stirring. Neither felt compelled to fill the silence with words, an unspoken understanding between them. He tucked a strand of hair behind her ear, allowing his fingers to linger against her cheek.

Before long, Royce watched Cordelia's eyes grow heavy, a deeper softening as she drifted to sleep. Her hand rested on his chest, directly over his heart, sensing his rhythms. He adjusted the sheets around her shoulders and memorized the furrow between her brows as she dreamed.

The sound of her steady breathing lulled him to sleep, and for the first time in years, he fell asleep without an agenda.

# Chapter Eighteen

The tennis club's locker rooms oozed luxury with mahogany lockers and cushioned benches. Cordelia stood in front of a full-length mirror, adjusting her deep blue tennis skirt, which stood out in a roomful of white. She smoothed an invisible wrinkle, her fingers betraying the nervous energy she worked hard to contain. It had been two weeks since Cassandra's dinner party, and now they faced off across the court.

Her phone buzzed. Marnie texted, reminding her she'd kill it, as always. Cordelia smiled, snapped a selfie, and sent it off to her. A heart reply came instantly, followed by one question, what's the latest on Daniel. The mention of his name triggered frustration. His texts had increased daily, more manipulative than the last, suggesting her support was crucial to his recovery. He needed her. Not anymore. He had Cary Anne.

As she tucked her phone away, the locker room door swung open with grand force. Cassandra entered. On her phone, she paused mid-conversation, annoyed someone occupied her favorite locker, and hung up without a goodbye.

"Cordelia," she said in a calculated tone. Her eyes assessed everyone in the room.

"Cassandra."

"Bold color choice. Most of us opt for traditional white."

Six months prior, as a new club member, the comment would've triggered self-doubt. Not anymore. Cordelia remained unfazed by her intimidation. "I find white to be so common, wouldn't you agree?"

A willowy blonde with a tennis bracelet that cost more than Cordelia's monthly rent leaned over with unexpected warmth. "That blue will photograph beautifully. I'm Olivia Benn, by the way. Are you singles or doubles?" She sat nearby, unpacking her sneakers from linen shoe bags.

"Nice to meet you, Cordelia Dyer. I'm playing mixed doubles with Richard Okoye."

"Aren't you lucky?" She glanced across the room. "Looks like you're overshadowed this year, Cassandra." Her voice lowered. "Typically, he partners with her for these things. They've won the charity cup three years running."

Cassandra's exterior hardened, which was hard to imagine, but she became statuesque in an unattractive way. "We decided to diversify this year, for the tournament's sake. More entertaining for the fans."

Cordelia's phone chimed. Daniel. He listed dates he'd be in London before heading to a rehab facility in the countryside. Out of all available locations, he had to choose England. Why? Adrenaline flooded her system with panic. Her fingers tightened around the phone, and her face flushed.

"Cordelia, dear, you look petrified. Everything alright?" Cassandra asked, as if she genuinely cared about Cordelia's distress.

"Yes, I'm fine." She dropped her phone into her bag. Daniel

would not disrupt her day or focus. "Just a friend back in New York."

As much as Cassandra pretended, her emotions read like an open book. "I hope it's nothing serious. We wouldn't want you distracted today." She clipped her smooth bob back. "Royce is very determined to win today. He's the perfect partner."

Olivia finished lacing her sneakers, tossed the bags into her locker, and grabbed her monogrammed designer tennis bag. "Good luck out there, Cordelia. Here's my number, let's chat soon." She handed her a card with a QR code and walked over to Cassandra, giving her a partial kiss on the cheek. "Be nice. I have a good feeling about this one."

Cassandra rolled her eyes and slipped on her white skirt. "Don't you have a match to get to?"

"Bye, ladies," Olivia shouted, heading out the door. Several other women followed behind, leaving Cordelia and Cassandra alone in the locker room.

Cordelia returned to the mirror, making final adjustments to her hair and mentally reviewing her pre-match routine. She gathered her racquet and water bottle, aware she was five minutes late meeting Richard. The rough grip tape reminded her she needed to buy a fresh roll. "See you on the court." Her hand paused on the cold brass door handle.

"Please do not say something sentimental."

"I wasn't." She turned to face Cassandra, who examined her outfit in the mirror. "I just wanted to say, good luck."

"Right. May the best players win."

As Cordelia headed toward the courts, her thoughts bounced between two uncomfortable truths—Daniel's arrival in London and Royce's unawareness of Daniel's fame. She'd kept the latter detail private, even as their relationship deepened, but the guilt of her omission weighed heavier. Yet Royce deserved to know the truth. But today she needed to focus on defeating Cassandra.

Cordelia stepped onto the bright green court and stretched beneath a large vinyl banner that announced the *12th Annual Chart Home Tennis Tournament - Supporting Disadvantaged Youth of London*. It hung prominently on the far wall. The smell of new tennis balls drifted in the air, as baskets of them lined the wall. Pre-match energy ran through her veins, a welcome shift from the social tension with Cassandra. At least on the court, skill is all that mattered.

Richard called and waved her to the other side of the court. He stood six feet tall with a vitality that oozed positivity. A headband held his short afro off his face, showing off his thoughtful smile. "Ready to make our beneficiaries proud?"

"That's the plan." They'd met during her second week in London, both having booked practice time with the ball machine. Being a gentleman, Richard gave her the court time, but suggested in the future they play together. Since then, they'd met weekly. Soon after, he convinced her to be his partner for the tournament, a charity he'd volunteered with since university, running summer tennis camps for the kids.

Across the court, Royce and Cassandra emerged from the clubhouse. Royce's stiff posture betrayed his discomfort despite Cassandra's confident grip on his arm. He moved like an awkward puppet across a stage. But his diplomatic mask fell away when his eyes greeted Cordelia with a smile, sending sparks through her body. She watched him in his white tennis shorts, her eyes drawn to his muscular legs. They were strong and lean, a reminder of how her skin felt against him in the darkness of his bedroom.

Cassandra stepped deliberately into Royce's line of sight,

disrupting the moment. Her hand curled around his bicep with a spider-like grip.

"She's in a mood today," Richard said, his voice low and deep.

Cordelia bounced a tennis ball against the strings of her racquet. She grunted.

"Whatever you do, don't let it throw you."

"Have you seen me thrown yet?"

He laughed, distracted by the match judge, "Riley!" They greeted with a warm handshake. "I hope those glasses of yours work better this year." Richard winked and joked with John Riley about last year's tournament.

Cordelia listened, but mentally found herself pulled back to Wimbledon, center court, five years earlier. Daniel, a charming jokester, had the crowd entertained during a set break, including the circuit's toughest umpire. The memory faded when Riley laughed at Richard's joke. She looked up and caught Royce watching her from across the court, a gaze that brought Cassandra's stream of chatter to a halt.

"All right, folks, let's get this match going." Riley clapped and barked encouragement.

Richard leaned close to Cordelia, squaring their shoulders to one another. "Cassandra's reactive and easily frustrated. More than anything, she hates losing control." His amiable smile remained, but Cordelia caught the gleam in his eye. "Use that to your advantage." Richard played to win, a quality she valued on the court.

As Cordelia took her position at the net, she welcomed the calm, the quiet just before the serve. Whatever social, work, or relationship issues waited outside the white lines, inside them, only the game mattered. The ball, the racquet, the strategy, all variables she could control. Skill and focus were her keys to victory.

Across the net, Cassandra settled into a classic ready position, a tiger stalking her prey. Her eyes narrowed with focus. She hunched over her racquet with elegant tension, baring her teeth. "Serve the ball, Richard." Cassandra hunted victory.

"Ready, Cordelia?" Richard called from behind her, bouncing the ball as he positioned his body.

Cordelia nodded. "Let's show them how it's done."

The ball met the strings with a thwack, signaling play, a dance of strength and will. The ball sailed over the net, and Cordelia's mind cleared. Game on.

Royce watched the ball arc over the net, landing exactly where Cordelia had intended. The placement forced Cassandra to lunge, sending the ball beyond the baseline. At one point, between serves, Royce caught Cordelia's eye and shifted his stance into a playful challenge, reminiscent of their table tennis match in Paris. In response, she flashed a determined smirk and twirled her racquet.

Richard served. Sneakers screeched. Racquets popped against the ball.

"Thirty-love," said John Riley.

Cordelia moved with athletic grace, an elegance that reminded him of the way she arched her back in the darkness of his bedroom. Royce shifted his weight and bounced on his toes, wishing the net no longer divided them.

"Royce," Cassandra hissed. "See, she's targeting me."

"It's strategy. And you're doing the same to her."

Cassandra growled in frustration. They lost the first set.

As they changed sides, Royce and Cordelia brushed past one another, letting their fingers intertwine.

"You're exceptional, Ms. Dyer."

"So are you, Lord Brownell." Her tongue moistened her lips.

"Enjoying yourself?"

"We're winning, of course I am."

Cassandra waited for him at the baseline. She leaned side-to-side and used her racquet as a stretching device. "Wake up, Royce, she's getting to you. I see it in your eyes."

"We're simply playing tennis, Cassandra."

"This is more than tennis, it's a competition. Surely you recognize that."

Rather than engage, Royce took his position at the baseline, bounced the ball three times in his pre-serve ritual, and listened to the rhythm variations of the ball bouncing between racquet and court. During the break, Cassandra had insisted they target Cordelia's backhand and force her into a corner, but Royce pushed her forehand. His strategy initially proved effective, but she read him and adapted, causing an unexpected surge of pride in him.

They were up four games to two, but Richard and Cordelia effortlessly targeted shots, and he watched them celebrate another win with a practiced high-five. "If I didn't know better, I'd say you two had those moves prepared."

"We have. Five months now, actually." Richard shouted across the court.

"Months?" Royce glanced at Cordelia, who adjusted her racquet strings. "You never mentioned knowing each other."

"You never asked." She shrugged and blew a kiss.

"I knew there was something off about her." Cassandra strolled behind him.

"Small world, mate. What can I say?" Richard chuckled and high-fived her again.

All along, she'd been connected to his world, moving adjacent to his own—Mayfair, the tennis club, Richard. Had fate orchestrated their meeting all along? He rejected the idea.

Cassandra cleared her throat. "If everyone is quite finished, we have a match to play. And win."

Royce nodded, but his focus returned to Cordelia, seeing her through a lens of destined connection. He settled into position. "Game on, Ms. Dyer, game on."

The third set began with renewed intensity, and both teams refused to concede the match. In less than an hour, the score stood at five to four. Sweat traced paths down Royce's spine, a welcome distraction from the pull of Cordelia's presence across the net. Cassandra targeted her, landing a serve directly on Cordelia's thigh. But Richard's final serve delivered an injury worse than that sting. Cordelia smashed the ball across the net and celebrated as it landed outside Cassandra's reach.

Privately, Royce applauded her. Their eyes met across the court, and in that moment, he knew he'd won the genuine match, the one that mattered.

# Chapter Nineteen

It had been three days since Cordelia and Richard won the tennis tournament, helping to raise over a million pounds for the charity. She arrived at BL London fifteen minutes early, greeted by the city's three a.m. hush. Her mind cycled through the day's production schedule. The cookbook's deadline loomed over her, while three special orders required her personal attention, making sleep a luxury she couldn't afford.

The bakery's side entrance swung open before she unlocked it, revealing bright lights emanating from the kitchen. She hesitated, holding her keys as a weapon, and looked around, wondering if someone waited in the shadows. When she stepped inside, the aggressive sound of metal-on-metal clanged, drawing her into the prep area. The air reeked of the bitter scent of burned chocolate. To her surprise, Jessica whisked by hand.

"Jessica? What the hell are you doing?"

Startled, she nearly dropped the stainless bowl. "Chef. I was just getting started on today's prep." Her voice stumbled on each word.

Moving closer, Cordelia noticed dark circles beneath Jessica's eyes and a slight tremor in her hands. In the bowl was a grainy, brown mess instead of a smooth ganache.

"Looks like your chocolate seized." Cordelia reached for the bowl.

"I know it seized." Jessica yanked the bowl back, sloshing chocolate onto the counter. "I can fix it myself. You don't always have to control everything."

"Excuse me?"

"You heard me." Jessica dumped the failed ganache and grabbed a fresh bowl. "I know it's hard for you to comprehend, but we can manage without you."

"That's uncalled for." Cordelia felt her professional mask slipping. "What the hell's gotten into you?"

"'You never let us forget, it's your kitchen, your way." Jessica faced her. Her eyes, raw and mournful. "You got the position. Congratulations. When will you stop reminding me?"

"What are you talking about? This position?"

"Yes. The job's yours, just like this kitchen. Congratulations."

"Is that what you're upset over?" Cordelia stepped closer. "Jessica, I've been here for almost a year. I don't consider this my kitchen, it's Bastien's."

"You act like it's yours."

"What's really bothering you, because I can't believe all of this is over me being executive."

"Well, it is. And it's time you knew how everyone felt."

Cordelia set her tote and coat down on a nearby stool. "By all means, enlighten me."

"You're here because you're the American girl on the rise. You're just a souvenir for him."

The words cut deeper than Cordelia expected, hitting insecurities that had more to do with Daniel and little to do with her career. Her throat tightened, and the emotions buried themselves. "I don't know what's gotten into you, or what you're on, so I'm gonna forget we had this conversation. Otherwise, you'd be out that door permanently."

Her heart raced, and she contemplated leaving. She felt less vulnerable walking the streets than there with Jessica's harsh words. The accusation exposed a fear she carried, that one day people would discover that beneath the confidence lived an uncertain girl.

"I've been here for over three years. I helped open this place, and I proved myself here. But you waltzed in from New York with your fancy techniques, that are no better than mine, and treated me like some first-year apprentice."

"Yet you still can't temper chocolate properly." Cordelia regretted the insult.

Jessica froze. "You know what? I'm done." She threw a chocolate-covered spatula down and reached for her pack. "Find another sous chef to micromanage. I quit."

"You can't quit," Cordelia exclaimed. "No one will hire you." Panic surged in her chest, thumping hard against her ribs.

"Watch me." Jessica yanked off her apron and hurled it at Cordelia's face.

"Seriously?" Cordelia grabbed a handful of flour from the prep station and threw it, hitting Jessica in the chest with a white cloud.

The kitchen fell silent. They stared at each other in shock.

"You are just." Jessica's words froze, and she glared at Cordelia.

"I'm sorry. It was a reaction. You threw your apron at me." Cordelia cringed at her own childish reaction.

A strangled sound escaped Jessica's throat, something between a laugh and a sob. She grabbed a handful of failed ganache out of the trash and flung it at Cordelia.

Lukewarm chocolate splattered across her white t-shirt. She

gasped, stunned by Jessica's reaction. "That's it. You really are fired!"

"I already quit, remember?" Jessica reached for a piping bag filled with pastry cream and lunged at Cordelia.

For several minutes, chaos turned the kitchen into a battlefield of flying ingredients. Butter and cocoa powder became weapons in their war. Cold, greasy trails slid down Cordelia's neck, and clouds of cocoa powder caught in her throat. Each breath tasted bitter.

Sanity penetrated Cordelia's anger when she slipped on spilled cream and glanced at the worktable, covered in a collage of food. "Wait." She ducked as Jessica aimed the piping bag at her face. "Stop. Jessica." Cordelia smeared her hand across the table, leaving fingermarks in the cocoa powder. "Enough."

Both women stood panting, surveying the disaster they'd created. A hysterical laugh bubbled up out of Jessica. "We've lost our minds." She plopped onto the floor, her body shaking with uncontrollable giggles.

"This isn't funny." Cordelia picked up two broken eggs on the floor. Her lip trembled, and she fought laughter. "I'm serious, Jessica. Look at this mess."

"Your hair," Jessica pointed, snorting and giggling. "Looks like the whipped cream monster got ya."

She touched the top of her head and realized there was a mound of cream slowly oozing down the sides. The irrational absurdity hit Cordelia. A burst, a growl escaped her mouth, and she laughed, gasping for breath. But as quickly as it began, it ended. An odd calm settled over the kitchen, and she settled onto the floor across from Jessica.

"I didn't really mean it," Jessica mumbled. "I wouldn't have quit."

"Well, I didn't mean it either. You're not fired." Cordelia picked eggshells off her black pants. "We both fucked up."

"Speak for yourself." She laughed, dusting flour from her shirt. "I was here early trying to develop something new, something to show you, you could trust me."

"I do trust you."

"Doesn't feel like it."

"If I didn't, you wouldn't have been given the Murray wedding."

"Then why do you double-check everything I do?"

"It's my job." Cordelia stopped, reflected on her words, and realized she'd micro-managed the kitchen. She'd done exactly what Bastien told her not to do—suppress others' creativity. "You know, you're very talented."

"Not like you. Or Sam."

"Yes, you are. You have skills that take years to master. I'm impressed."

"Impressed enough to give me a raise?" Her laugh was pungent like bitter herbs. "My parents' lease is up next week."

"Your parents?"

"Yeah, they're about to lose their temp house."

"Do you live with them?" Cordelia struggled to understand.

"Not anymore." Jessica rolled up her left sleeve and revealed a network of burn scars extending from wrist to shoulder. "House fire." She covered the scars. "Two years ago, they lost everything. I went back in for our dog. She still lives with them." She gestured at her arm. "It's worse on my shoulder and back."

"And your parents?"

"Dad has a limp after jumping from the second floor. Mums fine. They've been in temp housing while insurance sorts it out. I've been helping with their expenses. That's why I wanted the position, your job."

Cordelia imagined everything Jessica had been through, all the pain and grief, and then being passed over, when she carried heavy responsibility. All that pressure had finally exploded. "Why didn't you say anything?"

"You weren't here when it happened, and what was I supposed to say? 'Hey, new boss I know you don't know me, but could you pay me more because my life is a disastrous piece of shit?'" Jessica shook her head. "I don't think so."

"You're headed somewhere, and I don't believe it's disastrous." Cordelia thought of Jasper and Lucy. "You could've told me. We would've done something to help your family out."

Jessica looked up, surprised. "I'm not asking for favors."

"That's not what I'm saying. Listen, I admit I can get absorbed in things and not pay attention when you all are having personal issues. But it doesn't mean I don't care." Cordelia detected an internal shift, like an earthquake rattling inside of her. How many times had she criticized other chefs for putting career above relationships? She judged selfish ambition while committing the same crime. "I guess I've been so focused on proving myself that I haven't paid attention to anyone's needs."

"I haven't been the easiest. I kinda wanted you to fail. At first, but you do grow on people."

"Oh, thanks," Cordelia smirked. "Do you really think I'm a New York prima donna?"

Jessica chuckled. "Not all the time. I'm kidding. But you can be a dominatrix."

"Excuse me?"

"Controlling, you can be controlling. And don't deny it."

Despite herself, Cordelia laughed, glancing around the kitchen. "I haven't done anything this insane since. I don't know when, three?"

"You obviously needed it. You've been wound tight lately."

"Yes, I have." Cream dripped down her forehead. She used

the hem of her t-shirt to wipe it clean. "When's your parents' lease up?"

"Next Thursday."

"Let me see what we can do to help them." Cordelia stood, stretched, and offered Jessica her hand.

"What have you two done?" Sam said.

# Chapter Twenty

That evening, Royce leaned against the counter in Cordelia's kitchen, watching as she prepared dinner. Her expressive hands gestured as she recounted the confrontation with Jessica.

"And somehow, in the middle of that mess, we started listening to each other."

"I knew you'd eventually come to an understanding. Or kill each other."

"I'm telling you, the whole experience changed me. I've delegated more to her." She stirred a sauce on the cooktop and tapped the spoon, making sure it didn't splatter. The apartment smelled earthy and herbaceous, and steam rose from the pot. "Which means my cookbook can take priority." Cordelia leaned into him, pressing their hips together. "And more time for." Her voice softened, a reminder of the way she whispers his name during sex. A sweet taste lingered on her lips, and the warmth of her mouth invited him closer, like a siren's call.

The sauce began to bubble, distracting and pulling her away from his arms. "I've been meaning to talk to you about something," he said.

"What's that?"

"The foundation gala for my mum's charity is approaching." He kept his tone neutral, despite the weight of his father's call pressing on his shoulders. His fingers thumped against the counter, harmonizing with the simmering sauce.

"The one you mentioned a few weeks ago?"

"Yes. Well, Pop called earlier. Apparently, there will be specific media in attendance this year, and he requested I have a brief interview with them."

"Why you? Wouldn't they be more interested in your mother?"

"Well, yes, but apparently, an American journalist will be attending."

"American?"

"Yes. She's partnering with a New York organization, and they've invited him. Some guy from The New York Post."

"Oh. But why you?"

"I'm a board member. It shouldn't take long, but I wanted you to be aware."

Cordelia pulled vegetables from the refrigerator and placed them near the sink. "Okay. I guess that means you'll be late at the gala?" Her lips tightened as she rinsed the vegetables.

"Well, yes, but it means you'll be on your own for a bit. Cassandra will be there."

"Cassandra. Wait, I'm confused."

"Yes, she's attending. She attends every year."

"Alright. So she'll be draped all over you, all night. Is that what you're telling me?"

"No. I'm saying she can keep you company while I meet with the journalist."

Cordelia froze. The sauce on the cooktop bubbled, and water trickled from the faucet. "Wait, back up. Why would she need to keep me company?"

"She doesn't need to, but I thought."

"Wait, are you expecting me to be there?"

"Well, yes. I told you about it weeks ago."

The sound of her knife cut through carrots in sharp whacks. "Yes, you told me about it, but I didn't know you expected me to go."

"That's why I mentioned it. I thought you understood to add it to your calendar."

"Mentioning it and inviting me are two different things."

"No, when I told you, I was inviting you."

She chopped faster. "Maybe next time add the words 'you're invited' or 'please come with me', so I know."

"Noted." It jumped out firmer than intended. He approached her from behind, placing his hands on her hips. "I'd like you to join me."

Her knife snapped a carrot. The crisp sound echoed in the silence. Royce noticed a slight tremor in her fingers as she reached for another carrot. "I appreciate the invitation, but that's in two days."

"It would mean a great deal to have you there."

"Royce, I." She set the knife down and twisted in his arms, facing him. "The cookbook deadline is in two weeks. And I still have three recipes to test and the historical notes to revise."

"It's one evening, Cordelia. Surely the cookbook can wait a few hours."

"You of all people should understand." Her voice had that familiar edge whenever her work was challenged. "This isn't just any project. It's my first cookbook. And it's not just my reputation on the line. It's Bastien too."

"Yes, I understand." Royce countered gently. "It's easier to hide behind work than join the living."

Her eyes narrowed. "I'm not hiding. I'm being responsible." She refused to make eye contact.

"What are you afraid of, Cordelia?"

"Nothing. I'm just focused on my book."

"Not thirty minutes ago, you told me you delegated and had more time for us."

"And my cookbook."

"What are you not saying?" She spun around, returning to chopping vegetables. "If you're worried about socializing, I'll be by your side all night."

"Except when you're meeting with an American journalist."

'That's only five minutes, maybe twenty at the most, but I know you will charm everyone there. Look at how you've handled Cassandra."

"I didn't exactly charm her, now did I?"

Royce tugged at her hips, trying to get her to turn around. She resisted. "If it worries you that much, then join me in the interview."

"No." The knife clanked onto the cutting board, and Royce took a step backward. "I don't have anything to wear."

"What about the gown you wore to the symphony? You're stunning in it."

"I can't. Cassandra has seen me in it."

Royce burst out laughing. "Who cares? Everyone there has seen me in all of my tuxes."

"All?" She leaned against the counter and gripped the edge. "You have how many tuxes, and I have one gown. Do you see the difference?"

His eyes drifted from her furrowed brow to the white knuckles. If her hands had the strength, she'd crush the granite. "Is this because we had miscommunication, or is it something else?"

"Royce, don't analyze me." Her knee bobbed up and down as she tapped her pink fuzzy slippers. A strand of hair had fallen across her face, catching on an eyelash, but she seemed too focused to brush it away.

"I assure you, I'm not. But this isn't you."

"Oh my god, yes, it is."

"Fine." They held a gaze for a few seconds before Royce wrapped his arms around her waist. "If you don't want to go, I won't pressure you. But I'd like to have you there with me."

Cordelia's body softened, and vulnerability cracked the mask. "Your world's different. I mean, I'm sure Cassandra isn't a lone wolf in your circle."

"Not exactly. But there are nice people attending, like Olivia. You met her. And you know Richard."

"He's great. You're wonderful, and Cassandra's, unique. But Richard didn't grow up with a legacy and title. His parents are self-made. You, you and Cassandra grew up with unwritten rules and a stack of expectations that predate the Declaration of Independence."

He looked away, trying not to laugh, but he couldn't hold back. Although amused, her reference struck him, a reminder of the gap between their worlds. It wasn't merely wealth or title that separated them, but fundamental perspectives on heritage. Where she saw restrictions rooted in centuries of British aristocracy, he saw continuity. "You've been around my family, it's not that bad. Even my father can be genuine."

"No, but an entire room of them. I don't know."

"Then come with me and let me show you." Royce reached for her face. Her pouty lips distracted him. "Share this part of my life with me. It's important."

"But my deadline."

"Will still be there on Saturday. Just as my book will. My family obligations will always exist. If this is going to work, Cordelia, we need to find ways to integrate our lives, not compartmentalize them."

The silence stretched between them, heavy with unspoken concerns and patterns neither had fully addressed.

"Funny for you to say that when you're the one who secreted your life away." She smirked and batted her eyes.

"Are we going to revise that conversation?"

"No. But you did walk right into it."

Cordelia plopped her head onto his shoulder and exhaled. "Let me think about it?"

"Remember, it's in two days."

"I know, I know. But for the record, the cookbook isn't an excuse. It's a passion project."

"I understand." He kissed her forehead. "Just say, yes."

"Royce."

They kissed as the sauce bubbled and popped.

"I'll think about it. I promise."

Royce accepted her decision, though questions remained. For all her breakthrough with Jessica and talk of delegation, Cordelia still retreated to the kitchen when challenged.

"Now," she said, "taste this and tell me if you think it's ready." She tugged him closer to the cooktop.

"Is this a test?"

"No, but I can't be with someone who doesn't know the difference between basil and thyme." She held a steaming spoonful to his mouth.

"What if I fail?" He grinned and blew on the sauce.

"You won't. Now tell me what you think."

As Royce accepted the bite, he wondered about the conversation they weren't having, about priorities and patterns, about work as passion and shield. He recognized the irony, having spent years compartmentalizing and keeping his title separate from his career. Perhaps they were more alike than either wanted to admit. For now, the warmth in her eyes as she watched him taste her sauce was enough to quiet his questions.

# Chapter Twenty-One

Friday night at home left Cordelia staring at the cookbook manuscript on her laptop, untouched for over an hour. The words blurred together as her thoughts drifted to Royce at the charity gala happening at the Savoy. The soft white glow of her kitchen pendant light cast shadows onto the countertop, contrasting with the boldness of her laptop screen. She squinted, the words swimming in front of her as nighttime settled outside. She had planned to spend the evening working on her manuscript, determined to get ahead of deadlines. Instead, she kept checking her phone, waiting and hoping for a text from Royce. It was pointless to wait.

She closed the laptop, choosing to salvage her evening rather than waste it on anticipation. Images of chili-infused hot chocolate had teased her mind for days. The ingredients, things she could control, stood on the counter like a little army—a block of dark chocolate, vanilla beans, Bailey's, and Gavin's special chili spice.

Her phone rang, and her heart leapt. Before she saw the caller ID. Marnie, not Royce.

"Hey, how's life down under?" She put her on speaker and headed into the kitchen.

"A dream," Marnie said.

"Don't you open next week? I thought you were buried in prep."

" I am, but my Cordi radar pinged. What's wrong?"

"Nothing." The chocolate broke with a satisfying snap, releasing a rich aroma, and plopped into the warming milk. "What's up with that accent? You've been there two months, and your accent sounds like you've swallowed a crocodile."

"Says the woman whose fake British accent sounds like a gargling bird."

Cordelia laughed. "That's not even funny."

"Then why are you laughing?"

"Oh, shit." She grabbed a spoon and tried scooping lumps of spice from the pot. "I just dumped half of Gavin's chili."

"Wait, Gavin? You've seen him?"

"A few times. He's asked about you."

"And you're just now telling me this?"

Cordelia shifted her weight, leaning a hip against the counter as she traced swirls in the melting chocolate. Her shoulders, which had been tight all evening, softened as Marnie's voice filled the kitchen. "There wasn't much to tell. Royce and I ate there and."

"Ooh, how's Lord Gorgeous?" Marnie paused, mumbling to herself. "If you're not at work, then why aren't you with him? What's wrong?"

"My god, there's nothing wrong." She added sugar and scraped the vanilla pod into the pot, giving it a gentle stir. Steam rose in curls, carrying the sweet, nutty scent upward. She leaned in, closed her eyes, and let the spicy vapors caress her face and tickle her nose. "I spent many Friday nights without Daniel, and you never blinked. Why worry now?"

"Daniel-schmanuel, his idea of a date night was pizza and video games."

"Marnie. Cordelia squealed in laughter. "That's an exaggeration."

"Maybe, but he's no Earl, that's for sure."

"Royce isn't an Earl, not yet anyway. He has to inherit the title first."

"So, where is he? Why isn't *the Lord* there living up to the hype?"

Cordelia poured a shot of Bailey's into her mug and added some hot chocolate. "He's at his mom's foundation gala."

"And why aren't you with him?"'

"I needed to stay in and work on my recipes." Her voice skipped and stumbled.

"If that's true, then why do you sound disappointed?" There was a shuffling sound from Marnie. "Let's video chat. I want to see your face," she said.

Before Cordelia could protest, her phone screen shifted to an incoming video call. She reluctantly accepted, and Marnie's face appeared. Her platinum white hair revealed dark blonde roots, and bags framed her ice-blue eyes."

"You look exhausted."

"Love you too." Marnie studied Cordelia's expression. "Now tell me what's really going on."

The sofa enveloped her as she curled under a green wool throw blanket. "It's nothing. It's our crazy schedules. It's his title. And it's this." Cordelia shared an Instagram story with Marnie. The footage showcased Cassandra in a purple gown that minimized her 5'5' stature and highlighted her bust and slim hips. Off to one side, talking with Marcus was Royce, unmistakably handsome in his tux. Formal wear, she imagined peeling off him, like the unwrapping of a Christmas package.

"Clearly they're not together, so why does it bother you?"

"She's effortless. She belongs there. What if I don't?"

"Of course you do. You went to the symphony and impressed him. Remember? He chose you over her." No-nonsense Marnie provided a dose of reality whenever Cordelia felt like riding an emotional rollercoaster.

"Seeing this is a reminder." Cordelia sipped her hot chocolate, avoiding the conclusion.

"Of Daniel."

"Not just Daniel." Cordelia stretched out on the sofa and held the phone above her face. "It's my entire romantic history, which isn't saying much. It's either careers, or lifestyle, or something that creates issues. And then there's Royce, who's patient, understanding, and willing to accommodate my insane schedule. But how long before that patience runs out? How long before he realizes I'll never fit into the world of a Lord?"

"You're assuming you don't fit."

"No, I'm...I'm afraid I won't." Her legs curled under the blanket, and she picked at the wool fuzzies, flicking them onto the coffee table.

Marnie took a long sip of soda. The ice cubes clinked against the glass. "Have you talked to him about any of this?"

"No. I almost did the other night. He pushed for me to open up, but what am I supposed to say? 'I'm afraid of getting hurt if I don't fit into your social class?' That's attractive."

"Last time I checked, Lords are human too. If you don't talk to him, then you'll never know what he's thinking. And he won't know how you feel."

She groaned. "Why is dating so hard? Why can't it be like work, measurable?"

"Even that's outside your control. And humans aren't recipes."

"No, but it's a completely different world, and the pressure to be the best dressed or throw the best dinner party is too much. What if I try and fail? Then what, end up like I did with Daniel?"

"You didn't fail, he did."

"I know. But I don't want to be disappointed again."

"Don't you mean hurt?"

"That too." Her eyes pooled, but she held back the tears. "Why couldn't he just be Royce, the talented, hot writer I met in Paris?"

"He is, who happens to have a title." Marnie rattled her glass and drank the last of her soda." My point is, nothing is under our control. And you, of all people, know that the worthwhile things in life, the ones that truly matter, always involve risk."

Cordelia gazed past her face, remembering when Marnie had walked away from a head chef position to have Maisie. She sacrificed her opportunity, didn't resent Gavin's skyrocketing career, and still found happiness. Although she refused to tell him the truth, even she feared risk. "So, what are you saying is I should trust Royce?"

"Yes, exactly. I'm sure he can help you deal with all that uncontrollable pressure."

"If you're this wise, why aren't you taking your own advice?"

"What are you talking about?"

"Gavin. Why don't you trust him?"

Marnie's face shifted, and her confidence faltered. She stared off, looking away from the camera. Her voice had lost its overly opinionated edge. "It's not about trust, not exactly."

"Then what's it about?"

"It's." She sighed, running a hand through her platinum hair, revealing darker undertones. "Gavin and I were kids when we started seeing each other. My god, we all thought, you included, that after culinary school we'd conquer the world.

Well, you two are, but we've changed since then. We're different now."

Cordelia glanced at the sleek, modern hotel suite in the background, with all white surfaces and floor-to-ceiling windows of the Sydney Harbor. A half-eaten room service tray sat beside an open bottle of champagne. "Yes, but you still care about him. I see it whenever his name is mentioned."

"Clearly, the feelings are not mutual. He was perfectly fine leaving me in New York when he moved back to the UK. That's why I didn't tell him about the pregnancy." Her voice cracked slightly. "Do you know what it feels like to have someone you've built a life with just walk away?" She cleared her throat. "Sorry, I know you get it."

Cordelia adjusted the phone so Marnie could see her face better. "Maybe he thought that's what you wanted. You're not exactly an open book with your feelings."

"That's rich coming from you." She mumbled a laugh. "Now, he's famous, with multiple restaurants and TV appearances. But I have Maisie. So, our priorities don't align anymore."

"Have you asked him what his priorities are now?"

Marnie's eyes widened. "And risk Maisie getting attached to someone who might not stick around? I can't."

A bathroom door opened behind her, and Edward Gild walked out—tan, broad-shouldered, with a towel wrapped around his waist. He paused when he saw Marnie on a call, mouthed "Sorry," and disappeared into what Cordelia assumed to be the bedroom.

Marnie pursed her lips, popping them as she spoke. "Right. Enough about my ancient history. This is about you and Lord Gorgeous."

Cordelia drank the last of her hot chocolate, recognizing the deflection, as if she looked in a mirror. Whatever Marnie had gotten herself into with Edward, and whatever she felt for Gavin, remained behind her walls.

"Cordi, tell him how you're feeling."

"I'll see."

"For what it's worth, I think he's crazy about you."

They ended the call, and Cordelia scrolled through her photos from Dorset. She and Royce had taken a day trip to Old Harry Rocks, an adventure that challenged her fear of heights. Yet being vulnerable liberated her. His compassionate strength gave her the confidence to navigate the grassy trail and overcome her anxiety. In her favorite photo, the horizon stretched endlessly behind them, and a charcoal-colored sea met a somber sky, but there on the edge, they held each other happy, confident, connected.

Her phone chimed. Royce.

Wish you were here.

She smiled, feeling foolish for doubting herself. He didn't. Her fingers hovered over the keyboard, composing and deleting two different responses. The practiced reply felt like armor, safe but distant. Remembering Marnie's advice, she stepped outside the comfortable walls she'd built after Daniel and sent an honest reply. Her heart raced, but she ignored it.

Finding it hard to focus, thinking about you.

She hesitated before sending, the unusual vulnerability in her message making her finger hover over the screen. With a deep breath, she pressed send before she could reconsider.

Same. I'll call you when this concludes.

I'd like that.

She set the phone down, feeling lighter yet nervous. Her instinct advised protection and prioritizing the things she could control. But her sentimental heart whispered, reminding her of all she could gain with vulnerability. With renewed focus, Cordelia returned to her laptop and let the thoughts flow. With each recipe, she shared her memories, expressing herself to whoever read it.

# Chapter Twenty-Two

Royce knocked on Cordelia's door ten minutes past midnight, his tuxedo impeccable despite the long night. The cab ride from the gala had given him time to reflect, and he found himself unable to wait until morning to share his thoughts.

Cordelia opened the door in yoga pants and an oversized sweater. Her hair was pulled up, with strands tumbling around her face. "Royce. I thought you were going to call." She smiled through her surprise.

"Would you rather I leave?"

"No." Without hesitation, she pulled him inside. "I'm glad you're here."

The apartment smelled of chocolate and vanilla, with a hint of chili peppers. Her open laptop, which sat on the coffee table, was the primary source of light in the apartment. Beside it, a water bottle, an empty wine glass with cork remnants in the bottom, and a mug.

"Would you like tea? Water? Scotch?" She moved toward the kitchen and flipped on a couple of lamps. A haze of street light peeked through a half-closed curtain.

"Whatever you're having is fine." Royce moved further into the apartment, loosening his bow tie with one hand. "I apologize for coming by so late. I couldn't sleep. I needed to see you."

Cordelia dropped two tea bags into mugs and put the teakettle onto boil. As they waited for their tea, Royce shared details about the gala and the success of his mother's efforts. Before long, they moved to the living room, where they sat on opposite ends of the sofa facing one another.

"I had a conversation with my father this morning." He unbuttoned the top of his shirt, letting the night's obligations go. "One I've been turning over in my mind all day." Royce watched the steam rise and curl out of the mug. The subtle smell of chamomile calmed his nerves. "My father spent an hour on the phone explaining how I'm wasting my potential. He must've had a bulleted list of reasons, because he ran through my education, my network, and the future of the title. He gave an airtight sermon, and he had me convinced I needed to return to teaching."

"Wow, he's persistent." Cordelia's expression remained neutral, and non-judgmental.

"Relentless might be more fitting." Royce sipped his tea. "I was standing there tonight, surrounded by people I'd known my entire life. People with higher rank, more money, incredible legacies, and I had a moment of clarity. I watched them playing their roles, and when they thought no one was looking, I noticed something familiar. Desire. A thirst for authenticity, to experience themselves honestly, without pretense." Royce moved closer to Cordelia. "I realized I don't want to do that anymore. I want to be different. And I certainly do not want to subject my children, future children, to it."

Cordelia leaned forward, placing her hand on his knee. "Why did you leave in the first place? If you don't mind me asking."

Royce set his mug down, feeling a tightness in his chest whenever he thought too long about his departure. He'd avoided the conversation for over a year. "There was an incident." He contemplated his words. "Not directly involving me, but I bear responsibility nonetheless."

Cordelia's eyes remained fixed on him, creating a silent space for him to continue.

"My mentor, Gavin Andrews, who you unofficially met at the book signing, became involved with a graduate student. One of my students." The words tasted bitter on his tongue. Memories he'd worked to forget continued to haunt him. "Evie Lin. Brilliant researcher, with a promising career in archeology. She'd studied Roman artifacts since childhood, and she was going to be outstanding in the field. In light of her talent, I introduced them and encouraged her to seek his advice. They had a shared interest, and I thought he'd help advance her career."

Royce took a long sip of tea. "What I didn't know was that Gavin had a history of inappropriate relationships with students. The department had concealed the truth, moved previous students to different advisors, and silenced all complaints. There were rumors he'd done this at his previous university, too, but nothing proven. I learned after the fact, he collected vulnerable female students like trophies. Unfortunately, things deteriorated for Evie when he manipulated her academically and emotionally. She became desperate."

The memory of that night flashed like photos in his mind—the empty hallway, the sound of sobbing, Evie's ashen face streaked in grief.

"I found her after she'd taken a knife to her wrists." His voice tightened. "The ambulance got her to the hospital in time. I held her hand all night. I wanted her to know someone cared. And her parents' flight wouldn't arrive until the next day. When she told me what had happened, the extent of Gavin's misconduct, I went to the university dean. That's when I learned about the department's complicity. I resigned the next day. I couldn't be a part of an institution that protected predators at the expense of vulnerable students."

Cordelia's expression had shifted from curiosity to a somber blend of compassion and understanding. Her eyes teared, and she slid closer, resting her knee on his thigh. "Is that why they want you back? To guarantee Gavin's actions stay hidden?"

"Precisely." Royce met her gaze. "And my father, who sits on several academic boards, believes the incident was regrettable, including a professional overreaction on my part. He thinks I threw away a career over another man's indiscretions."

"And I assume, that's not how you see it."

"No." The weighted word summed up Royce's opinion of his father's assessment. "I introduced Evie to him. I vouched for his character. Yet, I failed to see what was happening." Sharing the story with her helped him process the guilt. "My father believes reputation is paramount. I believe it begins with integrity."

"That's why you didn't tell me?"

Royce nodded, feeling the softness of her hand. "With you, I just wanted to be myself, to see if that was enough."

"Oh, Royce. Of course, it is."

I should have explained sooner about the university situation, and the complexities that come with my family. I've been navigating two worlds for so long that I couldn't see the impact on you."

"Don't feel bad, I've done the same thing." Cordelia's fingers tightening around his hand. "I haven't exactly shared everything."

"We make quite the pair, don't we?" Royce offered a sheepish smile.

# Chapter Twenty-Three

Cordelia rested, curled against Royce's chest. She listened to the comforting rhythm of his heartbeat. His revelation about the university scandal lingered in her mind, not as a barrier, but a bridge that alleviated her relationship concerns. His fingers drew patterns on her back, a stimulating yet comforting sensation.

The early morning hours of quiet intimacy felt precious and precarious, a balance between worlds. He'd offered her trust, but to mirror his openness meant exposing herself to uncertainty. Her throat tightened and her stomach turned.

"What are you thinking?" Royce's voice rumbled in her ear.

Cordelia lifted her head to meet his gaze, finding patience rather than pressure. "How incredibly honest you've been with me, and I owe you the same."

"You don't owe me anything. Unless you perfected time travel and plan to leap into the future tomorrow, then I'd appreciate advanced notice."

She laughed. "As a matter of fact, Mr. Brownell, this is the future. We time traveled from 1731, and you forgot."

He rolled on top, "Then I guess you do owe me an explanation."

Royce teased and tickled the sides of her ribs, forcing her to laugh so hard she pleaded mercy. Catching her breath Cordelia gathered her thoughts, enjoying the warmth of his lips moving down her neck. Determination waned, and self-doubt set in, causing her to reconsider any revelations. She could let it go, save it for another day, and embrace the building heat between them. But that robbed them of sincerity.

She shifted from underneath him, insisting they needed to talk. Anticipation left her mouth dry, but Cordelia continued, telling him she wanted to share something with him. The gesture felt grand but important, an investment in their potential. She blurted, "I haven't been very open with you about my ex, Daniel." Her fingers fidgeted with the hem of her sweater. "It's why I'm cautious, which I know can be frustrating. But since we're opening up, I wanted to tell you what happened."

Royce rolled onto his side and propped himself up. She examined his eyes, wondering if she'd acted in haste, but he grinned and nodded, letting his hand rest on hers.

"I haven't been fully honest about how long we'd been together." Cordelia took a deep breath and relaxed her shoulders. She knew her story wasn't earth shattering or as emotionally heavy as his, but it had left scars. "When I said a few years, what I meant was eight. We were together for eight years."

Royce smirked and squeezed her hand. "That's a marriage for some people."

"I know, but we never...I've never been married, if that's what you're wondering."

"I wasn't, but obviously, it bothers you?" He sat up, their eyes meeting.

"No. I."

"Were you worried I'd walk out on you because there was someone before me?"

"No." A surge of foolishness ran through her. "It's not that. I mean, from what I've heard, you've had plenty of partners."

"I've had my share. Not eight years, but I don't see this as an issue for either of us."

Cordelia repositioned herself, wrapping her legs around Royce.

He pulled her tighter into his lap. "Clearly you're stressed over this, but I assure you, a prior relationship, whether six months, a year, or eight, isn't going to change my opinion of you."

Memories of Daniel washed across her mind, surfacing like waves rolling in at high tide. The whirlwind romance that began in Paris had fizzled within three years, yet she'd stayed another five as she transformed from partner to caretaker. They spiraled into a disappointing illusion and her loneliness found purpose in baking, propelling her career forward. Admitting the full truth, that she'd settled for a relationship that kept her emotionally safe but unfulfilled, felt too vulnerable, too close to confirming her deepest insecurities. She imagined Royce's reaction if he knew how long she'd chosen comfort over happiness.

She fidgeted and created physical space between them. Shouting from the street below provided a brief distraction, long enough for her to move closer to him again, grounding herself in his musky scent. "No, the eight years doesn't matter. It's everything prior to that, it's how it officially ended."

"You realize you're being cryptic right now, and I have no idea what you're trying to tell me."

"I know. Everything I want to share is swirling in my head."

"If you're not ready, then don't share it. But if you are, I'm listening."

"Eight, nine months ago I was still living in New York

sharing an apartment with him. He had a work trip, big event in California, and I was secretly interviewing for the position here. I knew he'd get upset even though, by that point, our lives were distant. The day I received the job offer is the same day he used my credit card for a hotel charge in Chicago. So, I called his phone, hoping it was card theft. But, a woman answered, one of my friends, and Daniel wouldn't take the call. He told her to hang up."

Royce inhaled sharply. "I'm sorry, Cordelia." He brushed a strand of hair from her eyes.

"That wasn't even the worst part. When I finally got him on the phone, didn't deny any of it, and instead, he blamed me for his cheating. He said I was emotionally unavailable." A boiling anger knotted in her chest, but with a forceful exhale, it subsided into resignation. "In one phone call, he cast me as the villain, a cold, career-obsessed woman who forced him into Cary Anne's bed, and for a while, I believed him."

He reached for her hand but pulled back. "I hope you know I don't see you as career obsessed."

"You've reminded me several times that I'm driven."

"Driven and obsessed are different dynamics. Your drive is inspiring, and Bastien's lucky to have you."

"Thank you." She held his hand between hers, feeling the texture of his skin. "I know I focus on work, a lot, but I love what I do."

"And you should be proud of your accomplishments. You've achieved more than most at thirty-four."

"Thirty-three." She playfully squeezed his hand.

"Right. Thirty-four in May?" He flinched playfully. "Alright, I won't forget." Royce grinned, his full lips pushing back into dimples. The thought of kissing him distracted her from the conversation.

She sighed and shifted back into his lap, wrapping her legs

around his waist. "It sounds so trivial when I say it out loud." Her voice pitched higher with embarrassment. "And you don't want to get me started on my mother issues." She chuckled, noticing the confused look on his face. "Yeah, that's a loaded story all on its own."

"Enlighten me."

"Are you sure? One emotional story isn't enough for you?"

"Try me."

"Okay, clearly you like baggage." She wrapped her arms around his neck. "When I was seven my mother decided she needed something different, a fresh start to life. So, she packed her bag, said goodbye and left my dad to raise James and me. She lives in Dallas, Texas, has retired as a flight attendant, married to a pilot, and I haven't seen or spoken to her since the day she left."

"Wow, that must've been difficult."

"Not an ideal family picture, but my dad filled the void."

His arms pulled her closer, offering a silent strength.

The admission felt shockingly vulnerable to her system, like exposing whipped cream to sunlight. She hadn't intended to reveal so much, yet her fears of abandonment dissolved in the gentle space he created.

"Cordelia, we're all shaped by our experiences. They question isn't whether those circumstances influence us, it's how we respond to them that defines us. And I assure you, your drive that's a result of their actions, isn't a negative thing."

She locked onto his eyes, searching for any sign of judgment or pity. Anything that would counter his words, but instead, she found a rare form of intimacy, the kind that sees her rough edges and doesn't try to change them.

"You're beautiful." His thumbs graced her collarbone, the callused edge catching slightly against her skin. She leaned into the touch, her body responding to the simple contact with a warmth that spread from her cheeks down to her core. "Even when you leave me waiting ten extra minutes at a restaurant or cancel our date because you spilt chocolate on your clothes, and even when you attend the symphony with an inflatable cushion."

"I had a good reason for that one." She rubbed her tailbone, remembering the shock to her bottom.

His dimples reappeared, sending a thrilling rush through her body. "And what about when I beat you to the top of the hill at Corfe Castle?"

"Even then."

"And what about the time I horrified Cassandra at her own dinner party?"

"Even then, especially then."

"You know, I'm still learning how we fit together, but I think you're pretty amazing Mr. Brownell."

Royce slid his hands beneath her hips and flipped her onto the sofa. "Promise me something."

"What's that?"

"If you're feeling overwhelmed, tell me. I can't read your mind, or your past. And I don't know about you, but I'm enjoying this."

"Me too. As long as we're making deals, if my work ever starts to interfere, tell me."

"Agreed."

She leaned up and kissed him. "And if you change your life to make all of them happy, I'll tell you."

"Agreed." His kiss, sensual and grand provoked her appetite for him. She pulled his hips into hers and lingered in the moment, until she had the urge to yawn. She fought it but finally gave in to exhaustion. The light slipping through the curtain crack had transitioned into sunlight.

"I should go." Royce said, glancing at his watch. "We both need rest, and if I stay, that's not going to be achievable."

Part of her wanted to ask him to keep her awake, to satisfy her carnal need, but she recognized the wisdom in his suggestion. Plus, they both needed time and space to process the emotional ground they'd covered.

He shoved his tie into a pocket and kissed her. "Remember, their actions don't define you."

After he'd left, Cordelia moved through the apartment with a strange sense of lightness. The cookbook manuscript still waited on her laptop, the deadline loomed, and the team still counted on her. All the demands of life remained the same, but something had shifted.

# Chapter Twenty-Four

Cordelia had been baking since midnight. Not because she needed three dozen black cherry rout cakes in her freezer, which held enough to supply a Christmas market. She baked because December 24th arrived with a gap, a missing link that disappeared when her father passed away three years earlier.

The absence of him seemed heavier with James and his family in Seattle. Marnie and Maisie had moved permanently to Sydney, where Christmas came with beach barbecues instead of snow.

She'd declined five invitations. Bastien and Jeannine. Two from suppliers. One from Sam. And the Countess had called three times, her voice warm with maternal insistence, leaving Cordelia feeling both welcomed and terrified.

She pulled the last batch from her oven. Three a.m., Christmas Eve. The scent of cinnamon and ginger filled her flat.

Her phone buzzed. Royce.

Why are all your apartment lights on?

She moved to the window. Outside on the pavement, a silhouetted figure waved up at her.

Stalking me?

Always. Want company?

They'd been together eight months. Eight months of dinners, stolen afternoons, nights that ended with sunrise. But Christmas meant something else. Things were getting real.

Bring milk.

I don't think I'll find a cow roaming at this hour.

Haha. True.

A minute later, he stood at her door, wearing joggers and the Cambridge sweatshirt she'd borrowed twice before. "I stopped by the twenty-four-hour cafe. Thought you could use this."

"How did you know?" She accepted a coffee in a holiday paper cup and breathed in the rich scent of roasted beans.

"Instinct."

In the kitchen, cooling racks covered every surface with cookies arranged in precise rows.

"Jane Austen's rout cakes, what do you think?" she explained. "They're going in the cookbook, well, a variation of them."

Royce bit into a cookie and chewed. His upper lip curled, and his face scrunched into an unpleasant expression.

"Seriously? You're joking."

He busted into laughter, affectionately grabbing her hand. "Yes, I'm joking. They're delicious. In fact, I'll have another one." Royce playfully grabbed a second cookie, dipping it into his coffee.

"Do you think your family will like them?" She rolled another ball of dough.

"They'll love them." He finished his cookie and washed his hands. "Teach me."

"How to roll dough?"

"Sure. Why not? It's the holidays, right?"

Cordelia found his chipper, early morning attitude surprising. "Why were you out so early?"

"When I can't sleep, I go for a run." Royce shared the stress of meeting publisher deadlines, something he still dreaded, even though it reminded him of his thesis deadlines.

Standing in front of him, with his arms stretched around her, and his breath on her cheek, she guided him on her rolling pin technique. She bit back a laugh when he used a ruler to ensure uniform cookie thickness.

"They don't have to be perfect," she said.

"Says the woman who made me whisk eggs for twenty minutes last week."

"That was different. We were making an omelet."

"And this?" He gestured at the precise rows of cooling cookies.

"This is your family."

Royce laughed. His rolling technique was erratic despite the effort. She didn't correct him. Something about his concentration, with his lips pressed together as he focused made her heart skip.

"Mum's excited you accepted her invitation."

"She called three times yesterday. Now I know where your persistence comes from."

"With my parents, it was inevitable."

When the timer dinged, Cordelia pulled out beautiful

golden cookies in various shapes. Royce's looked more like abstract art than holiday symbols.

Royce inspected the cookies, chuckled and tossed them back onto the pan.

"No one's perfect on their first try." She bit into one. "It tastes good."

She slid the next batch into the oven, set the timer, and wiped her hands. "Last batch. Twelve minutes." Cordelia led him into the living room and flipped on the TV. Royce yanked off his sweatshirt, adjusting the t-shirt underneath. The ripples of his abs grabbed her attention.

"What are watching?" His arms nested around her as they curled up together under a thick, knitted throw.

She scrolled through a selection of holiday movies. "Ooh, how about this one? They're stuck together at an inn with both of their ex's, and she's, haughty." On screen, a woman dressed in designer clothes stumbled through fake snow bumping into a handsome inn keeper.

"Let me guess, she's some corporate executive who never leaves the city, but when she does, she discovers the meaning of Christmas?"

"Obviously. And he's a single dad who makes furniture and coaches youth hockey."

"But what about the ex's?" His fingers traced patterns on her arm.

"Umm, I'll bet her ex is an introverted banker, and his is the town's former cheerleader."

"No, her ex was her boss, and his was the mayor."

"Oh, good one." She playfully patted his abs, feeling the hard muscles responding to her touch.

"Did you watch these growing up?"

"God no. Our Christmas eve entertainment was Dad

reading indigenous stories to us. And then in the morning we went to help out at a soup kitchen."

"Really?"

"Every year. He said if we were fortunate enough to have food, we should share it." She shifted to see his face. "James and I would help serve breakfast, then prep lunch. Gifts came at night."

"Even Santa?"

"Even Santa. He convinced us Santa made special evening deliveries for families who spent mornings helping others." She smiled at the memory. "What about you? Full English breakfast and presents at dawn?"

"Close. Sausages from the village butcher, Mum's Swedish-style pancakes, her once a year splurge, and yes, a tree full of presents."

"I bet it was obscene."

"Pretty much. But on Christmas Eve we'd attend the choir service at the village church, and have dinner at the pub. You know, the little one on High Street next to the florist?"

"That one? I can't imagine your father ever stepping foot in there."

"He'll surprise you sometimes. He grew up with the Cutchers".

She burrowed deeper into his warmth. On screen, the executive had discovered the inn was being foreclosed.

"She'll save it." Cordelia predicted.

"While learning to love again."

"After some contrived misunderstanding in act three."

"Involving his precocious child who orchestrates their reconciliation."

They watched in comfortable silence. His thumb traced infinity patterns on her hip. The apartment smelled of ginger and coffee and him.

"I could get used to this." he said.

"Bad movies and artistic cookies?"

"You. Here. Us."

The timer chimed before she could respond. She returned with two warm cookies, settling back into his arms.

"These are perfect."

"Unlike yours."

"Mine have character."

"Is that what you call it?"

His lips rested on her temple. "Like a fine wine, distinct and unforgettable."

"They're definitely unforgettable." Cordelia jumped up, grabbed her phone, and snapped a photo of Royce's cookies—trees with limbs that spread like a spider's web. "They're now immortalized."

"If these impress you, wait till next year."

Next year. The words flowed from his lips as if he'd planned their future. After Daniel, the assumption of permanence should've triggered a need to retreat, but it didn't. Her heart didn't jump. Her stomach didn't seize up. Instead, she plopped beside him, wrapped her arms around his waist, and listened as he talked about the movie.

On screen, snow began to fall as the executive realized she loved the inn keeper. Cordelia rolled her eyes but didn't change the channel. Royce's arms tightened around her.

"Let's skip Hayton today."

"We can't, your mother would never forgive me, or you."

"I'll tell her we're both violently ill, and can't make it."

"Royce Brownell, you can't lie to your mother." She flipped into his lap, straddling him. "We're going to Hayton with all these cookies and enjoy a traditional Christmas with your family."

He squeezed her hips. "I'd rather make a new tradition with you."

An alarm rang in Cordelia's bedroom, distracting her from Royce's affection. "We have to go." She jumped up and pulled him off the sofa. "You need to go home. And make yourself presentable. It's Christmas morning, babe."

Royce lifted her to his hips as her thighs wrapped around his torso. "This means something to you." His voice sounded surprised, contemplative. She saw the moment he understood Christmas meant something to them as a couple, because her grief and joy were becoming part of his landscape too.

"Yes, it does."

"Then to Hayton we'll go." His tone deepened into a raspy sound. "As you desire, Ms. Dyer."

# Chapter Twenty-Five

Three weeks after Christmas at Hayton, Royce navigated the oak-paneled corridors of the Private Club, brushing his fingertips along the polished wood as he passed, the texture a constraining comfort, like the rituals he'd once embraced without question. The scent of leather and citrus permeated the air, as much a part of the atmosphere as the whispered conversations and clinking crystal. His footsteps slowed as he approached the dining room, shoulders tensing beneath his tailored jacket.

The maître d' nodded as Royce entered the dining room. "Lord Brownell, your father is already seated at your usual table."

"Thank you, Harrison. How was your daughter's ballet recital?"

Harrison's stern professional mask slipped, revealing surprise. "She was a very convincing swan. Thank you for asking."

"Excellent. Tell her congratulations."

Royce continued into the dining room, spotting his father at the window table with red leather chairs, a high-profile spot where they met for lunch every Tuesday for the past four and a half years.

The Earl marked his book with a monogrammed silver clip as Royce approached. "Why are you late?" he asked without looking up. His voice carried a particular blend of judicial authority and paternal disapproval.

Royce felt the tightness in his chest, a response since childhood, as if his father's disapproval compressed the air around him. "Hello, Pop." Royce settled into the chair opposite his father, refusing to be drawn into their pattern of accusation and defense. "I was detained by the ancient and sacred ritual of London traffic."

"I thought you walked here."

"I did."

The Earl cut his eyes up. "Punctuality is a matter of planning, not circumstance."

"Ah yes, the family motto. I believe it's embroidered on the crest, just under the stern falcon."

"It's a peregrine." The Earl narrowed his eyes. "Are you mocking our family?"

"No, Pop. Never." Royce settled into his chair. "But you must admit some of our traditions are ripe for mocking. Like Grandfather always insisting the butter be served at precisely five-and-a-half degrees Celsius, or how the staff measures each garland at Christmas, ensuring perfect symmetry."

A waiter appeared beside the table, placing a gin and tonic in front of Royce, his standing order that required no verbal confirmation. At the club, routine was religion.

"You're being impertinent. That girl's influence isn't very promising." The Earl took a careful sip of his scotch, the amber liquid catching the afternoon light.

"Let's leave Cordelia out of this." The memory of Lang dropping the bag of flour, and engulfing Cordelia and Sam in a cloud of white followed by Cordelia's laughter left him in a lighter mood.

"Your mother seems to think she's good for you." The Earl swirled and sipped his scotch again, his expression a teetering balance between interest and judgment.

"Mum reads people well. She also thought you needed a cat to improve your disposition and look how that turned out."

The Earl's mouth twitched. Sir Albert, their British Shorthair, had made Hayton Manor its home and since then it paraded around, ignoring everyone but The Earl. Instead of softening his temperament, it reinforced it. "Sir Albert recognizes natural authority."

"He's essentially you in cat form."

The Earl cleared his throat. "We were discussing the American, not my cat."

"Were we? I thought we were discussing punctuality." Royce looked around the room and gestured at the table setting. "Don't you ever get tired of this place? We've attended state events with less ceremony than here."

"Proper standards are not ceremony," The Earl insisted. "They're the foundation of a civilized society."

"Right." Royce sipped his drink. "Without the correct fork, society would crumble into chaos."

The Earl cleared his throat and methodically aligned his silverware with the edge of the table. "I will say, the American."

"Her name is Cordelia." Royce straightened his own utensils as they shimmered against the crisp white tablecloth, catching himself mirror the inherited habit, that revealed more about their connection than words expressed.

"I will say, Cordelia surprised me. I expected her to be another one of your fortune seekers, but it seems she has a head on her shoulders."

"You contradict yourself."

"How so?"

"You say she's a poor influence but smart, however, you recognize she's not a fortune hunter. If she's an intelligent woman who's not interested in wealth, then how is she a bad influence?"

The Earl squared his forks off. "Do you intend to marry her?"

"I hadn't given it thought, but if I do, at some point, you'll know after Cordelia."

A gentleness washed over The Earl's face, a rare glimpse at warmth, reminding Royce of childhood moments when his father revealed the man behind the title.

A server approached with their first course—consommé for the Earl, and seasonal soup for Royce. He watched his father examine the amber consommé with a critical eye, smelling it for clarity.

"Is it satisfactory, Pop? Or should we call the chef out for a formal inquiry?"

The Earl looked up and narrowed his eyes. "Very ill-mannered, Royce. You find this amusing?"

"Some of it, yes. You must admit, it's funny how you pretend to read the menu every week, yet order the same meal. For a decade."

"Traditions provide stability."

"They're also amusing. Like the toast your brother gives every New Years. He pours the brandy, sniffs it for exactly fifteen seconds, swirls it, sniffs again, and then recites the exact same speech."

A reluctant smile emerged on The Earl's face. "It is tedious."

"It's comical. Just as absurd as measuring garland or serving two kinds of meat at Christmas just because some ancestor did it under the Tudors. And even you must admit that Grandfather's thirty-minute lectures on the proper way to fold a pocket square was excessive."

The Earl's spoon paused halfway to his mouth. "You sound like your mother."

"Thank you."

"You've become rather outspoken lately."

"Occupational hazard, I guess."

"And you find this... refreshing?"

"I do. I also find it refreshing when you drop the persona and just act like my father."

The Earl glanced up from his soup and gave a single nod.

"Remember when you taught Marcus and me to skip stones on the pond? Or when you let us build that makeshift fort that violated at least a dozen of Grandfather's landscaping rules?"

A crocked smile flickered across The Earl's face. "Your grandfather was livid when he saw what you'd erected beneath his favorite oak."

"Yet you defended us. Remember, you told him that tradition shouldn't stifle creativity."

"Did I say?"

"You did. That should be the family motto."

"That's a bit extreme. And impractical."

"I disagree. Tradition has its place, but it shouldn't be a prison. It shouldn't prevent us from forming meaningful connections or pursuing our passions." Royce leaned forward, bridging the distance between them. "Listen, Pop, I want us to end this animosity. We used to be close, remember? We talked and didn't despise each other."

"Despise is harsh."

"We both know it's heading to that if we don't solve this issue."

The Earl repositioned his flatware, bringing each remaining piece to the edge of the table with meticulous attention. The practice annoyed Royce, yet as Cordelia had pointed out, he himself did it when anxious.

"Yes, well, I agree it's been difficult this past year. But only because you left the university," The Earl said, emphasizing the last four words.

"Pop. You need to stop demanding I do everything according to your expectations. You need to respect my decisions and listen to me."

"Son, I expect things from you because you represent this family." The Earl's voice carried the weight of centuries, of portraits lining the halls of Hayton, and of responsibilities that transcended individual desires.

"I know, but there won't be a family if you keep demanding I be your puppet."

"Is that what you believe?" For the first time, genuine surprise broke through The Earl's facade.

"Yes. You don't give me room to be myself. I need all of your demands to end. I need your unfounded hostility toward Cordelia to end. And if you won't, then I'll step aside and let Marcus have the title."

The threat, more real than he'd ever articulated before, hung in the air like a weighted balloon. The Earl stared into his scotch. A faint nod acknowledged the ultimatum.

"I need to focus on my career and my life." Royce softened his tone, letting a deep warmth come through. "Can you trust me to do what's best for myself and the family?"

The Earl finished his scotch, glanced at his watch, and stood. "It's 13:45. I have a meeting at 14:30."

"Pop." Royce rose to his feet, unwilling to let the conversation end with this unresolved tension.

The Earl placed his napkin in the chair and paused, his expression momentarily shifted between man and title, father and Earl. "We'll conclude this conversation next week. And let it be clear, Royce, I will never despise you. Quite the contrary, actually." Then, with a glint of unexpected humor, he added, "Though I might require you to explain to your mother why Sir Albert has taken to sleeping on my dress shirts. She seems to think I'm encouraging him."

"Noted." Royce smiled at his father, aware they'd crossed an impasse, one he wasn't sure they'd ever fully conquer.

The Earl turned and walked away, his posture stiff and impeccable, although Royce thought he detected an air of ease in his father's step that hadn't seen in years.

Royce remained at the table, finishing his lunch as he contemplated the subtle shift in their relationship. He'd stood his ground, and while no resolution had been reached, something had changed. His father had at least acknowledged the possibility of further conversation, a small victory in the ongoing battle between tradition and personal happiness.

His phone vibrated with a text from Cordelia.

Emma told me Marcus can't keep a secret and told you about the birthday party. Pretend to be surprised, okay?

I have no idea what you're talking about ;-)

Sharpen those acting skills, Mr. Brownell. x

The simple message, with its casual intimacy and the small 'x', reminded him precisely why this confrontation with his father became necessary. What he was building with Cordelia, a balance of respect and passion, had overflowed into his everyday life. The realization settled into clarity. Her influence hadn't weakened his connection to family as his father feared but strengthened his ability to authentically stand within it.

Royce wanted to sustain the legacy, but not at the cost of personal respect.

He slid the phone into his jacket pocket and glanced around the room, observing men who abided by the tradition of dress jackets, whispered sideways conversations, and dining on the same food their fathers had eaten.

As he left the club, stepping from its hushed atmosphere into London's vibrant afternoon, Royce felt liberated. For the first time since he could remember, he looked forward the next Tuesday lunch with his father. Perhaps he'd suggest they skip the club altogether and try somewhere new, someplace modern where tables aren't precise and the napkins came in colors other than white. The thought of his father agreeing to culinary anarchy was almost worth breaking with tradition.

Almost.

# Chapter Twenty-Six

The rhythmic whirl of machinery and chattering voices at BL London had quieted after the day's production. As nighttime settled over the shop, Cordelia appreciated that the loudest sound was a soft scratch of her pencil against paper as she noted revisions on the eclairs. She rubbed her neck, feeling the day's tension stored in her shoulders.

A sharp knock on the front window startled her from concentration. Cordelia glanced at her watch. Nine p.m. Expecting to find a confused tourist who had missed the CLOSED sign, she walked to the front empty handed. Instead, Cassandra peered through the glass, her red manicured nails rapped like an impatient child.

Cordelia hesitated, calculating the cost of interruption against the potential benefits of improving her relationship with someone who held influence in Royce's life, whether guilt or encouragement. "We're closed." She opened the door and offered a flat grin.

"Obviously." Cassandra swept inside without waiting for an invitation, her presence commanded compliance despite her petite stature. "But I saw the light on and knew you were working."

The presumption carried a blend of entitlement and directness that characterized every encounter. Cassandra appraised the shop front, "I was hoping to speak with you privately."

"Does it look like anyone else is here?"

"Of course not. Is this an inconvenient time?"

"I'm working on the cookbook. The deadline is pressing, but what's up?"

"This won't take long." Cassandra reached into her designer handbag and withdrew a folded newspaper page and handed it to Cordelia. Her entire faced squinted. "I thought you should see this." Her oversized diamond tennis bracelet caught the streetlight and sent rainbow streaks outward.

Cordelia accepted the page, immediately noticing it was from the Sunday society section. Near the bottom, a photograph showed she and Royce at the charity tennis tournament. His hand rested on her hip. They laughed. He whispered in her ear. An intimate moment, caught in black-and-white. The caption read Lord Royce Brownell with pastry chef Cordelia Dyer at the Chart Home charity tournament. Has London's most eligible bachelor been taken off the market?

"Thank you for sharing this, but one, it's old news, and two, I'm not sure why you felt the need to personally deliver it." Cordelia kept her tone neutral despite the discomfort of seeing their private moment publicized like a dating show. She handed it back to Cassandra.

"You can keep it. It's actually rather good of you two, rather genuine. Don't you agree?" The complexity of her voice carried tones of reluctance and admiration. Cordelia struggled to decipher the meaning.

"Is there something you want to say, Cassandra?" Cordelia placed the clipping on the counter, refusing to play games.

"I want to discuss Royce."

"And?"

"Let me be frank." She removed her black trench coat, draping it over her arm. "He's become quite invested in you, quickly. More than I've seen him do with anyone."

Her opinion, delivered with precision, carried an air of disapproval that reminded Cordelia of the dinner party. "And you feel it's your duty to say something because...?"

"Because he's deeply private about his feelings, and, I've seen him retreat to Paris too many times when he's hurt." Cassandra's tone revealed a soft concern beneath her cold exterior.

"Paris?"

"Yes, he goes there to escape the gossip. He's not as immune as he appears."

"I'm aware of that. Royce and I have been quite open with each other about our respective vulnerabilities."

Cassandra's face tightened, leaving tiny lines around her eyes, and her lips puckered with what appeared to be pain or jealousy. "How refreshing." She glanced around the bakery, examining the cold marble counter. "Do you have somewhere we can sit? Standing is so adversarial."

"There's more?"

"Of course there's more."

Cordelia hesitated and gestured toward the kitchen. "Would you like tea?"

"That would be lovely, thank you."

The simple task of preparing tea gave Cordelia a moment to ground herself. When she returned to the kitchen prep area, Cassandra examined framed articles about BL London's awards at the International Pastry Competition on a staff wall.

"Impressive credentials. I see it in your work."

"Thank you." Cordelia said, handing off a mug to Cassandra. "Sorry for the bag, it's all we had."

"I prefer my tea this way, shocking I know." She held the tea bag up and dunked it three times. "I haven't been entirely fair to you. My behavior at dinner and the tournament has been rather," Cassandra's confident composure wavered. "Rather territorial and in reflection, not entirely kind."

"Wow, that's unexpected, but appreciated, if you're apologizing?"

"Please let me finish before I change my mind." She traced the rim of her teacup with one perfectly manicured finger.

Cordelia could only imagine the struggle Cassandra's ego endured confessing that her actions were less than perfect.

"Royce has been my constant through very difficult periods. There was a time when I thought, when I hoped, he and I might become more than friends. Despite my utterly embarrassing attempts over the years, Royce has never seen me in that way. And I've watched your relationship develop, admittedly resenting you, wondering why you, and not me."

"And?" Emotionally Cordelia felt compassion and discomfort, listening to Cassandra seek answers for something only Royce could answer.

"I care about Royce and want to see him happy, even if it isn't with me."

Before Cordelia could respond a sharp knock on the front window interrupted them. Taylor Henson, dressed in athletic attire with a bag slung across her body, peered in, her determined face pressed against the glass. She answered the door, "How can I help you?"

"Hello, again, Ms. Dyer. I hadn't heard from, and it's very important that we speak. I need your interview so I can finish this piece on Daniel's recovery and return to tennis."

"Ms. Henson, As I said, I have nothing to contribute, and you'd be better off talking with Cary Anne, or Daniel himself."

"Taylor. I did, and he said," She read from her phone. "Cordelia has always been my biggest support, the one to get me through rough times."

"Well, he's mistaken."

Taylor pushed her way into the shop. "Just give me five minutes, and then I'll let you go on with your life."

"Fine. Ask your questions, but I doubt I can contribute much."

Fifteen minutes passed before Cordelia scooted Taylor out of the shop. When she turned for the kitchen, she found Cassandra staring with a glazed look of surprise.

"Daniel Montali? The tennis player with those shirtless cologne ads?"

"Yes."

"That must've been incredible."

Cordelia hesitated, fumbling for a response. "It's not always what it seems, Cassandra."

"It never is. Mind if I ask why?"

A sharp laugh escaped Cordelia. "Let's just say it started out fun and ended with a dramatic revelation that killed a dying relationship."

Cassandra's face transitioned from confused to shocked. "He cheated on you?"

"Wow, you must be good at puzzles."

Cassandra remained silent, looking past Cordelia. Her red nails clicked on her mug. "I know the look, the signs. My fiancé cheated on me. With my mother."

The confession landed like a physical blow. Cordelia stared, robbed of speech by the revelation. Contradictory emotions rose up—sympathy for the betrayal, and embarrassment for quickly assuming the worst about Cassandra.

"It was a year-long affair." Cassandra's words spilled out like an open dam. "I discovered it the night before our wedding. Called everything off, of course. And I never told my father why. It would've destroyed him." Pain echoed in her voice. "Our scandals aren't so different, are they?"

The shared experience of betrayal created an immediate and unexpected bond between them. Their competitive tension dissolved, replaced by a silent understanding, a silent wound.

"No one understands unless they've been through it." Cordelia said, quietly mumbling her words. She reached for Cassandra's hand and squeezed it, offering compassion.

"Exactly. It made me question everything, my judgment, my worth, and if whether I even knew what love meant."

"I wondered if I'd ever be able to trust anyone again."

"This is why Royce is so important to me. He was there when everything fell apart that night, the only person who knows the full truth. He's been my constant." She traced the pattern on the ceramic mug. "I'm not sure I would've survived it without him."

The revelation provided Cordelia with a new perspective on the bond between Royce and Cassandra. They had a foundation of incredible support during a profound crisis, and an awareness she'd misjudged the situation.

Cassandra sandwiched Cordelia's hand between hers. "I can see why Royce is drawn to you."

"Well, I."

"Does he know about Daniel?"

"A little? He knows what happened, but he doesn't know it's the Daniel Montali."

"You need to tell him the full story before he hears it elsewhere."

Cordelia sighed. "I know, I know. It just felt irrelevant, and now we're in a great place, but it's starting to come up, especially with Daniel texting again."

"You still communicate with him?"

"More like, he communicates with me. I keep telling him to stop, but he's relentless."

"Cordelia, trust me when I say this," Cassandra scooted her stool closer. "Secrets never end well. And if Royce discovers Daniel's full identity from a newspaper article or gossip, it'll be far more disruptive than hearing it directly from you."

"I know you're right."

"Don't wait." She stood and drank the last of her tea. "I'd like us to be friends."

The offer, so different from their previous interactions, surprised Cordelia, who'd assumed the conversation was a brief reprieve from their adversarial relationship. Yet she found herself appreciating Cassandra's interruption. "I'd like that. But what about when Royce is around? Friends?"

"One step at a time." Cassandra snorted a laugh. "I'm joking, of course, darling."

As Cassandra prepared to step out the door, she turned, and said, "Whatever Daniel did or said, don't hold that against Royce. And don't break his heart."

"I don't plan to, but thanks for the advice."

"That's what friends are for." She pressed a quick kiss to Cordelia's cheek, her signature perfume lingered, leaving a cloud of sugary essence in the air. "Goodbye, darling, and thanks for the tea."

After Cassandra departed, Cordelia returned to her notes, yet her concentration had been shattered. Her mind felt like an overwhipped egg whites on the verge of collapse. Every thought circled and fear mingled with determination. She retrieved the newspaper clipping and studied the photo that had started the evening's chain of events. Cassandra was right, they both appeared happy. A bright glow radiated across their faces. The emotions the photographer captured in that moment with Royce contrasted sharply with what she felt each time Daniel reappeared.

But the shock of the night, Cassandra's candid and raw disclosures. For a woman who'd been a rival to reveal herself without knowing how it would be received, suggested she was either brave or desperate. Cordelia chose bravery.

Cordelia reached for her phone, knowing there'd never be a perfect moment. She texted Royce, telling him she wanted to see him, and returned to her recipes while she waited.

# Chapter Twenty-Seven

The gravel driveway crunched beneath the tires as Royce pulled up to Hayton Manor. The familiar scent of damp earth filled the car as he rolled down the window, bringing with it memories of childhood foot races across the lawn and dinners in the great hall. Winter had stripped the gardens bare, leaving exposed branches silhouetted against the pale afternoon sky. He glanced at Cordelia beside him, watching her take in the landscape as it transformed from parkland to gardens surrounding the house. Despite her previous visit months earlier, he noticed a nervousness in her expression.

"You're quiet," he said, stealing another glance at her profile. "And beautiful."

She blushed, placing her hand in his lap.

"Nervous?"

"No. I just hope my hostess skills can keep up with your mother's. We've been planning this party for months." She smoothed an imaginary wrinkle from her blue dress. "And remember, it's a surprise."

"Don't worry, I have it all planned out, Mum won't have a

clue." The car braked and Royce threw his hands to his face, pretending to be shocked.

"That's your plan? That face? I've seen better acting from statues." She laughed, blotting her eyes to keep from smearing her makeup.

"What? I'll have you know I acted in many prep school plays. And I was told I had unexplored abilities."

"Are you sure that was meant as a compliment?"

"Come to think of it, I don't know. Pop said it."

"I'm sure he did." Cordelia patted his cheek, still chuckling from Royce's earlier expression. "You'll fool them all."

They pulled up to the entrance where valets waited. "Showtime." He kissed the back of her hand. "Ready?"

"For your performance? Absolutely."

He handed off the keys to a young man, wrapped his arm around Cordelia's waist, and escorted her inside, where guests mingled in the entrance hall and adjoining sitting rooms. Royce kept a protective hand at the small of Cordelia's back as he guided her through introductions, noting the slight tension in her posture as she committed names and titles to memory. Pride swelled as she navigated each exchange with hospitality, and any disconnect he'd felt between obligation and desire narrowed with each handshake.

The countess greeted them and wished Royce happy belated birthday. She embraced Cordelia with a motherly affection she seemed to reserve for Emma, and now Cordelia. "So happy both of you could make it out."

Royce noted the quick conspiratorial glance between the two of them. He enjoyed witnessing their growing friendship. It had taken on a life independent of him.

Before entering the front sitting room, they were joined by Marcus, Emma, and Ada Rose. At five months, she recognized their faces, smiling and carrying on babbling conversations with

Cordelia, who argued anytime someone called her a natural. She had an easy rapport with everyone they spoke with, asking questions, and finding common ground with them. When it came to hosting, Cordelia proved herself to be gracious and well-spoken.

Across the room, Royce spotted his father towering above two men in conversation. The Earl's gaze shifted from the conversation to Cordelia who spoke with village neighbors, the local stationers. The shop had been in their family for almost one hundred years and was one of his favorite places to retreat from the estate. His chin dipped and based on the slightly lifted corner of his mouth, The Earl approved.

"Follow me." Royce took Cordelia's hand and guided her through a maze of rooms and behind a paneled door, where they entered the family's private hallway. Lining the walls, photos chronicled several generations of Brownells, and the narrow space had been Royce's refuge since he was a boy.

As soon as the door closed, he pulled her into himself. The corridor smelled of pine, and mingled with Cordelia's floral cologne, creating a scent of refuge, where past and present merged into new adventure. "You're incredibly charming, and I might add, making me anxious." His hands brushed down her back and arms.

"Did I say something wrong? It's the Duke of Evenshire, right? Or is it Benshire, and I called him Evenshire? Oh, god, please tell me I didn't screw up."

"You're doing fantastic, and for the record, it's the Duke of Evenshire, the Earl of Leyford, and Lord Benshire. Don't worry, everyone screws up occasionally."

"Then why are you anxious?"

He closed the gap between their mouths. "I'm anxious to have you to myself."

"And why is that?"

Royce's hands unbuttoned the top disk. Neither said anything, they kept their eyes locked onto each other. He released the second one.

Cordelia leaned closer, letting her lips barely rest on his, "You'll have to wait for the rest until later tonight." Her parted mouth rested on his, inviting him to share a sensual, but brief kiss.

A few minutes later they returned to the crowded hall just as a harpist began playing.

"Please tell me this wasn't your idea?" Royce said.

"If it was?"

"I'd tell you it's exactly what I wanted to hear at my surprise party."

"So, you'd lie to me?"

"I'd call it, supporting your efforts."

"Lucky for you, it was Marcus' suggestion. He said you loved the harp."

"Of course he did. And he probably told you I despise the violin?"

"Yes. Was he wrong?" She burst into laughter. "I'm kidding. Not about Marcus suggesting it. He did say you disliked the harp, but she's saving to attend music school in London, and we couldn't say no."

"As I said, it's exactly what I wanted to hear."

Cassandra waved from across the room. He felt Cordelia's arm stiffen.

"Play nice," he whispered.

"Tell her that." The razor edge to her voice sounded duller, softer.

The Duke of Evenshire stepped directly in front of them, and cornered Royce, hoping to discuss the latest pottery finds in Yorkshire. Cassandra called Cordelia over and introduced her to several supporters of the countess' charities. While he continued the conversation, Royce kept Cordelia in his peripheral vision, watching as she fielded a barrage of questions by the women. Occasionally she'd make eye contact with him, biting her lip, signaling her deepest thoughts.

When Royce re-engaged in the conversation the duke had finished a story about the discovery of a sunken Viking ship off the eastern shores. During the conversation he lost track of Cordelia, and by time he extricated himself, she and Cassandra had disappeared. The unexpected pairing caused a moment of concern, after all, their history of tension hardly suggested voluntary companionship.

"If you're looking for Cordelia, she and Cassandra slipped out about fifteen minutes ago," Olivia said. "Headed toward the east wing, I believe."

Thanking her, Royce made his way through the gathering, scanning rooms as he passed. His search was interrupted by his father's measured voice from an adjoining doorway.

"A word, Royce."

The Earl stood alone in his study, flipping the pages of a book under his thumb. "Happy birthday, son." He poured two glasses of Scotch from a crystal decanter on a side table. "Ms. Dyer seems to have impressed quite a few of the guests."

"Are you that surprised? She helped in the planning."

"So, you did know." He eased into his leather chair with practiced dignity. "Your mother was certain she'd managed to surprise you."

Royce took a sip before responding. "Marcus told me."

The Earl's deep chuckle shook his body. "That boy never can keep a secret."

The conversation was interrupted by a knock as Marcus entered. "I knew you two would be in here hiding out."

Both replied, "We're not hiding."

"Well, whatever you call it, mum is gathering everyone in

the formal living room for toasts." He opened the door wider and waited for them.

The Earl nodded and touched the Scotch to his lips without taking a full sip. "It seems your surprise awaits. Don't disappoint her."

"Not planning on it." Royce tipped back his glass and finished off his drink.

The three men made their way toward the living room, passing the harpist who plucked long melodic notes that evoked summer days spent watching clouds pass overhead, youthful and carefree. Royce scanned the crowd and spotted Cordelia near a wall of tall windows, engaged in conversation with Emma and Cassandra. An interesting blend of personalities, each one representing different aspects of his life.

Cordelia glanced up, as if sensing his eyes on her. She moistened her lips and blew a faint kiss. Another simple exchange, a private moment reminder that their relationship could no longer be defined as casual.

Moving to join her, Royce caught Cassandra weaving through the guests and greeting a society columnist. Their eyes met, and Cassandra looked away without offering a smile or nod, unusual behavior for her. When he passed by, Royce overheard Cassandra say she wasn't ready to discuss the situation.

He joined Cordelia, Emma, and Ada Rose by the windows. Her fingers intertwined with his, a small gesture that anchored him. Whatever social currents swirled around them, they had created something real, something secure. He squeezed her hand, silently communicating what he wasn't yet ready to say aloud.

# Chapter Twenty-Eight

The afternoon at Hayton Manor had been a beautiful blur of celebration and complicated social dynamics, but she'd successfully navigated it all. Cordelia sighed with relief as she unlocked the door to her London apartment, Royce following close behind with an overnight bag. The familiar scent of her own space, a blend of jasmine, citrus, and remnants of cookies she'd baked for Jasper and Lucy, welcomed her home.

Her shoulders relaxed the moment the door closed behind them, the weight of social performance finally lifted. The soft glow of an entry lamp cast gentle shadows across the angular lines of her space. Modest compared to Hayton's grandness, but none-the-less filled with textures and objects that represented her life. A handwoven throw blanket draped across the arm of her sofa, purchased when she first moved to New York City. Cookbooks stacked by the window, a collection that began when she was only eight. And the worn leather ottoman permanently imprinted from her feet after long satisfying kitchen shifts. Each element spoke of comfort rather than presentation, of a life lived, not just displayed.

She ran her fingertips along the wall as she walked in, a habitual gesture of homecoming that grounded her after hours in Royce's world. Not that his world wasn't becoming increasingly comfortable, but here she knew every creak in the floorboards, every draft by the windows, every quirk and flaw that made the space unmistakably hers.

"I have to admit, I love this little place." She dropped her keys on a side table and kicked off her heels. "Don't get me wrong, Hayton is spectacular, but."

"But it's not home." Royce set his bag and shoes beside the table. "I understand, and I grew up there."

"It's just a lot of space. I still get lost in all those rooms."

The unspoken understanding between them was one of the many things that had deepened her feelings for him over the months they'd been together. She especially appreciated how he knew when to rescue her from long conversations, like the one with Lady Benshire who detailed the process of pruning roses as if it was a garden club lecture.

"Tea? Or something stronger?" She moved toward the kitchen, not waiting for his reply, and filled the kettle with water. "Did you hear Mrs. Northfield's twenty-minute description of the car pileup on the M25? Morbid."

"Tea." Royce agreed with a laugh, propping his feet onto the marble top coffee table. "You handled her well, although you turned a bit pale at one point."

"Self-preservation." She prepared two mugs with tea bags, and tested the water, anxious for the kettle to boil.

"One of these days, I need to teach you how to make a proper pot."

"Who has time?"

"You'll thank me for it."

"Maybe. I kinda like the bags. And tea pots, as pretty as they are, are a pain to clean."

Royce laughed. "This coming from a chef."

"Even Cassandra prefers bags. Cassandra. Who knew."

When she joined him in the living room, the top buttons of his shirt were undone, and only one lamp remained on, creating a pool of warm light around the sofa. She handed him the mug, dashed into her bedroom, and returned with a blue and gold wrapped package. "Happy birthday." Cordelia handed the gift to him, proud of her selection. "I hope you like it."

He accepted the gift, "You shouldn't have gotten me anything."

"Yes, I should've, now open it." Cordelia had spent two hours searching one shop for the perfect gift, examining each shelf in the two-story bookstore.

Royce slid his finger between the tape and paper, carefully unwrapping a tissue wrapped book, a signed first-edition John le Carré *The Spy Who Came in From the Cold.* "This is incredible."

He ran his fingers over the cover and opened to the title page where the author's signature flowed across the paper. The book's subtle aroma of aged paper and dusty shelves drifted into the air. "I can't believe you found this, have you read it?"

"No, but it looks good."

"Le Carré is a genuis. How did you find this? Where?"

"Through a dealer in Soho. You really like it?" Cordelia watched his reaction, pleased with her decision.

"Yes. And you remembered our conversation. I'm honestly speechless, thank you." Royce expressed his feelings with a kiss, letting her feel the depth of his appreciation. Tired, they lounged on the sofa and continued their conversation about Mrs. Northfield, noting her fascination with auto accidents. "They always were a bizarre family, now I know why." His fingertips caressed Cordelia's skin. "What were you, Emma, and Cassandra plotting this afternoon?"

"Nothing, just talking."

"Since when have you and Cassandra just talked?"

"I don't know, but we did." She cut her eyes up at him. "Would you prefer us to be enemies again?"

"No."

Cordelia changed the subject, mentioning she wanted to plan a trip to Venice. She hoped that would be enough to distract his curiosity.

"Speaking of trips, I have something for you."

"For me?" Cordelia raised an eyebrow, surprised. "What is it?"

Royce placed his mug on the side table and reached into his pocket. "It's a little piece of Paris."

"Why did you get me something, it's your birthday?"

"Do I need a reason?"

Flustered, Cordelia accepted the palm size gift wrapped in one of Royce's monogrammed handkerchiefs. A warmth flooded her body, "Can I keep the wrapping?"

"Yes, sure."

Her heart raced as she peeled back each corner of the cotton fabric, revealing an engraved silver bracelet. Cordelia held her breath as she read the inscription, *We met in Paris...* "Royce," Her "finger ran across the lettering. "It's beautiful."

"Our story, our beginning." He fastened it around her wrist, letting his hand linger and caress her skin. "A reminder that it all started with our collision on Rue Hautefeuille."

The cool silver contrasted her skin as his fingers worked the clasp. Memories of their meeting resurfaced, including the smell of the filthy truck that engulfed her in dust. But Paris had a way of orchestrating chance encounters, a random act of kindness set everything into motion, and then, the city of love let fate weave in the rest. Cordelia rotated her wrist, watching as the engraved words caught the light at different angles.

What struck her most wasn't just the thoughtfulness of the gift, but its quiet confidence. Not diamonds or some grand statement, but something personal and meaningful. Royce had selected a gift that represented him as much as her.

Royce ran his hand underneath Cordelia's palm, like he memorized the texture of her skin as it brushed across with the lightest of touch.

She crawled into his lap and kissed him. The sentimental gift, acknowledging their journey together without pressure to define it with a title or name touched deep within. At times she wanted him to say the words, to define her as his partner or girlfriend, but the past had taught her, definitions mean nothing. She'd rather have devotion over a label.

If she listened to Cassandra, Cordelia would use the moment to tell him about Daniel, to clear the air completely, before they moved forward. Cassandra's advice, even at Hayton, echoed the same speech, to tell Royce before someone else does. The fear haunted her. "Royce, there's something I've been wanting to talk to you about." Her fingers traced the bracelet's surface.

"What is it?"

The words formed in her mind—My ex is Daniel Montali, the tennis player—simple and straightforward. Yet before she could voice them, she found herself distracted by the warmth of Royce's hand on her thigh. His gaze focused, waiting.

"I," She found herself leaning forward, magnetically drawn closer. "I wanted to tell you, there's a lot of." Their lips met in a kiss that deepened beyond her initial intention.

Royce responded, his free hand cradled her face with a tenderness that made her heart ache, and the conversation she'd planned dissolved under the heat building between them. Rational thought gave way to desire.

When they broke apart, breathless, Cordelia said, "I wanted to say thank you." She gestured to the bracelet. "It's perfect."

"You're welcome." Royce unbuttoned her dress, exposing her black bra. His thumb brushed across the lace, teasing her nipple. Her breath caught.

Fueled by desire, she unbuttoned his shirt, and eased him backwards, feeling the way his tongue moistened his lips. He was her aphrodisiac.

"Was there anything else you wanted to say?"

She shook her head, "Nothing."

They moved to the bedroom, leaving her dress behind. Their bodies touched as established lovers, yet beneath the rhythm of familiarity lay a sense of wonder, as if knowing created deeper mysteries waiting to be solved.

The city sounds faded away, held outside the bedroom windows. Distant traffic, passing voices, and the urban melody she'd grown accustomed to were replaced by the symphony of their breathing, and the subtle rustling of sheets. His cologne, now warmed and altered, mingled with the traces of her perfume, creating their own intimate signature.

In these moments, their individuality within the walls of their relationship revealed themselves, but not as differences that on the surface appeared to divide. Somehow, backgrounds, experiences, and social circles created a compelling tension, a space where each of them discovered something unexpected in the other.

As his palms felt the curve of her hips, Cordelia surrendered to the contradiction at the heart of their connection, a physical knowing that deepened the mystery rather than exhausted it. Each time they came together like this, barriers dissolved, yet new territories emerged, emotional landscapes waiting to be explored.

Later, they lay tangled in the sheets, feeling the afterglow within their cocoon. Cordelia rested her head on Royce's abdomen, struggling to keep her mind from the unfinished conversation.

"Royce, what I said earlier."

Contented, his fingers played lazily with her hair, and he replied with a drowsy mumble.

"There's something I want to say." She gathered her courage.

He shifted slightly, giving her his full attention despite their relaxed position. "I'm listening."

"It's about my last relationship"

Royce's hand continued its gentle movement through her hair, the steady contact reassuring. "Cordelia, I don't need to know the details. Clearly, it was painful, but I assume, I hope you've moved past it."

"Yes, but there's more to it." Cordelia lifted her head, meeting his gaze directly. "He has a reputation."

Royce's expression showed interest, but without reaction. What she'd feared subsided. "In culinary circles? Don't tell me it's Gavin."

"No. God no, I'd never."

The shrill of her phone cut through the moment, startling both of them. "I should get that." She apologized and raced into the living room, wrapping Royce's shirt around her. Cordelia answered Jessica's call and in less than five minutes untangled the staffing issue due to a cold circulating among the team. When she returned to the bedroom, Royce had propped himself up with a stack of pillows, partially covered by the sheet.

"Everything alright?"

"Yes. But let's not talk about it." She dropped his shirt to the floor and crawled into bed. "This is our space, and I don't want anything invading it."

In the darkness with only city light filtering through the curtains, Cordelia spotted his smile, the insatiable one—the unspoken, dimple grin that pulled her back into his arms. The warmth of his chest quieted her mind. Royce kissed her with insistence, intending to arouse her body to an explosion. She was already there. His hands journeyed, making all conversation impossible as sensations overtook thought. She moaned. He exhaled. Their bodies found a passionate flow, a rhythm of knowing.

As she straddled him, their moves became slower, more deliberate. Their lips touched, infusing emotion into urgency. The bracelet on her wrist reflected the light as her hands moved across Royce's shoulders. Her body released. She found safety.

The warm weight of Royce's arm around her waist and the steady rhythm of his breathing against her hair made it difficult to disrupt the peaceful moment with unfinished revelations. Besides, she refused to let Daniel overshadow what she and Royce shared. Despite Cassandra's warning, although too important to ignore, Cordelia decided she'd tell Royce over breakfast, when it was acceptable to let the outside world in.

"What's weighing you down?" Royce murmured against her hair, not as close to sleep as she'd assumed.

The question offered another opportunity, another chance to tell Royce the full truth. She turned in his arms and faced him, finding his sleepy eyes waiting. "I'm happy you're here. And I wouldn't want to be anywhere else."

"Me either. But whatever it was you wanted to say earlier, it doesn't matter. It's behind us."

"Yes, it is." Her fingers traced his jawline.

"Get some sleep." Royce pressed a kiss to her forehead. "Whatever it is, work or past, we'll figure it out together. That's what partners do."

A term that defined their relationship. Partners. One word, one important word, and with it came a basket of emotions. Tiredness took over, and she mentally filed away her concerns for the next day's consideration, including the Daniel revelation. As Royce said, they'd face them together, their foundation now set. Her last thought before drifting off was a mixture of contentment and resolution. Partners. Not just lovers or companions but equals invested in each other's lives. Everything had changed.

# Chapter Twenty-Nine

Morning light filtered through Cordelia's bedroom curtains, painting stripes of yellowish white across the tangled sheets. The sounds of London filtered back in, and the sky had a unique quality to it, a muted blue with hints of brightness. She stretched, the silver bracelet catching the light as her arm extended. The weight of it felt unfamiliar but pleasant, a tangible reminder of the previous night's intimacy, both physical and emotional.

Cordelia studied Royce's face for a moment as he slept, struck by the contrast between his public composure and private vulnerability.

Careful not to wake him, she slipped from the bed and pulled on her Missoni robe, a plush gift to herself when she moved to London. A glance at the bedside clock showed it was just after seven, giving her plenty of time to make coffee and breakfast. Then she'd tell Royce the last of her secrets, before they spent the day at St. Paul's Cathedral, exploring like tourists.

In the kitchen, she did her usual routine, grind beans, boil water, and assemble the French press. She really needed to buy a machine to make things move faster.

Just as she poured the water over the coffee grounds, someone knocked at the door. She peered into the bedroom and saw Royce still sleeping. The knock came again. She glanced at her phone, nothing from Jessica. It was too early for the neighbors to disturb her. Baffled, she tightened the belt of her robe, moved to the door, and peered through the peephole. Daniel Montali. It couldn't be. He said he'd be in London, but she hadn't agreed to see him. How did he find her? She peered again, barely pressing against the door, and hoping he'd leave if she didn't answer. Shit. He leaned against the stair railing, holding an enormous bouquet of flowers, dressed in one of his Italian suits.

Her heart pounded. The panic surged, causing her hands to shake, and a cold chill swept through her body, leaving her fingers tingling and her mouth dry. She tiptoed away from the door and stood in the foyer. Her mind couldn't process the cosmically bad timing of his appearance. Of all days for him to show up. Really bad timing. She had to think. Royce slept in her bedroom. Daniel stood at her door. The conversation she'd rehearsed would happen under the worst possible circumstances. Dammit, Cassandra's prediction came true.

She took another step backward and tripped over her heels, left in the foyer from the night before. Her body bumped the side table and thumped the wall. Shit.

Daniel knocked harder. Busted, she couldn't ignore him any longer, besides the scent of coffee filled the apartment. With a deep breath, she cracked the door and poked her head out.

"Daniel." She kept her voice low. "What are you doing here? It's seven in the morning."

His white, smug smile, the one that had graced sportswear ads and magazine covers, the grin that made women blush, flashed across his tan face."Del, babe. My flight got moved up. I arrived last night." He held out the flowers. "And I needed to see you right away."

"This really isn't a good time." Cordelia refused the flowers. "I have company."

"Got it. But this can't wait, Cordelia. And I think you'll want to hear what I have to say."

Before she could respond, Royce's voice came from behind her.

"Cordelia? Who's at the door?"

She turned to find him standing in the living room, dressed only in his trousers. His hand ran through his tousled hair, alert but from the furrow of his brow, confused.

The moment stretched like taffy on a rack.

Cordelia opened the door and motioned at Daniel. "Stay right here. You're not coming in any further, got it." She positioned herself between the two men. "Royce, this is Daniel Montali." Her confidence plummeted. "He." But she saw it in his eyes, the connection.

"The tennis player?"

Daniel stepped forward, but Cordelia's hand pressed him back. She cringed, touching him. Her eyes locked onto Royce, who darted his eyes around, resting them on the flowers.

"Sorry to intrude." He extended his hand to Royce, the same handshake he offered the media. "As she said, Daniel Montali. And you are?"

"Royce Brownell." His aristocratic training kicked in as he accepted the handshake. His expression revealed nothing, just a stoic mask above a very stiff posture. "How kind, he brought you flowers." His tone hinged on pompous annoyance.

The men squared off, and she braced for a cock fight. The contrast between them couldn't have been more obvious.

Daniel, with his athletic build consumed, while Royce, shirtless and surprised, maintained quiet assurance.

Royce moved beside Cordelia, placing his hand on the small of her back. "Are you going to let him in?"

"No."

Daniel cleared his throat. "I apologize for disturbing you this early. He turned his attention back to Cordelia. "But I need five minutes of your time. It's important."

The tension trapped Cordelia between past and present. "I already told you, it's not a good time. I'll text you tomorrow, and we'll meet for coffee."

"Perhaps I should give you some privacy," Royce said, his voice in the neutral tone he relied on for uncomfortable situations. The Earl taught him well.

"No." Cordelia grabbed his hand. "Whatever he has to say can be said with you here." Her instinctive response gripped Royce's arm.

"Mind if we sit? This is better if we sit."

Reluctant but conceding, Cordelia gestured toward the living room, hyperaware of the clues scattered around the room —Royce's jacket draped over a chair, two half-finished tea mugs on the coffee table, and of course Royce, shirtless with messy hair. Unmistakable signs of her current relationship.

Royce took a seat on the sofa, while Daniel remained standing. Cordelia positioned herself next to Royce, feeling his arm wrap behind her.

"I'll be direct. The injury has given me time to think about my life and my priorities. And I realized I'd chased the wrong things, like endorsements and sponsors. But I forgot about what really matters."

The way Daniel talked was how he played, one point, one idea at a time, always approaching that crucial match point, and knowing when to strike.

"I made mistakes with us, Del." He began to slowly pace around the room.

"Del?" Royce whispered.

Cordelia nodded. "Ignore it."

"Mistakes that I really regret, like you. When I lost you, I lost the one person who saw me as more than just a tennis player. Who always challenged me on and off the court."

"Well, not quite, we never played together, remember?"

"You always challenged me to be a better person." His memorized speech didn't miss a beat, but he displayed a newfound sincerity, reminiscent of the guy she'd initially known. But she doubted he'd eradicated the self-absorbed athlete from his personality.

"Daniel, that's nice to hear, but it's in the past, and we've both moved on."

"Have we? I haven't. Not really." He pulled a small velvet box from his pocket, the significance of which was immediately apparent.

"No. Put that away."

"I'm going to get my shirt." Royce left the room.

"I should've done this years ago, before I let my ambition drive you away."

"Daniel, stop. You did it years ago, and I said no." Cordelia felt her lungs constrict. She gasped. All the air in the room vanished. Daniel lowered himself to one knee, and she wondered if she was asleep, trapped in a nightmare.

"Cordelia Dyer," he opened the box to reveal a large emerald-cut diamond ring, bigger than the one he'd presented the last two times he proposed. "Will you marry me? Give me, give us the second chance we deserve?"

The absurdity of the moment wasn't lost on her, Daniel proposing in her living room with Royce, her lover and partner, present to witness the whole damn thing.

"Daniel. This is wrong. I'm with Royce, you're with Cary Anne."

Daniel glanced at Royce, who stood near the bedroom buttoning his shirt. He moved closer to Cordelia. "I understand you've moved on temporarily. But what we had was special, Cordelia. The kind people search their whole lives for."

Cordelia jumped up. "No. No, no. That's not what it was."

"I know I hurt you." Daniel stood, attempting to touch Cordelia's hand. "The situation with Cary Anne was inexcusable. But people make mistakes, and I've changed."

"That's great to hear. But that has nothing to do with my life now."

Royce walked back into the living room and stood near Cordelia.

"Listen, man, I know you're with her right now, and I'm sure you didn't expect this."

"Not hardly." Royce placed his hands in his pockets. "It's been a lot for everyone. Why don't you give Cordelia some time?"

"No. I don't need time." Cordelia cut her eyes at Royce. "I don't need any time. I need space." She looked back at Daniel. "You said what you needed to, and my answer is no. It's always been no. But you know who'll say yes? Cary Anne. Now, can you leave, so I can get my life back on track?"

"Yeah, I should go." He slipped the ring box back into his pocket. "Sorry for the intrusion. I hope you'll keep the flowers. They're pretty, just like you."

"Daniel, please."

He moved toward the door, paused, and turned back. "I meant what I said about realizing what matters." With that, he left.

Cordelia faced Royce, bracing for a reaction. With his hands in his pockets, he rocked on his heels. The silence between them pressed against her chest. She searched his face for a sign of his feelings. Dealing with anger, jealousy, or disappointment would almost be easier to face than quiet calm.

"So, Daniel Montali is your ex."

"Yes. That's what I was going to tell you last night."

"Remarkable timing, wouldn't you say?"

"Terrible timing." Cordelia searched his face for clues to how he really felt. "Royce, I'm sorry you found out like this. I've wanted to tell you for weeks."

"Then why didn't you?" His voice lacked accusation. "Why withhold it?"

"Initially, I didn't mention him because it didn't seem relevant. I mean, everyone has past relationships that end badly. But then." She paused, drawing in a deep breath. "A reporter contacted me about his recovery and comeback. She wanted my perspective as his former partner, and that's when I realized I needed to tell you the full story, before you heard it elsewhere."

"A reporter. And Cassandra knows?"

"Yes. She showed up at the bakery when Cassandra was there. We were coming to an agreement, and she showed up. That's how Cassandra found out."

Royce's expression altered, first surprise, then a flicker of hurt. "Cassandra's known for a week?"

"She encouraged me to tell you. Actually, insisting."

"And you planned to tell me last night, before."

"Right." Cordelia moved closer, relieved he didn't back away. Instead, he folded his arms across his chest. "Royce, I'm so sorry." She met his gaze. "I was afraid of how it would change things between us. Afraid you'd see me differently."

"Because you dated a famous athlete?"

"No. Because of how it ended. How it affected me."

"I already know all of that. Why would you hide this minor detail from me?"

"I don't know."

"Yes, you do, Cordelia. Tell me the truth. Why did you hide his status?"

Cordelia fidgeted with the robe's belt, rubbing the soft fabric between her fingers. "Like I said, at first, I didn't think it mattered. You were Paris, something casual. But then we came back here, and we had the symphony. It all escalated, my feelings escalated. And I thought, at that point, if you knew, it would create a negative opinion."

"Why?"

"I thought you'd see me as a relationship failure."

"That's your logic?"

I thought you'd wonder why I stayed with someone who made me feel invisible." Her voice broke. "Why would I accept being known as his girlfriend for years? And then I wondered, if I told you, would you think I was weak for staying or wonder about my motives with you." Her thumb rubbed the edge of the bracelet." I was afraid either way. And I'm sorry."

"I need time to think." Royce put his coat and shoes on, preparing to leave. "This was a double standard, and I lamented over not telling you about my family. Yet all the while, you kept your own secret, which wasn't much of a secret. And why? Because you thought I'd judge you?" Royce walked to the door, grabbing his overnight bag, and paused. "What do you think this conveys, Cordelia?"

"Royce, don't leave yet. Let's talk this out."

"As you said earlier, I need space." He paused in the foyer, and Cordelia watched his back muscles expand and contract as he let out several deep breaths. "For the record, I never would've said you were weak, until now."

The unfairness of it crashed into her. She'd been trying to find the right moment, the right words, and Daniel stole that from her. Anger flared. But it wasn't directed at Daniel. She's the one who'd waited too long. Her choice. Her omission. Her consequences.

# Chapter Thirty

Royce walked.

With no destination in mind, just one deliberate step after another, he moved away from Cordelia's apartment building. London's streets were beginning to stir with Sunday morning activity, faceless figures wrapped in their private worlds, oblivious to his internal turmoil.

A light mist settled over the city, leaving a sheen on his skin. He welcomed the winter's coolness, a temporary balm for the burning sensation in his chest, which began when Daniel knelt in Cordelia's living room, revealing a ring and dangling a proposal.

Daniel Montali. Grand Slam champion. Sports icon. A man Royce had watched on television was now permanently linked in his mind to Cordelia, in ways he couldn't have imagined an hour ago.

What gnawed at him wasn't the celebrity, but the realization that Cordelia had deliberately kept a significant part of her past hidden. She'd allowed him to share his life, his family, and his home while maintaining one small yet critical omission.

Eight years. She'd been with him for eight years, her longest relationship, while his had barely lasted twelve months. Their relationship had reached nine months, and already their lives had become intertwined. Yet she'd omitted this piece of herself. Not once, in all their conversations about building trust, had she shared that part of her history.

The mist thickened into rain, but Royce didn't seek shelter. He welcomed the discomfort as the morning's scene replayed in his mind.

An artist huddled beneath an enormous umbrella in a small park, sketching the rain's pooling pattern and capturing the beauty born from discomfort. Royce sat on a wet bench, ignoring the dampness seeping through his clothes. He checked his phone, noting Cordelia's silence, and found himself remembering their time in Paris.

They'd shared a brief kiss on the Petit Pont bridge the night before he returned to London. They had stopped there, one of Royce's favorite spots in the city, as they strolled to Ile de la Cité. He had asked her to close her eyes and listen to the surrounding sounds. She described the various pitches of voices, the multitude of languages, tires squealing to a halt, and a jogger's feet pounding the pavement.

When he told her to imagine standing at that spot in 885 CE, she thought he was putting her through some relationship test, but Cordelia laughed and played along. As they let their imaginations escape through time, she listened to his tale of Rollo laying siege to Paris, and the impending life-or-death moment about to unfold. When they opened their eyes and kissed, she'd said, "How terrifying it must've been to see the Vikings coming and know something worse than death approached." When he asked her to clarify, she said, "That changed the Parisian's identity forever."

Royce had been impressed with Cordelia's ability to see the humanity in the story, and now he understood why. She'd lived through her own siege, her own identity transformation. But she hadn't trusted him enough to share it.

He came to three conclusions, curious how she'd answer his questions. Had her concealment been about protecting herself from revisiting old wounds? Or controlling how he perceived her? But the question he dreaded to hear was that she kept it secret because she expected their relationship to fail. Her response determined their future.

The rain stopped, leaving a silence in the park, and drawing his attention back to the surroundings—droplets of water clung to leaves, puddles reflected the brightening sky, and the air smelled of damp.

His phone vibrated. Cordelia. She'd sent over a photo he'd taken at Hayton Manor, she and Marcus laughing. He studied her face in the image, the unguarded joy in her expression created a physical ache in his chest, a reminder of what they'd built together and what now hung in precarious balance.

Royce remained in the park for another hour, listening to the emerging birds and watching people pass through the park. She'd sent a second text, requesting he call her. He waited, giving both of them time to determine the value of the relationship. Maybe Daniel had been right, you don't appreciate something until it's no longer yours.

As he left the park, feeling the heaviness of his waterlogged shoes, he sent Cordelia a text.

I need time. But I'll call.

He knew for certain that he loved her, but without trust and vulnerability, the emotions would fade. Both had made mistakes, and she was a complicated woman, afraid of judgment, who had hidden parts of herself away. The clarity of his emotions didn't erase the hurt or questions, but it gave him reason to confront the challenges.

Cordelia stared at her phone, thumbs hovering above the screen as she reread Royce's text for the fifth time. He needed time, but the question was, when would he call?

The brief message appeared after two hours of sending desperate voicemails and texts. Each minute of his silence had felt like a verdict, her imagination constructing elaborate scenarios of permanent separation while her rational mind fought to maintain perspective. Her worry felt unfamiliar, the sensation of urgent pursuit, and she realized she'd never chased after anything other than her career. But with Royce, she'd put herself on a cliff, stared into the dark waters, and jumped.

She glanced at the Sunday afternoon bustle at the coffee shop, which provided a welcome distraction from the suffocating silence of her apartment. She'd escaped to the BL Kitchen, but found the carousel of questions too much to bear, plus she found the whirl of mixers enhanced her thoughts.

"Mind if I sit?"

The voice jolted her as she watched a toddler lick its whipped cream and chocolate mustache. Daniel stood beside the table, holding two steaming cups of coffee.

"I thought you could use this." Without waiting, he made himself comfortable.

"Why are you always showing up unannounced?" Her voice snapped as she glanced around to ensure no one had heard. The last thing she needed was to be spotted with Daniel hours after his disastrous appearance.

"I saw you through the window and thought you could use some company." He slid a cup closer to her. "Earl Grey, splash of milk, no sugar. Some things don't change, right?"

"And some things shouldn't reappear without warning."

Daniel cradled his cup between his hands. "I owe you an apology, better than the one this morning."

"You think?" Cordelia leaned forward, softening her tone. "And what the hell were you thinking? Proposing after fifteen months?"

"I had no idea you were in a relationship." He mirrored her actions. "Are you sure he's the right one for you?"

"That's none of your business, is it?" Cordelia's eyebrows emphasized her frustration at the situation. She leaned back and sipped the drink Daniel offered her. "It's good, thank you."

"Del, I'm really sorry I hurt you. I'm a changed man, I swear it. I haven't cheated once on Cary Anne."

Cordelia froze, squinting at him. "And I'm supposed to be proud of you for that?"

"I didn't mean. It's nothing against you."

"Then I would say she's earned that ring."

"She's been amazing through all of this." Daniel picked at the cardboard sleeve of his cup.

"I've heard. Does she know what you're doing? What you did this morning?" Cordelia studied his face, trying to understand Daniel.

"So, I see life's treating you well, and you're still the Executive Pastry Chef. You've done well for yourself, Cordelia."

"Yes, I have." The silver bracelet on her wrist caught the light as she reached for her cup. The engraved words shimmered, taking her thoughts back to the Petit Pont bridge, and the vibrant taste of pears on his lips after sharing a bottle of Chardonnay.

"I promise you, the man I was then—selfish and entitled, consumed with ambition—that's not me anymore. The doctors said I might never play again. Do you know what that's like? Tennis is all I have, it's who I am. Without it, I'm just." He stared into his coffee. "That's why I needed to fix us. Next to tennis, you're the only real thing I've ever had. I want a second chance, Del, that's all I'm asking."

A few years back, his growth might have meant something to her. It might have earned him what he wanted. But like him, she'd changed. The weight of Royce's brief message remained unanswered. Daniel's late self-awareness meant nothing.

"Give it some thought? Please?" Daniel inched his fingers across the table, reaching for her hand.

"Daniel, I've given you my answer. Even in New York, I said no." They sat in the silence, looking into each other's eyes. For Cordelia, it was a moment to close the door to the past, but she saw longing in Daniel's expression.

"Royce seems like a nice guy."

"He is. And now, thanks to all of this, I don't know where we stand."

"I'm really sorry. I didn't think you might have someone over." Daniel's knee shook, rattling the table. "You, okay?"

A simple question, but it forced her to confront an uncomfortable truth. "I don't know. Will I be okay if there's no more of us? Yes. I'll survive. I still have my job, which I love, but it'll just be one more broken relationship."

"You still hide behind those walls, don't you?"

"Oh my god, are you an analyst now?" She chuckled.

"Hey, if I can face it, you can too."

She picked at the loose thread on her father's old watch-band. When he passed, it was the first memento she kept of him, even though the leather was tattered and the analog face had long gone out of style. Royce had given her a smart watch for

Christmas, but she preferred her father's watch even though she had to manually wind it each morning.

"Wow, you still wear that thing?"

"Some things don't change, remember?" They shared a laugh, a reminder that beneath the hurt, a friendship had once lived. "I'm sorry I've been rude. But I was really shocked this morning."

"I get it. I wish I hadn't been too late."

Cordelia smirked and nodded. "Don't you see? Your persistence is what makes you so good on the court."

Daniel laughed. "Yeah, I guess it does. You're happy with Royce?"

"Yes. I'm very."

"In love?"

The words, delivered by the person whose actions had created the current crisis, provided a moment of clarity for Cordelia. She loved Royce. She loved him for the person he was, and for who she was because of knowing him. But her unwillingness to be honest might have cost her a valuable commodity, his trust. "Yes, in love."

Daniel nodded, "Then I hope he doesn't let you go, ever. You're pretty special, Del."

"You are too, Daniel, for the right woman. And I think that's Cary Anne."

"She doesn't know I'm seeing you."

"Well, you might want to confess. Do you love her?"

"I think so. I can see myself having a family with her. Is that love?"

Cordelia threw her head back. "Please tell me you're joking. Of course, that's love."

Daniel chuckled. "Yeah, I do, but I think I needed to get you out of my system first."

Cordelia watched Daniel leave the coffee shop minutes

later, relieved to feel closure on her past. In some ways, she felt her self-protective patterns walk out the door with him.

She glanced at her phone, re-reading Royce's text. For the first time since he'd left that morning, a fragile sense of hope took shape. She would give him the time he needed. And then, perhaps, they could rebuild trust.

# Chapter Thirty-One

The Heathrow terminal surged with morning travelers. A sea of activity surrounded Royce, who stood motionless, staring at the departure board without seeing it. A leather overnight bag pressed against his shoulder, a reminder of his decision to put space between London and himself.

His phone vibrated again. Six times in the last thirty minutes. A quick glance confirmed what he already knew, another concerned person calling to check on him. This one, Marcus. He slid the phone back into his pocket and headed for the gate.

"Brownell."

Royce recognized Richard's deep voice before spotting him pushing through a pack of ambling travelers. They greeted each other, exchanging observations about Richard's impeccable suit and tie, an attire he preferred to avoid.

"Get my messages?" Richard asked, gesturing to a nearby coffee stand.

"No." Royce joined him in the short queue. "You're off to Frankfurt?"

"Yes, not as exciting as Paris, but the beer's better." A toddler wobbled in front of them, distracting their attention. "Cassandra called me."

"Of course she did." Royce placed his bag between his feet, unsurprised yet irritated. "Since when did she become Cordelia's confidante?"

"Apparently, after Daniel showed up with a ring, you walked out." Richard never lacked for words. "Any particular reason you're heading to Paris today?"

"Like I said yesterday, additional research for the book,"

"Without your notes?" His skeptical expression revealed his thoughts.

"What? The timing's coincidental." Royce smoothed the front of his sweater and crossed his arms.

"That's bollocks, and we both know it." Richard accepted his coffee, nodding thanks to the barista. "You always disappear when things get complicated. Remember when you lost the big debate at university, or what about when you broke things off with Leigh?"

"That was different," Royce protested, though the parallels weren't inaccurate. "What did Cassandra tell you?"

A family wheeled matching luggage around them, the parents argued in hushed tones while the children trailed behind, slurping sodas.

"Enough to know that you've discovered Cordelia has an impressive ex she never mentioned. Although I'm not sure how that warrants the sudden trip."

"She kept Daniel's identity from me for nine months, after criticizing me for not immediately disclosing my title."

"Ah, so this is about hypocrisy, not jealousy?" Richard raised an eyebrow.

"It's about trust." Royce corrected, ignoring the jab. "She deliberately concealed who he was."

"And you've never withheld anything about your past relationships?"

Royce fell silent, uncomfortable and aware of his own selective disclosures. His relationship with Leigh had ended badly, with her accusations of emotional games.

"So, how does it feel, knowing her ex is a celebrity?"

"From what I saw, there's no competition." Royce slung his bag over the other shoulder as they walked toward their gates.

"If he's not a threat, then why Paris?"

"As I've said to everyone, I need some distance to think."

They navigated around a tour group wearing matching red hats and clutching identical guidebooks.

"And what exactly will that accomplish?" Richard asked, his tone more curious than accusatory.

"Perspective. I need to determine whether this changes everything or nothing."

"Have you asked her why she didn't tell you?" Richard paused, facing Royce.

"You know me, that's the first thing I'll ask."

A hurried woman collided with Royce's shoulder, sending his bag sliding to the floor. "Watch where you're standing," she snapped, rushing toward the gates.

"Open your eyes, why don't you?" Royce retrieved his bag and dusted it off.

They approached Richard's gate, where a growing line of travelers waited, many with expressions of resignation and impatience.

"Look," Richard said, "I understand you stand by your principles, and I've watched you stubbornly take a stance, at personal cost. But sometimes people have reasons for withholding things. Remember, Evie?"

"Paris helps me think." Royce glanced at his watch.

"Does it? Or does it help you avoid decisions?" He adjusted his carry-on strap. "Just think about it."

Royce nodded. "I'll call you tomorrow."

"Call her, not me." They buddy hugged, and then Richard joined the boarding queue.

As Royce walked to his own gate, he remembered a museum cocktail party a few weeks earlier. He and Cordelia had strolled into an empty gallery exhibiting 18th-century fashion, where a paneled door had been left open. She pulled him into the storage room, and before he knew it, they'd abandoned discretion, their bodies pressed against the wall, satisfying a desire that had been building all evening. The encounter ended abruptly when another couple entered the gallery, but Cordelia's scent remained with him for the rest of the night.

He presented his boarding pass and took a last look at the terminal that stretched behind him. Somewhere out there, Cordelia faced their situation alone, making him momentarily hesitate. But then the memory of Daniel's proposal resurfaced, along with the shock on her face. The uncertainty plagued him, wondering if her shock was embarrassment over the situation, or something deeper? The inability to read her expression had splintered his confidence, leaving him stuck in assumptions.

After taking his seat, Royce removed his phone from his pocket. Three missed calls, including Cassandra, Emma, and Cordelia. His mother had texted, asking if he was joining them for dinner on Sunday. She never slows down. He replied, 'yes', assuring her he'd be back in a couple of days.

Royce looked around the cabin and noticed how the ordinary concerns of life continued, even when internally it all felt surreal. He stared at Cordelia's name on the screen, preparing to send a message, but instead, he switched the phone to airplane mode and stowed it back in his pocket.

As the plane sped down the runway, Royce made a decision.

He'd give himself three days in Paris. No more hiding behind research. After that, he and Cordelia would face whatever future they had together.

The bakery buzzed that morning, and Cordelia declared chaos as the word of the day. The upcoming petit fours order for the Gartz wedding had been mismanaged, proof of Jessica's inexperience in independently handling staff scheduling. Cordelia spent the morning reviewing the process and re-teaching her the system. After an hour review and lots of note taking, Jessica understood.

"I'm sorry about this. It won't happen again."

"We all make mistakes, Jessica. The main thing is to learn from it."

Cordelia reflected on her words, realizing she needed to listen to her own advice. How would she recover from her own mistakes? She'd thrown herself into work, focusing on several team disputes and correcting shipping orders. It seemed easier than facing the emotional turmoil that had built since Royce walked out of her apartment. Cordelia recognized the pattern, but it seemed easier to go with it, especially with her work demands. She could offer solutions to Jessica's scheduling errors, but couldn't apply the same methodical approach to her personal miscalculations. Avoidance only postponed the inevitable.

Her phone buzzed. Emma. One of her newly discovered lifelines. With Marnie halfway around the globe, having friends nearby provided a sense of security.

Marcus spoke to him. He's in Paris. No surprise. How are you?

Cordelia waited sixty seconds before replying. She thanked Emma and assured her that work had consumed her time and thoughts. Even now, she wasn't ready to fully expose herself.

In the kitchen, Sam tempered chocolate for bonbons. His tall frame hunched over the marble slab as he pushed the chocolate into a glossy texture. His thick red hair, perpetually disheveled despite the bakery's standards, peeked out from underneath his hair net, letting wayward strands fall across his forehead.

"Jessica asked me to help remake the petit fours and said I needed to be here at 4 a.m. tomorrow instead of seven. Is that true?"

"Is that a problem?"

"No, but I thought you had to approve all changes."

"I did."

Sam's blue eyes assessed her as if he read her mind. "Four is fine." He re-focused on the chocolate. "I would've pulled those petit fours before they over browned. She gets distracted when she's managing multiple projects."

"Wait. What are you talking about? Over browned?"

"The petit fours, she left them in too long and they overcooked."

Cordelia called Lang over from a nearby mixer. "Let's put that workshop to use. Take over for Sam, please." She cut her eyes at him. "In my office, please."

He closed the door and sat across from her. Cordelia rapped her fingers on the desk. "Are you telling me she burnt them? She herself overcooked them?"

"Yes, Chef. I told her they needed to be pulled, but like I said, she struggles to manage multiple projects."

"I understood there was a staffing issue."

"That's not quite accurate."

The subtle undermining of Jessica wasn't lost on Cordelia.

Despite being good friends and working under Jessica, Sam had never fully accepted her authority. His exceptional skill with chocolate, particularly his handcrafted truffles, had developed its own following among customers, giving him leverage with Cordelia.

"Was it or was it not a staffing issue that caused problems?"

"No, Chef."

Cordelia reflected. "She identified the problem as short staffed and developed a solution where she prepared the petit fours, leaving the eclairs and macarons to you and the team. But you were short-staffed, so she had to assist you."

"That's incorrect. Chef. She prepared the petit fours and the macarons, leaving the eclairs to me. She put Lang and the others on mixing and sheeting dough for the shop." Sam's leg bobbed up and down, knocking into the desk. "I suggested she pull them, but that didn't sit well with her. I knew they'd come out burned."

"Well, thanks for letting me know." Cordelia twirled a pen between her fingers. "How's your application coming for the chocolatier program in France?" She deliberately changed the subject.

Sam was ambitious, a quality Cordelia appreciated. He pursued one of the most renowned apprenticeships in chocolate, where only two candidates were selected annually. Cordelia had assisted him in refining his portfolio, allowing him to transition from pastry to chocolate during his shifts.

"Submitted it last week. My sister-in-law helped with the final presentation." His body relaxed as soon as he mentioned her."

"When will you hear back?"

"Eight weeks." The conversation detoured, discussing his brother and sister-in-law, who were about to become first-time parents. As a proud uncle, he shared how he'd spent all of his off time the past two weeks helping them prepare the nursery. Cordelia's mind drifted out of the conversation, thinking about Ada Rose and Hayton Manor. Sam eventually weaved things back to the apprenticeship. "So I need to put some space between myself and Elsie."

Cordelia pieced together the bits she'd heard and understood. Sam's dating life made sense. He compared every woman he dated to an unattainable standard, and he preferred working holidays over spending time at family gatherings. She thought it was drive, but it was emotional protection.

"I guess distance is sometimes necessary."

Sam met her eyes. "Is that what you're doing?

The question caught her off guard. She stumbled for words. "I don't think that's relevant to work."

"It is when you've practically slept here since Sunday. And you check your phone every two minutes. And."

"'Of course I'm checking my phone.' She immediately felt bad for her snappish tone. But underneath the regret, a sharp frustration rose, an annoyance that her private life had become workplace gossip.

"Sorry, but we've all noticed."

"We?"

"Yes, we."

"Good to know." She dropped her pen on the desk. "I'm sure Lang could use some help. Four tomorrow, then. And thanks for your honesty."

Sam nodded and left, but echoes of their conversation remained. Cordelia listened to the muffled kitchen activity and reflected, not just on Sam's observations, but on how it made her feel. Complex questions about escapism and fear dashed through her mind, creating a tightness in her abdomen. The stark reality between her professional control and emotional avoidance had served and limited her, a protective maze for anyone to navigate.

After re-reading Emma's text, she typed out a new reply, an honest one. The simple act of acknowledging her feelings rather than hiding them felt like a revolt against her own patterns.

Thanks for letting me know. I miss him.

Emma immediately replied, inviting Cordelia to Hayton Manor for a visit, insisting Ada Rose would enjoy the company. She considered the invitation and accepted the offer. Royce needed Paris, but maybe she needed Hayton. Not to escape life, but to face what really mattered.

# Chapter Thirty-Two

Cordelia's hands tightened around the steering wheel as she navigated the final stretch of country road leading to Hayton Manor. The rental car's navigation system had guided her through the soothing countryside, but the technology failed to calm the butterflies that had taken up residence in her stomach since she'd left London an hour earlier.

A box of delicate orange-scented madeleines sat seat belted to the passenger seat alongside her tote and a gift for Ada Rose. She'd risen at dawn to prepare the cakes, one of the first pastries she'd learned to bake, and now a symbol of family for her.

Emma had responded to her message with surprised enthusiasm, suggesting an early afternoon arrival, but failed to disclose who all would be at the house. Cordelia hoped to avoid The Earl.

The stone gates of Hayton Manor appeared just as her phone dinged with a message from Emma, apologizing for changing plans. Apparently, she'd dashed into London to assist her parents and would be delayed meeting Cordelia at the house.

The Earl and Countess look forward to seeing you.

She stopped the car, her mind ping-ponged between options. For a moment, she considered turning around, retreating to London, rather than facing Royce's parents alone. But she'd driven this far, and fleeing wouldn't alleviate the panic, so she put the car in drive and continued toward the house.

Cordelia approached the door, noting again the long-standing traditions that resonated behind the carved family crest. With madeleines in hand, she waited for someone to answer, her heart palpitations banging like the old brass door knocker.

Jerry, the middle-aged personal secretary for the family, answered the door, dressed in dark jeans and a t-shirt. He greeted her with the toothiest grin. "Ms. Dyer, so good to see you again." He gestured her to come inside. "Forgive the way I look. I've been in the attic sorting through old clothes for charity."

"I hope I'm not disturbing anyone. I know Emma and Ada Rose went into the city, unexpectedly."

"Not at all, the Earl and Countess are eager to see you again."

He escorted her through several hallways leading to the kitchen and family den. The prospect of facing them alone still created conflicting feelings for her. She wanted to present herself confidently, even without Royce there, but she found the Earl's judgment difficult to navigate. She could hear Marnie's voice saying, *Just be yourself and let him figure out his own attitude. It's his problem.* Cordelia puckered her lips, trying to hide the giggles.

They entered the room and found the Earl relaxing on the sofa, reading a newspaper, with his feet stretched onto the coffee table. His slippers lay precisely aligned next to the sofa.

"Sir, Ms. Dyer's here."

The Earl stood, greeting her with a flat smile. "Ms. Dyer. Nice to see you again. I'm afraid the countess is on a call and will join us later."

"I'm sorry to intrude, Lord Thornbury. I didn't get Emma's message until I was pulling into the drive."

"Please do not apologize. The countess will be happy to see you." He gestured for her to sit in a club chair near a window that overlooked the garden.

Cordelia glanced towards the door, weighing the social awkwardness of declining versus accepting. "I brought these for you all." She handed him the box. "They're madeleines, orange-cardamom. I hope you enjoy them."

"Thank you, very kind."

Natural light flooded the room, highlighting a sofa table covered in family photos. A comforting scent of smokiness lingered from the fireplace. From where Cordelia sat, she spotted a youthful photo of Royce. He grinned with thick glasses perched on the bump in his nose. He must have been nine or ten years old, based on the middle school awkward pose.

"Royce was what you Americans call a late bloomer. He was twelve when we took the boys to Rome."

"Did you say twelve?"

"Yes." The Earl glanced over his shoulder, picked up the photo, and examined it. The corner of his mouth lifted. One of the few times she'd seen him smile. "Six months later, Royce went from 152 to 180 centimeters. That would be almost a foot by your calculations."

"I didn't know. And he wore glasses?"

"The magic of surgery." The Earl paused and picked up another photo. "This is Royce at sixteen. My friend, Dr. Josh

Rankin, invited him on his first student archaeological dig. Did he tell you about it?"

"No. I mean, he said he was sixteen when he decided to study archaeology, but that was about it."

"Yes. Well, Dr. Rankin gave me this photo after Royce completed a week in the field. He called to say Royce had the skills for the work. Said he displayed an inquisitive, analytical mind." The Earl held out the photo, giving Cordelia a closer view of Royce, covered in dirt up to his knees, holding a long-crusted item. After placing the picture back in its exact spot, the Earl stood, jutted his chin outward, and rattled a few pocket coins. "Well, then, can I interest you in a cup of tea to go along with those cakes?"

Within minutes, the Earl had filled a tea kettle with water, waiting for it to boil on the cooktop. "What's your preference?"

"I'm fine with whatever you're having." Cordelia remembered the night Royce made her tea and the events that transpired.

The Earl tucked in his chin and looked at her. "I'll ask again, what's your preference?"

"Earl Grey with a twist of lemon, no sugar, no milk, but a drop of honey, if you have it." Cordelia rambled off her order as if she were at a Starbucks back in the States.

He pointed at the commercial fridge. "Lemon slices are in there. Help yourself."

While the Earl prepared a teapot, Cordelia rummaged through the fridge looking for the lemons. She found them behind a container of strawberry yogurt, a bowl of half-eaten cereal flakes, and a dish that looked like lasagna. Cautiously, she sniffed the mystery dish as she reached for a container, detecting black truffle and crispy onions. She peeked under the foil, curious to discover that a thin layer of fried onions covered the top of the pasta dish.

"Were you able to find them?"

Cordelia grabbed the lemons and popped her head out of the fridge. "Yes, Sir. Right here."

"Very good. Bring them over."

After the Earl had timed the tea to perfection, they returned to the family den, sipping tea from hearty mugs. Their angled club chairs faced each other while providing a picturesque view of the garden.

"How's your tea?"

"Very good, thank you." Cordelia peered at him over the rim of her mug.

"Royce tells me you were raised by your father, an academic, historian, if I remember correctly?"

"Yes."

"And your mother?"

"She...she moved back east when I was young. I haven't seen her since. My parents were very different from each other. I'm more like my father."

"Did Royce tell you his mother had been raised in London due to her father's diplomatic career?"

Cordelia nodded. Her knuckles turned white from gripping the mug.

"We met at Oxford. She had planned to become a human rights lawyer, dividing her time between London and India. She loves law, but she loves people even more so." His eyes warmed with an affection. "I didn't fit her plans, but I was determined to take her on a date. So, for an entire year, every week I asked her to dinner, and every week she refused me. Finally, she said yes, but insisted it was only one date to reward my persistence. A month later, she met my father. They had a conversation just like you and I are having right now."

Cordelia watched his fingers tap against the mug, noticing they had the same shape as Royce's—broad and long. The similarity, a physical reminder that, despite their differences, Royce carried pieces of this man within him. The patches of peppery hair near the Earl's knuckles distinguished him from Royce.

"You see, my father doubted if she could live up to the expectations of the role. He scrutinized her, but she never tried to justify herself or our relationship. She did not ask to be given a chance."

" I see. Did she know she wanted to be with you when they met?"

"The countess will tell you that conversation decided for her, but I know she decided after that first date." The Earl grinned and chuckled. "She'll never admit it."

"And what about your father? Did he change his mind?"

"Yes, he did. Because he saw a woman who was confidently engaged with him. She didn't question herself, and she never accepted his doubt as anything more than an opportunity. And she still does."

"Sounds like Royce."

"She graduated at the top of our class and achieved all of her goals, even after marriage."

"Impressive. I didn't know that about the countess." Cordelia cut her eyes out the window. A gardener clipped hedges near the terrace. He clipped and bagged, clipped and bagged. She rested the mug on her thigh.

The Earl dropped another cube of sugar into his tea, clicking the spoon as he stirred. "I don't tell many people this, but I think you'll understand. Pursuing my wife that year has been the best decision of my life."

"Do you mind if I ask you a question?"

He nodded, giving approval.

"Then, why are you so hard on Royce about doing what makes him happy?"

"There are times Royce needs guidance."

"But you didn't."

"No. We were surer of ourselves back then."

"Well, I think Royce is very self-assured."

"Do you?"

"I do. Despite the circumstances, I do."

The Earl crossed his legs and smoothed the fabric of his trousers.

"Since we're being honest with each other, and I hope you won't take offense at what I'm about to say," she said, drawing a long breath.

"Is that the opening to your argument?"

"I guess it is." Cordelia cracked a laugh, realizing he was attempting to be funny. "Sir, you've pressured him to give up something he loves to do, just because you think teaching is a better route for him. But when I saw you with that photo, you looked like a proud father. Not a controlling one."

"I see. Is that how you perceive me, Ms. Dyer? Controlling?"

"Not really. I think you're proud, but I also think you demand a lot of him. But have you read his book?"

"Not yet."

"Well, you should. It's excellent. You can feel his passion for research and history."

"I'll take that under advisement." His demeanor hardened, as if she'd hit a nerve.

Cordelia began watching the gardener, holding the mug close to her chest.

"Would you like more tea?"

"No, thank you."

"Ms. Dyer, I appreciate you being forthright with me, few people do." The Earl poured himself more tea and dunked a madeleine into his mug. "Tell me about your career. Have you always enjoyed pastries?"

"As long as I can remember. Baking is something I'm good at, and it makes people happy."

He finished his madeleine and grabbed another one. "And what did you bake when you were young?"

"At first, just cookies, and then I expanded into cakes and madeleines. They were my father's favorite, out of everything I baked."

The Earl nodded as he finished the second one. He leaned forward, about to grab a third one, when Lucie, the house-keeper, entered the kitchen. She stopped and tucked a feather duster behind her back when she saw the Earl. "I'm sorry, Sir."

"It's not a problem, Lucie. We will be done soon."

"Yes, Sir. Thank you." She pushed open the oversized swing door that led into the butler's pantry and disappeared.

"Would you like to stay for dinner, Ms. Dyer? I know it would please the countess..."

"Oh, if it's not an inconvenience."

"I wouldn't ask if it were."

"Right. Then I'd love to stay for dinner."

They examined each other's smiles, silently coming to an understanding, a mutual recognition of the other's place in Royce's life.

# Chapter Thirty-Three

Cordelia stared out the train window as the French countryside blurred past. The ride had been smooth, but since talking with the Earl, her thoughts remained a churning pool of uncertainty.

She'd coordinated the trip in less than twenty-four hours, a surprisingly smooth accomplishment encouraged by Emma and Marcus. Her fingers outlined the bracelet's edges on her wrist, watching as sunlight reflected off the inscription.

After returning to London Wednesday evening, she'd spent the night staring at her ceiling, fragments of conversation with the Earl, with Emma, with Sam, and even with Jessica. By dawn, she'd made her decision. If Royce needed Paris, then she would find him there.

By eight a.m. she had packed and called Bastien, explaining her need for a few days of personal leave. True to his nature, he'd chuckled and shared his sage advice about love trumping food. When she resisted the word, he laughed some more and said, "My dear, you are clearly in love. Embrace it."

As the train approached Gare du Nord, Cordelia rehearsed what she might say when and if she found him. She had no guarantee she would find him, no certainty he'd listen, but the alternative of returning to London without trying remained unthinkable. Her courage outweighed her fear.

The station bustled with energy as she pushed her way through the crowd. She grabbed a taxi and hurried to her hotel in the 4th district.

Her phone buzzed. Marnie.

You on the train?

No, a taxi. On the way to the hotel.

Go get him, Cordi!

What if he's not ready to talk?

Then he's an idiot. Text me after. x

The brief exchange grounded her. Marnie, even fifteen thousand kilometers away, knew what she needed to hear.

The city remained the same, and Paris wrapped itself around her, offering familiar sounds. The scent of coffee wafted on the street, and the pavement seemed to whisper reminders of conversations that had shaped them as a couple.

When she arrived at Boulevard Saint-Germain, the evening light stretched long shadows across the pavement. Cordelia breezed past ambling tourists, tucking the hem of her peach sweater into her black trousers. She spotted the green awning and cafe tables where they'd had their first shared bottle of wine. A single red light kept her from where she hoped he'd be, where she knew he'd dine, because Cordelia knew one thing, she knew Royce—he maintained his habits, even in Paris.

. . .

Through the window, she saw him. Her breath caught, and she pressed her hand against the door handle. He sat alone with an open notebook and a half-empty wineglass, splitting his attention between writing and people watching. The glow of a bistro lamp warmed his profile.

When she entered, several waiters greeted her with nods, while delivering drinks and food to occupied tables. She stopped every few tables, pretending to check her phone, postponing the moment that would determine everything. His cologne reached her as she approached the table. The scent that used to linger on her pillows. "Is this seat taken?"

Royce looked up. His pen froze mid-sentence. An unreadable expression, followed by a dimpled smile. "Cordelia."

"I hope I'm not interrupting."

He closed the notebook. "Not at all." His voice remained neutral, but friendly. "Please, sit."

Cordelia settled into the chair opposite him, while he motioned to the waiter for another glass of wine. Her hands tingled. Her heart pounded. A physical reaction she fought to control. As she looked around the room, every detail became sharp, like the light caught in the dark flecks of his eyes, or the habit of running fingers through his hair. And the way he repositioned the collar of his V-neck sweater as if it needed adjusting.

"You're in Paris," Royce said after the waiter departed.

"Yes." She met his eyes. "And so are you."

"Well, now that we've established that." He aligned his pen beside the notebook, centering it on the seam. "It's good to see you." His hands remained on his side of the table, his fingers open, waiting to be embraced.

"I had tea with your father yesterday."

Royce's eyebrows lifted. "I heard." She watched his eyes move around her face, as if he were reading a book. "You impressed him."

"He made tea for me, and we shared madeleines." Confidence washed over her, and for the first time in days, she let herself fully smile, feeling the internal glow. "He told me how he pursued your mother for a year before she agreed to one date."

"Ah, the famous story. Consider yourself one of his chosen ones. He doesn't share that with just anyone."

The waiter returned with Cordelia's wine, creating a momentary interruption. When he departed, the silence between them landed like a flat tennis ball. She was relieved to have the wine.

"Why are you here, Cordelia?" Royce's tone was gentle, but direct.

She took a deep breath, gathering her answer. "Because I realized something after talking with your father." Her fingers traced the condensation on her wine glass. "I've spent my life creating distance with people, professionally pushing while hiding. All because I wanted to avoid what I felt from my mother and then from Daniel. But now, I can see those patterns pushed you away when what I wanted was for you to stay, to fully know me."

Royce's jaw tightened. He picked up his pen, set it down, and aligned it with the edge of the notebook. When he finally looked up, a raw sadness flickered in his eyes.

"I didn't tell you about Daniel because I was protecting myself. It had nothing to do with deceiving you." The words rolled off her tongue, and although painful, they provided liberation. "I was afraid you'd see me differently, knowing I'd stayed in a relationship that made me feel invisible for so long."

She met his gaze, anticipating a debate, but he waited and listened. "By hiding myself from you, I created exactly what I feared." Her voice stumbled, and she swallowed before continuing. "And now I'm here, chasing you to Paris like some desperate." She shook her head. "I don't even know." Her voice steadied despite feeling exposed and tender. "Yes, I do. I came to Paris because the alternative was unacceptable, and I wasn't going to lose us out of pride or fear." She gripped her wine glass and sipped. "Even if you tell me it's too late."

The tension in Royce's jaw softened, and his shoulders seemed to open.

Confidence to continue sharing her feelings grew in Cordelia. "I almost turned around twice. Once at St. Pancras, when I told myself, coming was impulsive and reckless. And the second time, a minute ago, outside the bistro when I first saw you." She scanned his face, his body, searching for a reaction.

His thumb rapped on the table a few times, stopped, and rapped again.

"For a moment, I thought, what if he doesn't want me here? What if I've missed my opportunity?" Her voice caught. "But then, I remembered what your father said, about pursuing what matters, and I couldn't live with the regret of not trying."

He relaxed into his chair, giving a brief chuckle. "Pop's pearls of wisdom."

"Royce, I'm willing to risk heartache to win you back."

His fingers gripped the wine glass stem, twisting it between his fingers. He seemed deep in thought, watching the swirling wine. She waited, looking for a sign. Finally, he let out an audible sigh.

"Cordelia, when I left London, I told myself I needed a fresh perspective and some clarity over the situation, and our relationship. I thought intellectually distancing myself from you would provide answers that the emotional proximity couldn't." His voice had a reserved cadence, reminding her of their first dinner together at that same bistro. "But Paris didn't offer the escape I expected."

He gestured toward the bustling Parisian street outside. "Every corner reminded me of you. This bistro, the park, the river, you're tied to all of it."

A sense of hope emerged, and she offered him a brief smile. She wanted to leap across the table and touch him.

"I spent three days convinced I was processing what happened, analyzing trust and disclosure like historical evidence. In reality, I missed you." He dropped his voice lower and leaned forward. "I came here the last two nights, telling myself it was a convenient location, but truthfully, I was here waiting for you. I wanted you to walk through that door and find me." His fingers tightened around the glass.

Nervous energy flooded Cordelia's body. Her hands fidgeted with her napkin.

"I wanted to put our relationship into a chart, run a formula, and find solutions. It didn't work this time." He smirked, his magnetic eyes holding her captive. "I kept telling myself that trust isn't," He rubbed his temple. "That you don't deserve... Christ, Cordelia. I want to stay angry. And it would be simpler."

"I understand the feelings."

"I know what we've built is based on consistency, and showing up in difficulties, not avoiding them. I've been ridiculously stubborn." He reached for her hand, caressing the back. "Your omission hurt." The words snapped, but he softened his voice. "I thought about my past relationships, about how I handled those situations, and I must admit, I did the same thing. I retreated instead of fighting for what mattered, which now, is you."

His thumb rubbed the edge of the bracelet, and she wondered if he remembered choosing the words. And did they still mean something to him? For her, his simple touch felt like coming home after a long journey, yet more precious, especially after almost losing it.

"So, where do we go from here?" The question scraped against her throat. She needed to know, even if the answer destroyed her hope.

"I don't know." The honesty hung between them. "I want to say home, together. But I need to know this won't happen again, not just the secret, but the emotional running, from both of us."

Cordelia felt the warmth drain from her face. This was it. The moment where he'd choose them or choose self-protection. She forced herself to meet his eyes. "I can't promise I won't make mistakes. But I can promise I won't run or hide from them again."

He studied her face for a long moment, and she saw the decision spread across his face. "Let's go home, together. But we do this properly, no more half-measures."

"Agreed. No more secrets."

Royce walked around the table and embraced Cordelia with a kiss. "I'm sorry I overreacted."

"I'm sorry I held back." A tingling sensation ran down her spine, and her heartbeat skipped like a child dancing through a field of wildflowers.

"Perhaps we should start with dinner."

Cordelia agreed with a smile and a kiss.

As he signaled the waiter, Cordelia reflected on the journey that had brought them to this moment, from their collision on Rue Hautefeuille to their day trips outside London, and the blending of their lives. She marveled at how a brief interaction with a stranger could lead to love.

The waiter delivered a charcuterie board, and as they

nibbled on the food, Cordelia noticed Royce's eyes lingered on her hands when she reached for the bread. His gaze drifted to her lips.

Their fingers brushed together as they reached for the same piece of cheese, and both held the touch longer than normal. The soft texture of his skin against hers created a heat that spread up her arm, reminding her body of what she'd tried to suppress. The sensation ignited memories of their night in the kitchen at Hayton, when his hand skimmed across her breasts.

"I've missed this," Royce said.

"The food?"

"You."

As dinner progressed, the distance between them shrank. Royce leaned forward whenever she spoke, his attention completely focused on her. Cordelia caught herself mirroring his posture, drawn closer to him despite the table between them. Their conversation once again flowed easily, and the initial tension gave way to new pressure. The kind charged with anticipation rather than uncertainty.

When the waiter cleared their plates and asked about dessert, Royce looked at Cordelia, questioning with his eyes.

"I think I've had enough for now." She held his gaze. "But dessert later sounds perfect."

As they left the bistro, Cordelia felt the familiar touch of Royce's hand at the small of her back, a gentle pressure that teased her body. Nighttime had descended on Paris, yet the boulevard remained busy with life. They strolled, intertwining their hands, and refusing to break their connection when people pushed past.

"Where are you staying?" His voice sounded expectant rather than curious.

"Same place as you."

He pulled her against a wrought-iron fence covered in ivy and held her close. "Did you get a room?"

"Just in case."

"In the same hotel?"

"You weren't getting away that easily."

"Shall we?"

"Definitely." Contentment descended over Cordelia. Her willingness to reconnect with him wasn't about having a perfect resolution or erasing mistakes, it was about embracing the challenges to create a strong foundation. In one sense, Paris offered herself as a retreat, an illusory hideaway in which to find clarity. But maybe that had been the point all along, that distance wasn't about running away. It was about gaining perspective on what mattered and discovering that love was worth the trials, rather than fearing its loss.

# Chapter Thirty-Four

The door to Royce's suite closed with a soft click that echoed through his entire body. Located on the île Saint-Louis, the hotel was his favorite place to stay when in Paris. The suite enjoyed natural light, with tall windows overlooking the Seine. A blend of historic architecture and modern furnishings, creating elegant shadows from the moonlight. As the door closed, Royce's attention narrowed, obsessively focusing on her.

Cordelia faced him, her back against the door, and whatever restraint they'd maintained during the walk from the bridge instantly evaporated. The space between them disappeared as Royce moved closer, his hands finding her face with desperate control.

"Cordelia." He breathed against her lips. Her name held a suppressed longing, a realization of what he'd almost lost.

Their kiss was nothing like the gentle reunion they'd shared on the bridge. This was hunger, pure and desperate. Only a week of separation, but all the uncertainty dissolved, leaving an explosive connection. Her hands fisted in his shirt, pulling him closer. He pressed her against the door, his body covering hers with an intense protection.

Royce's fingers traced the line of her throat, reacquainting himself with the softness of her skin. "I thought I'd lost this," He whispered. "I thought I'd lost you."

"Never." Cordelia breathed, her hands working at the buttons of his shirt. "I'm here, right here."

The simple words teased him, igniting his desire, creating a frenzy in his body. His mouth found hers again, more demanding now, as his hands mapped the curves of her body, feeling her breast through the fitted sweater that had tormented him all evening. She responded with matching intensity, her fingers finally succeeding with his shirt buttons. She pushed the fabric from his shoulders.

Cool air hit his chest as the shirt fell to the floor, landing near his jacket. Cordelia's palms pressed against his skin, her touch burning trails of sensation that made him gasp against her mouth.

"Too many clothes." She said, reading his thoughts.

Royce found the zipper of her trousers, drawing it down with reverent slowness despite the urgency coursing through his veins. The black fabric pooled at her feet, revealing pink lace undergarments.

"Beautiful." His whispered voice conveyed his need for her. So beautiful."

The mirror on the side panel reflected their silhouettes in the lamplight. Their curves created an artistic composition. Royce paused. His hands framed her face. He studied her expression with a new intensity, a depth he'd never experienced before.

"What are you thinking?" Cordelia's pulse raced under his touch.

"I love you." The three words emerged without hesitation or

constraint. "I love you, Cordelia." The words suspended between them, transforming everything. She saw the vulnerability in his eyes, not just desire, but the risk of offering his heart. His complete heart.

"I love you, Royce." Heat spiraled through her body, pooling low in her belly. When he lifted her, she wrapped her legs around his waist, feeling the solid strength of him against her softness. The few steps to the bed felt like crossing a gateway, heading into territory they'd only glimpsed before.

Cordelia had forgotten how his touch could completely unravel her. His hands roamed her body, gentle but insistent. He took his time exploring, retracing every curve he'd committed to memory. When her back pressed into the plush bed, the cool linens warmed against her heated skin. She felt herself surrender to a craving she'd suppressed during their separation.

"My god, I missed you." She gasped as his mouth traced a path between her breasts. "Every night, I missed us."

He responded without words, eloquently communicating his insatiable appetite. Their bodies shared the same desperate language. They intertwined and moved together with determination.

Their clothes, scattered across the rug, created a trail of abandonment. Their shadows danced in the dim light.

When they claimed each other, relief and pleasure mingled in their sounds. Time seemed to suspend itself. Every touch tingled beneath her hands, discovery and recognition, feeling the defined muscles of his abdomen. His skin was warm and slightly damp from their exertion. She tasted the faint salt of sweat when she kissed his shoulder. As she mapped the hollows of his torso, he shuddered beneath her caress, revealing a sensitive spot just below his ribs.

"I dreamed about this." She confessed, resting her head on

his shoulder. Her breathy, deep tone hung on each word. "Every night since you left."

"So did I." His hands glided across her body, worshipping every curve with reverent attention. "But imagination is under-rated." He rolled on top of her and hovered his mouth above hers. "I prefer the real thing."

They kissed, immersing themselves in tenderness. Each kiss a seductive longing. The bed yielded and absorbed their passion. Against her back, the sheets whispered as her hips moved.

Not long after, steam filled the marble bathroom as hot water cascaded over their entwined bodies. Cordelia's back pressed against the cool tile as Royce massaged soap across her chest, playfully popping the bubbles to reveal the orbs hidden beneath.

"Is this what you call research?" She tilted her head back and let the water streak through the soap.

"Yes, I believe in being hands-on."

"I like your methods." Maintaining eye contact, Cordelia grabbed the bar of soap from him and lathered her hands. Steam surrounded them, a sanctuary.

The cool air of the bedroom was a sharp contrast to the bathroom's warmth as their damp bodies slid under the sheets, holding each other close.

"Your hair looks golden in this light."

"Flatterer. You do realize you've already scored?"

"Banking them for the future, the near future." When Royce smiled, water droplets rolled down his cheeks.

"Awfully confident, Mr. Brownell."

"Based on the faint, little gasp you made in the shower, I think you'll beg me for more."

She broke into laughter, "Oh my god, that's got to be the cheesiest thing I've ever heard you say."

"That's only the beginning. I can get very cheeky. Want to hear more?" He pinned her to the mattress. "Your skin is like a rare manuscript, and I plan to spend hours examining every detail."

Her laughter shook the mattress. "Wait, wait, I have one. "Your hips provide excellent room service. I'll be sure to order again."

Comfortable in the silence, Cordelia curled against Royce's chest, her partially damp hair flopping over his arm. She listened to the steady rhythm of his heartbeat, remembering a similar night in her apartment. Instead of hearing London outside the window, she listened to the gentle lapping of the Seine whenever boats cut through the calm waters. And distant Parisian nightlife occasionally harmonized with Royce's soft, steady breathing.

"There's something we need to discuss." His fingers traced circular patterns on her bare shoulder.

"What now? Please don't tell me you have an ex who's about to show up and propose?"

"Now you've gone and spoiled my surprise."

"Haha. Cute. What do we need to discuss?"

"London. Balancing our work schedules better. And I'm wondering, can you tolerate Sunday dinners with my family? In particular, my father?"

Cordelia propped herself up on her elbow and looked at him. She noted the playful spark in his eyes, something she'd missed. The look disarmed her. "Is this an official, hang out with the parents offer? Because technically, I already did that on my own."

"Technically, you ambushed my father with madeleines and charm." Royce flashed a snarky grin. "There's a difference between strategic reconnaissance and formal presentation."

She laughed, the sound bubbling up carefree and light. "Strategic reconnaissance? Is that what we're calling it?"

"Well, what would you call showing up at my family estate with baked goods?"

"I didn't just show up. Emma invited me but canceled right before I arrived."

His thumb traced her lower lip. "Pop described you as refreshingly direct, which in The Earl's language translates to terrifying but effective."

"He didn't call me that, did he? Terrifying?"

"That's what he said, if the translation's correct."

"Well, I like terrifying, but effective." Cordelia nipped at his thumb. "Almost as much as refreshingly direct."

"Mm, both suit you." Royce's expression shifted, flattening out his smile into a grin that resembled the Earl's. "What are you thinking about London? About us, practically speaking?"

Cordelia considered the question, her fingers drew lines on the planes of his chest. "I'm thinking Jessica might be ready for more responsibility at the bakery. And I'm thinking your flat is closer to work than mine. But most of all, I'm thinking I'd like to wake up next to you more often."

"More often?" Royce raised an eyebrow. "Not every day?"

"Wow, confident and cocky, Lord Brownell." Her smile undermined the bluntness. "Are you asking me to move in?"

"It's a prime location, and."

"I know, but I haven't agreed to move in with you yet."

"Yet. I like that word. It implies that with the power of my persuasion, you'll say yes."

"It implies ongoing negotiation," Cordelia said. "I have terms."

"I'm listening." His hands settled at her waist, stroking the soft skin in a way that made concentration difficult.

"First, I need to have space to work sometimes, especially on my cookbooks. Second, Sunday dinners with your family cannot become a weekly performance review of my suitability. Third." She paused, suddenly serious. "We have to agree, no, promise that we'll talk when things get complicated. No more retreating to Paris for either of us." The words felt like a vow, more binding than any formal promise they might negotiate.

"Agreed on all counts," Royce said without hesitation. "Though I reserve the right to occasionally retreat to Paris with you, for research purposes."

"Research purposes. I think I can handle that."

"Purely academic. I promise." Royce slid her beneath him with a movement that was anything but scholarly. "Speaking of research, I believe I have more investigating to do."

"Now?" she laughed. Her body responded to his touch that ran down her thigh. "We just."

"Thorough research requires multiple data points." His mouth found a sensitive spot at the base of her neck.

"You're finding all of them tonight." She giggled.

His mouth drifted to the sensitive spot below her ear. "I'm thorough."

"Thank God for academic rigor."

Much later, the morning filtered through the windows. Cordelia felt a contentment she'd never experienced before. Not just satisfaction or happiness, but a bone-deep sense of rightness.

The Egyptian cotton sheets created a cocoon of warmth and satisfied exhaustion. Outside, Paris woke, and the sound of delivery trucks and early commuters starting their day.

"I should probably call Jessica." Cordelia felt the burden of responsibility, but didn't get up to grab her phone. She rested beside Royce, feeling secure in his arms. "I need to let her know I might be delayed returning to London."

"Might be? That sounds ominous."

"You're a voracious researcher, and I thought you might need to conduct some more." She straddled him.

"Well done. I think you topped me for the cheeky prize."

"Face it, you'll never win against me."

"I believe you're right. But I have a mountain of research I need to complete." Royce gave her a wicked grin.

"And from what I understand, these investigations can get lengthy." Her fingernails walked up his chest.

Cordelia realized this was what she'd longed for, a beautiful blend of passion and companionship, a joy of being at home with someone, no matter their location. "Royce?"

"Mm?" His response vibrated against her chest.

"I love you. Just in case that wasn't clear."

She felt his body smile against her temple. "I love you, too. Rather desperately."

"Desperately?" Cordelia tilted her head to look at him. "That doesn't sound very Lord-like."

"Would you rather I say, I adore you, Ms. Dyer, or my loins ache for you?"

"Actually, that sizzles." She laughed and traced the lines of his face, feeling the day-old stubble on his cheeks.

As the morning unfolded around them, it brought with it the promise of a London return and the realities of building a life together, Cordelia looked forward to the complexities of it all. The negotiations and compromises, the Sunday dinners and late-night conversations, the daily choice to love each other despite and because of their imperfections.

It would be messy and wonderful and nothing like the self-preservation she once believed kept her safe. It would be honest, and that made all the difference. For the first time in her life, the unknown felt like a promise rather than a threat.

# Chapter Thirty-Five

The dining room at Wonder sparkled under the medieval vault's arched ceiling, candlelight casting dancing shadows across stone walls. Royce checked his watch, 6:30 p.m., ninety minutes before Cordelia arrived for what she believed was an intimate birthday dinner.

"The cake's perfect and in cold storage," Jessica said, busting through the door. "And Sam's been rehearsing his lines all day. But I have to tell ya, he's adding some wild pauses that make him sound like he's auditioning for Shakespeare."

Royce chuckled and gestured, letting her know it wasn't a problem. "And Cordelia suspects nothing?"

"Nothing. I'll admit, keeping your secret has been torture. Do you know how many times I almost blew it? Take yesterday, I started to say birthday three times and had to turn it into the birth of a new macaron flavor."

He smiled, agreeing with her relief that the secret-keeping was nearly over. "You've been brilliant. I couldn't have done this without your and Sam's help."

Jessica placed her hands on her hips and puffed her chest out. She proudly nodded.

"She'll be shocked you managed it." She gestured at the elegant setup. "The Chef I met nine months ago would've bolted at a surprise party. But now." She shrugged. "Last week, she actually left before seven. Twice. And without checking production schedules seventeen times before getting out the door."

The door swung open as Marcus entered, carrying an elaborate arrangement of orange blossoms and roses. "Where does this botanical explosion go?"

Royce and Jessica both appeared stunned at the size.

"I know, it's colossal. Emma insisted it's tasteful and significant. I do what she tells me." Marcus grinned at Royce, a knowing, brotherly look.

"There, central table. She'll love them. What would we do without Emma?" Royce paused as he shifted chairs. "When Cordelia was young, living in California, they'd pick and bring them home. They were a favorite of her father's."

Marcus positioned the flowers, then stepped back. "That's very romantic of you to remember. Sickeningly romantic, honestly."

Before Royce could respond, Richard appeared with Cassandra, whose emerald cocktail dress complemented her personality.

"We're early," Richard announced. "Cassandra insisted on arriving ahead of time to prevent any catastrophes."

"I merely suggested punctuality might be appreciated." She kissed Royce's cheek, her expression warm. "Although everything appears surprisingly organized. I'm impressed you pulled this off. Bravo."

"Congratulate me after the evening's done. I thought I said, muted attire. I know you're friends now, but I don't need you trying to upstage the guest of honor."

"Never, darling. Besides, she'll always shine brighter in your eyes. Isn't that all that matters?"

Royce patted her arm and ran his fingers through his hair. "Let's hope she agrees."

"You know, she will." Richard and Royce bro-hugged.

The restaurant staff arrived with champagne as more guests filtered in. The Earl and Countess made their characteristically punctual entrance, followed by Emma, who immediately commandeered the gift table. She handed Ada Rose off to Marcus, slinging the diaper bag over his shoulder. Bastien and Jeannine arrived last, having traveled from Paris specifically for the occasion.

"Well done, Royce. She deserves this after a long year." Bastien said, surveying the gathering. "Our girl is blossoming into a wonderful chef."

A text from Sam.

She's on her way. I'm following her. I don't think she knows I'm on her trail.

"Is he a spy now? I've created a monster." Royce stepped to the center of the room. "She'll be here in a few minutes. Let's prepare."

As guests arranged themselves, Royce positioned himself near the door, surprised by the flutter of nervousness in his chest. He resisted smiling, imagining a class full of students. The image tempered his expression. His pulse quickened when he heard approaching voices.

Darius led Cordelia through Wonder's main lounge, past tables nestled in stone alcoves, and up an open staircase.

"Special table for you tonight, reserved upstairs in the vault room. Royce is already waiting."

His booming voice and word choice seemed odd to her, but Darius had always been a bit theatrical.

When she reached the top of the stairs, an eruption of familiar faces shouted, "Surprise!" Her smile froze as she processed the situation. Jessica beamed. The Earl and Countess clapped. The list continued—Marcus, Ada Rose, and Emma, Bastien and Jeannine, who she'd believed were on holiday in Mallorca, Richard and Cassandra, and other colleagues from the bakery and publisher.

Royce stepped closer. He kissed her cheek and whispered, "Happy birthday, love." His dimpled smile radiated with satisfaction. "Surprised?"

"Slightly." The surprise might've once triggered panic, but she felt pleased and overwhelmed at the effort this represented, a warmth seeing everyone gathered to celebrate her.

"Happy birthday, Cordelia." Royce announced, taking her hand. The group echoed him.

"How did you manage to pull this off without me knowing?"

"It wasn't easy," Jessica admitted, approaching with champagne. "Especially when you're obsessively checking every custom order."

"Hey, I'm better. I only do that twice a day now." She and Jessica tapped glasses.

As Cordelia circulated, accepting congratulations, she noticed the thoughtful details Royce had placed around the room. On a small gift table, he'd added framed photos of her with the BL London team, her favorite supplier rep, and her editor. "Oh my god, that's why Sam was obsessively taking Polaroid photos."

She paused and smelled the roses and orange blossoms. Framed photos peeked out from underneath. She felt tears bubbling up and quickly wiped them away. There was a selfie of her and Royce on the Petit Pont bridge right after they kissed, another one of Marnie and Maisie in New York City, and one of her brother, James, and her father. Cordelia picked it up, hugged it, and looked around for Royce, who chatted with Bastien and Jeannine. The weight of the gold frame transported her back to her father's office, where the exact photo had sat on his desk beside stacks of graded papers and coffee-stained research notes.

"He's been planning this for weeks." Emma hugged her from behind. "Called me five times about those flowers. They're shipped in from California."

The image of Royce methodically organizing everything sent a warm, melting sensation that radiated to her toes.

"Yes, but Pop's the one who suggested the idea," Marcus added.

"Seriously?" Cordelia said, her voice squeaking. "He thought of this?"

"Ask Royce, that's what he said when he approached us about it."

The Earl's thoughtfulness left her momentarily speechless. When he and the Countess approached, his formal stiffness had softened, like the day he shared the *courting story* with her.

"Ms. Dyer, happy birthday. You look lovely tonight, dear."

"Glowing, I would say." The Countess hugged Cordelia and whispered, "He's lucky to have you, and so are we."

"Thank you." Cordelia stepped back, dabbed her eyes, and slightly curtsied. "Thank you both for coming. It means a great deal."

The Earl chuckled. "No, my dear, save your curtsies for the King." He patted her shoulder. "And we wouldn't have missed it." Despite spending Sunday dinners with them for the past three months, his warmth still caught Cordelia off guard.

Richard gave a toast, teasing Royce about his former culinary ignorance while praising Cordelia's achievements. All evening, the celebration flowed naturally. The medieval stone walls absorbed their laughter, creating a deep, warm sound that made every conversation intimate. Conversations ranged from bakery discussions with Bastien to warm exchanges with Emma, who she now considered one of her closest friends.

When she found a quiet moment, Cordelia surveyed the gathering with a childlike amusement and wonder. Her professional world merged seamlessly with personal connections, and the aristocratic sphere that once had intimidated her now represented a warm, extended family.

"Come with me. There's something I'd like to show you." Royce guided her to a small wrapped package in the corner.

Inside was an elegant blue leather portfolio with two tickets to Venice, Italy. Royce had organized everything, flights, five-star accommodations, and research credentials for the Biblioteca Marciana archives.

"Your editor knew someone who knew an archivist there, and arranged the credentials."

"Really? When?" Cordelia scanned the tickets. "Next month? I can't go next month. I have interns starting."

"Bastien's handling it."

"Bastien? I can't ask him to manage interns. He's the boss."

"He offered."

"Oh. Really? Just so I can go to Venice?"

"Yes." Royce wrapped his arms around her waist, pulling her closer. The gesture felt both protective and possessive, and she realized how much she trusted him with her happiness. An unfathomable idea a year ago. "Think about it, next month, we'll be in Venice, just the two of us." His lips rested on her cheek.

"I've never been there."

"You'll love it." The back of his fingers grazed her jaw. "We'll live like Venetians for two weeks."

"Two weeks?" She wrapped her arms around his neck. "Seriously? Two weeks?"

"No phone calls to the bakery. No checking in. They can manage. Agreed?"

"Royce, that's a long time. You can't ask me to go two weeks without checking in."

"You might be so busy researching that you forget about the bakery." His thumb held her chin.

"That'll never happen. And you do remember we're in a roomful of people?"

"I hadn't forgotten." The sweet taste of his lips lingered on her mouth. "So, it's settled. We're going to Venice for two solid weeks of research." He winked, playful and sensual.

"Yes."

"Oh, and there's more." Royce handed her another envelope with two invitations to a masked gala at Palazzo Pisani Moretta. "It's a benefit for the Venice Historical Preservation Society. A former colleague is the curator there."

"Seriously? That's incredible."

"Don't worry about a gown. I commissioned costumes from a local atelier. We have fittings the day after arrival."

"My god, you've been busy."

"It wasn't easy, but we managed."

"I guess secrets come in handy sometimes." Cordelia cleared her throat and wiped a single tear that pooled under her eye. "Everything, Royce, all of it. I can't tell you what it means. I'm speechless."

They shared a kiss before Sam interrupted, insisting on giving his toast before guests left. Cordelia agreed, moving to the center of the room, where Sam gave his theatrical speech.

As the evening wound down, guests departed with warm

farewells. The Earl's parting comment about reviewing estate kitchen records before their Venice trip carried professional respect alongside personal acceptance.

Alone in the gradually emptying room, Cordelia turned to Royce. "Thank you for the orange blossoms. For coordinating with Bastien. For knowing me well enough to risk a surprise party."

"Three months ago, I wouldn't have attempted it."

"Three months ago, I might not have welcomed it." She took his hand. "But here we are."

"Venice. Research day and night, a masked gala, and one very romantic gondola ride."

"You have outrageous demands, Ms. Dyer."

"Then you should consider yourself lucky."

"I do." Royce traced circles on her palm.

She lost herself in the reality of the night. Appreciation washed over Cordelia, and every time she tried to speak, the words lodged in her throat. All she could do was kiss him, letting her body convey what her heart felt.

As London's lights blurred past the car windows, she reflected on the journey from their Paris collision to this moment. The cookbook's success marked a professional milestone. The thoughtful celebration demonstrated connections she'd once guarded against. And Venice promised new adventures personally and professional.

Another chapter began. The story they were writing together had found its rhythm, neither perfect nor complete, but genuine in all the ways that mattered most to her. And with Venice's winding canals sand mysterious, romantic streets, she imagined a sweet feast ahead. An adventure to savor.

# Gift

**A Sweet Thank You from the Author**

Dear Reader,

You have made this story complete by choosing to share in Cordelia and Royce's journey. Thank you for spending time in their world, from that fateful collision on Rue Hautefeuille to the kitchen of BL London and the grand halls of Hayton Manor.

Your support means everything to an author, and I'm delighted to offer you a small token of my appreciation.

**Your Exclusive Gift Awaits**

As a special thank you, I've created a downloadable bookmark featuring Cordelia and Royce on the book cover.

**Download Your Free Bookmark Here:** https://Book Hip.com/KLFVZPM

Print it on cardstock for best results, and let it transport you back to those Parisian bistros and moonlit walks along the Seine whenever you open your next book.

P.S. Keep an eye out for Book Two, where we follow Cordelia & Royce to Venice Italy. Release date - August 28, 2025

# Stay Connected

**Stay Connected for More Sweet Escapes**

Loved Cordelia and Royce's story? Their journey continues, and I'd love to share what's next with you:

**Join my Reader's Club** for exclusive bonus scenes, author's musings, recipes, and be the first to know about upcoming releases.

**Sign up at:** https://shannonsteevesauthor.substack.com/subscribe

You'll also receive:

- A bonus chapter of Cordelia's life in New York
- Cordelia's recipe for those irresistible orange-cardamom madeleines
- Early cover reveals and pre-order pricing
- Monthly letters with behind-the-scenes stories, research, travel, and more

# Reviews

**One More Thing...**

If Cordelia and Royce's story touched your heart, please consider leaving a review on Amazon, Goodreads, or your favorite book platform. Your words help other readers discover their next favorite escape, and they mean the world to me as I write the next chapter in this series.

Thank you again for choosing this book. Like the perfect macaron, the best stories are meant to be savored and shared.

With heartfelt gratitude and warmest wishes,
**Shannon Steeves**

# Book Two - We Danced in Venice

# Acknowledgments

Every book is a journey, and I'm grateful to the incredible people who helped me navigate the journey, from that first spark of an idea to the story you hold in your hands.

First and foremost, my deepest gratitude to Reedsy, Tom Bromley, and the writing group who provided feedback, support, and encouragement, while helping me to develop as a writer.

To my editor, Steffi Waters, whose keen editorial eye and unwavering belief in Cordelia and Royce's story made this book infinitely better. Thank you for pushing me to dig deeper and for knowing exactly when to add "more interiority." Your patience is legendary.

Special thanks to Katarina (nskvsky) for creating a cover that captures the romance and style perfectly.

Additional special thanks goes out to my social media manager, Adriana Bernal, for putting up with my revolving ideas. You've been a blessing all these months! Thank you.

To my brilliant beta readers and critique partners: Lena, Langdon, Jim, and Jörgen—who provided insight and honesty, pushing me to challenge myself. You remind me that the writing process may be solitary, but the journey is never lonely.

My husband, Ford, deserves medals for living with a writer. Thank you for supporting and encouraging me to never give up! To my children and grandchildren, you inspire me daily and remind me why happily ever afters matter.

To every librarian, bookseller, book blogger, and bookstagrammer who champions romance novels, you are the true heroes of the literary world.

Finally, to you, my readers, thank you for choosing Cordelia and Royce's story. Thank you for believing in second chances, stolen moments in Parisian cafés, and the transformative power of love (and excellent pastries). Your support makes this journey possible. I'm thrilled to have your support, and you all encourage me every day!

Any errors in French pastry techniques, British aristocratic protocols, or tennis match scoring are entirely my own, probably because I was too distracted imagining the next kiss scene.

With gratitude and love,

*Shannon*

# About the Author

Shannon believes every great love story requires passion, trust in the characters to guide the story, and the right amount of spark to make it unforgettable.

She's a lifelong student of literature and history, in particular, England's past, from pre-Roman Celts to the Norman invasion, and Victorian society, which she weaves into her contemporary love stories. When she's not crafting strong feminine heroes and new book boyfriends, you'll find her in her kitchen attempting to perfect the elusive croissant or planning her next historical research trip.

An avid tennis and F1 fan with a bucket list that includes all four Grand Slam tournaments and the Monaco Grand Prix, she brings the same passion for competition and precision to her writing that she does to the court, though she admits she's better at writing match points than scoring them.

She currently lives in Atlanta, GA, where she treasures time with her husband, adult children, and four grandchildren who keep her young at heart and provide endless inspiration for storytelling. Her German Shepherd serves as both hiking companion and patient listener during plot brainstorming sessions. Between researching and planning her next adventure, she's working on her next romance, because she firmly believes that love is the element that carries us through life's journey.

Connect with her at shannonsteeves.com or shannonsteevesauthor.substack.com/subscribe for updates, bonus scenes, Cordelia's recipes, and tales from Royce's latest historical discoveries.

Find me on Instagram *@shannon.steeves.author* or TikTok *@s.steeves.author*